EIGHTEEN LIVES

DOVE CALDERWOOD

Published by Inspired Quill: October 2018

First Edition

Contact the author through their website:
www.dovecalderwood.com

Chief Editor: Rebecca Hall
Cover Design: Victoria Huelin
Typeset in Minion Pro

Paperback ISBN: 978-1-908600-69-1
eBook ISBN: 978-1-908600-70-7
Print Edition

Printed in the United Kingdom
1 2 3 4 5 6 7 8 9 10

Inspired Quill Publishing, UK
Business Reg. No. 7592847
www.inspired-quill.com

For my family

CHAPTER ONE

London, England
1700s

MY SISTER'S BREATH rasped in her small frame. I leaned forward, waiting, praying for the rise of her chest. When at last it came, my shoulders slumped, and I finally allowed the air trapped in my lungs to escape. Isabel still lived.

Our parents' hushed voices traveled with the draft from the hall, under Isabel's door. They spoke with the town doctor. I doubted they knew I could hear them. Or perhaps they were so desperate it didn't matter who listened.

"Doctor—" My mother's voice cracked. "Doctor, can she—I mean, will…will my daughter live?"

The old wooden floorboards moaned—the doctor shifting his weight? I barely made out his deep sigh. "Isabel appears to have inflammation of the meninges."

Taking a slow, unsteady breath, Mother asked what

the strange phrase meant.

The doctor must have set down his bag, the rattling instruments inside created macabre music. "The cause is not known, but what the fates bring for this condition is quite dire, especially for one so young."

Silence smothered the room, save Mother's hiccupping sobs.

My nostrils flared. With my trembling hand tightened into a fist, my fingernails jabbed my palm.

No …

At last Father spoke in tear-thickened words, piercing that terrible quiet. "Is there anything we can do to ease her suffering?"

"Your presence by her side until the end is the best medicine. Staying close will comfort the child. Let her know you are there, should she cry out to you. I am sorry."

With that, the doctor's voice stopped. His shuffling footsteps echoed down the hall, and the door closed behind them, snuffing out any hope for Isabel's recovery.

Isabel's decline had happened so fast. Only three days prior, she'd seemed absolutely healthy. The next morning, she rose complaining of a strong pain in her head. By evening, her skin felt blistering hot. One day later, she fell into the deep slumber she now fought.

I brushed strands of damp hair away from my sister's face. Again, she let out a soft groan.

Her pale grey eyes fluttered open—the first time in what felt like days. I gasped, daring to hope, "Isabel?"

"Anna," she moaned, looking up at me through droopy eyelids.

"Is the pain severe?" With misty eyes, I asked, "What can I fetch for you?"

I winced as she coughed. How her face shone with a layer of sweat! "…it's so cold…our quilt… please…"

As I snatched up the quilt from Isabel's desk across the room, a gentle breeze blew, causing the air to chill. The scent of candle-wax wafted throughout the dim room. Through the casement, the dark haze of evening replaced the afternoon sunlight. Upon my return to her side, my sister's skin shone a ghostly white. Her arms seemed thinner than even the day before. Were I to grip them, my slender fingers would fit snugly around the whole of her upper arms like a mourning band.

With the quilt snugged around her shoulders, I again beseeched our Lord, praying for help. For a moment, I considered calling our parents. But the sight of their youngest in this state, the quilt's colors so bright against her faded pallor… their minds would surely latch onto that image forever.

"Better?" I asked, struggling to hide concern, and guilt at my choice.

"Better." Despite the quilt's aid, Isabel shivered still. "Thank you, Anna," she whimpered, the frailest of smiles lighting her face.

Now, my gaze fell upon the quilt failing to warm my sister. A wave of bittersweet nostalgia swept over me.

Sewing felt such a monotonous chore, but Isabel seemed always eager to practice the techniques our mother taught us. She asked every day until I conceded to help her make this silly thing. A breath caught in my chest. In truth, spending time together had made the whole affair much less tortuous.

The room around us blurred with my tears while I ran my fingers over our initials, stitched on the bottom corner of the quilt, a little attempt at being grown in her handiwork. Isabel would make a wonderful seamstress someday, with such an eye for things like that…

Someday.

Yet…the vision of her lying in a cold, dark tomb… gooseflesh crept up my arms. The hairs on my neck prickled and an uncontrolled shiver wracked my body. Suddenly, a frosty burst of air stole up from behind me, brushing at my hair, a glimpse of a grave's chill… We were not alone.

I turned, expecting to see Mother or Father stepping though the door. Instead, a shadow lurked in the room's corner. My entire body trembled as the vague outline of arms reached toward me and disembodied legs stepped forward. This seemed a ghostly presence, its shade not extending across the walls or floor. Instead, it coalesced, and hung, lingering a chair's height above the floorboards.

I spun, searching for the source, but found nothing.

In my peripheral vision, I saw Isabel's eyelids flutter at the change in the room, then slide shut. She sank into the bed, arms limp at her sides.

Instinctively, my hands flew to Isabel's, clutching them tightly.

No. Not Yet.

When I turned again, the spectre advanced toward her bedside. My racing pulse caused my command to stutter. "C-come no closer!" I demanded, "What are you? What do you seek?"

The shadow drifted closer, gesturing. I recoiled despite myself, betraying the horror swelling in me. Any doubt as to the name of this spirit vanished.

I gazed upon Death.

I launched my body forward, covering Isabel's with mine. My arms wrapped around her petite torso, holding her against me. She lay quite still. Only a muffled cough escaped her lips. "No! Please. She is but six years old. Spirit, you must be mistaken!"

"It is her fate."

Once the first tear escaped, others quickly flowed, streaming down my cheeks. "Please, do not do this!"

"It must be done."

My resolve strengthened. Loosening one of my arms' grip on Isabel, I swiped at my cheeks, banishing those traitorous tears. "I will not let you take her."

The shadow lengthened, darkening a larger area around her bed. Silence crowded the room, then a whisper echoed, offering, "One need only be willing to take her place, to change the child's fate."

My mouth ran dry. *Exchange my life for Isabel's?* "Yes."

"I must warn you—it comes at a price greater than death." The voice did not barter, but demanded outright, "Do you agree?"

I paid little heed to Death's warning. In that moment, the only important thing was saving my baby sister. "Aye."

The shadow morphed again before engulfing me.

EVERYTHING VANISHED. A cold, stinging sensation crept into my fingertips, spreading up my arms little by little. *Whatever is happening, Isabel must not know how excruciating this is. Be brave for her.* Were those thoughts mine or the foul entity's echoes? I did not stop to consider. With teeth grit, my screams remained locked in my chest. Invisible hands clutched my lungs, laboring my breath. Biting cold continued coursing through my body. Frigid tears drifted down my cheek.

Our Father, who art in heaven, hallowed be thy name.... Thy kingdom come, thy will be done...Mother, Father, someone—anyone! Please spare me this agony!

Pain increased tenfold, as if my body were falling apart. An icicle shattered upon a stone beyond the casement. When my mouth opened to cry out, I found I'd become mute; the room remained silent.

What within me could I conjure to escape this consuming pain? Memories? Yes. The day of Isabel's birth. She lay swaddled, tiny, perfect, with beautiful stormy grey eyes—they matched mine exactly. I loved her at once, and promised Mother I would watch over her all her days.

Mercifully, with the beauty of that single memory to carry me, the pain eventually vanished. Yet, I still could not see—darkness engulfed all. Silence threatened to swallow me whole. I tried moving, but a flexible, yet somehow sturdy substance held me captive. No matter how frantically I tried, puncturing it seemed impossible. The temperature felt pleasantly warm, wherever realm I'd been forced into. The temperateness might have offered comfort if my heart weren't speeding with panic.

Am I encased? What is this thick, murky miasma?

It appeared to be a brume of some sort, yet my lungs were not screaming for air.

I lay resting, for how long I could not tell. With a jerk, these bonds constricted, pushing me toward a light far too brilliant for my mortal eyes.

CHAPTER TWO

Idaho Falls, Idaho
Modern Day

MY TIME IN this life was running out. The possibility of my imminent demise, during my walk to the bus stop, loomed overhead. Halfway across the street, a flash of black hurtling toward me grabbed my attention. Screeching tires and the stink of burnt rubber gave little warning. A car skidded to a stop a foot in front of me, drenching my clothes with slushified snow.

Ugh. I haven't even made it to school yet...today already sucks.

The driver's white-knuckled hands gripped the steering wheel to the point I swore it would snap in half. "Are you trying to get yourself killed?" he yelled.

"Kill *myself*?" Gritting my teeth, I swung my bag at his BMW, hammering it on the hood with a satisfying *bang*. "I'm in the pedestrian crossing, you idiot! You almost killed me."

His eyes, so huge they might burst out of his skull, stayed transfixed on the bag-sized dent that now blemished his hood, for the first time I felt happy to have such a ridiculously oversized science textbook. My nostrils flared.

Kill myself. Yeah, like I really want to go through childhood all over again. Eighteen times is enough, thank you very much.

I braced to swing my bag again, but he'd reversed a few feet, swerved around me, and sped off, probably heading to something more important than my life.

"Don't worry about me," I called after him. "Really. I'm just someone you nearly squashed. *Have a nice day!*"

Brushing the splattery mess off my chest as I waited for the bus proved more difficult than I'd hoped. The stuff was everywhere. When I climbed aboard, it was stuffed to the brim with kids.

"Anyone else smell wet pooch?" one of the boys behind me snarked, "Must be Poodle."

Of course, the other two beside him snickered, shushing each other.

Don't engage. Keep your head down. Be normal.

Poodle—my unofficial, *unapproved* nickname. In this current life, *blessed* with wildly curly hair, its shade resembling desiccated wheat grass on a summer afternoon, I got it every day. The bus lurched to a stop in front of the place I considered my personal purgatory: Idaho Falls High School. Home of the Tigers. And one drenched, dirty poodle.

THE MOMENT MY foot stepped through the door, a crowd of faceless students swept me up into their chaos. Any struggle seemed futile. My shoulder slammed into a locker, its combination lock digging into my ribs. When I probed my side, a pained hiss escaped.

Teens are so disrespectful. Try growing up in Ireland in 1700, then cry about having it rough.

The school bell echoed down the halls. I raced toward my locker, late and sopping. The moment the bell stopped pealing, morning announcements started up.

Why do Mondays exist? I rubbed my forehead.

God, I wish electronics weren't banned during class time. At least then I could use my iPod to block out the annoying monotone. Following the rules can be so frustrating sometimes.

Turning right down the hallway, there leaned my friend, Alexis, waiting against my locker with a precocious smirk. Her bright red hair, styled in choppy layers, lay enviably tucked flat behind her ears. Black makeup circled her rounded brown eyes, naturally meshing with the dark, stereotypical Goth attire she wore.

"Hey, Heather. Sent in your ISU stuff yet?"

"Hi, Alex. Er… no, I haven't, actually."

She fidgeted with her hoodie's zipper. "Might wanna hurry. Take too long and we won't be able to go together."

Water dripped onto my shoe when I tossed my jacket

into my locker. *Great. Thanks, BMW asshole.* "Good point. I'll start filling out an application later."

"God, I can still remember us vowing to go to Idaho State together. What ten-year-olds make those sorts of plans?" She stared at the ground for a moment before clearing her throat, then looked up at me with misty eyes. "Sorry, started feeling old for a second." Her mouth stretched into a grin with a forced edge to it; it didn't reach her eyes. "Anyway, now we're gonna make it happen."

"Yeah." How could I tell her I couldn't keep my word, even though I wanted to? My nineteenth birthday came right before the start of fall semester. I'd never reached that age in any of my lives. It could happen some random Tuesday, it could happen the day I turn eighteen, it could even happen at 11:59 pm on the eve of my nineteenth birthday. A macabre part of my brain wondered how it would happen this time.

Will I be killed by a mugger? Hit by a car?

I hated the unfairness of it all. If I had to begin my life over ad infinitum, couldn't I at least live complete lives? I wanted to know what it was like to grow old. To watch my grandchildren play while I relaxed on the porch. Maybe remember what it felt like to hold the comforting hope of seeing my loved ones again someday.

Alex's voice pulled me from my reverie. "Well, it'll happen if I can get my grades together, at least. My next report card might be covered with Ds." *Might!* "And I don't think my parents will laugh if I say they stand for

Delightful."

Eager to aim my thoughts down a cheerier avenue, I teased, "You're gonna blow racists' minds, not living up to the stereotype. Bet they can't even fathom a Japanese girl getting anything other than an A."

She gave me a rough slap on the arm for my joke, then with a laugh threw her head back. "It'd be a nice change from people asking how to make egg rolls or General Tso's chicken."

"That's true." I leaned forward, giving Alex an enormous hug. "I'm so sorry you have to put up with shit like that."

"Thanks."

"If they were gonna insult you, they could at least get their facts straight."

"Damn straight. I don't know how anyone can tolerate the nasty shit that white people say is Asian food."

"At least your mom makes authentic cuisine. It's amazing. I'd eat it all the time if I could."

"You should come over for dinner this weekend. My mom got a new agemono nabe."

I grinned. "That sounds great!"

As we climbed to the second floor and turned a corner, I spied a couple by the vending machine, their lips glued together... rank sucking noises coming from their clench. I only just managed to avoid staring while we tried getting past.

Unfortunately, the girl spotted me, breaking her

embrace. My stomach dropped upon recognizing Tiffany, one of the cheerleaders. Most girls on the squad weren't too bad, but since fourth grade, Tiffany'd made sure to torture me. Every chance she got.

"Look, Tim. It's the Dorky Duo." She sneered. "Miss Teacher's Pet and the Asian freak trying to be the singer from Paramore. News flash, loser, it's not 2007 anymore."

We walked past. Over her shoulder, Alex shot an obscene gesture at Tiffany.

We slipped through the classroom door in time for the final bell. English with Mrs. Anders. I took my seat next to Alex. I shivered—the temperature'd plummeted, making me pull my hoodie tighter around myself. In the back of my mind nagged a sense of déjà vu, but I ignored it.

It's January in Idaho. Of course it's cold.

Alex snatched up my day planner and began her usual routine of doodling. I leaned closer, trying to see what she'd drawn.

"Nuh-uh," she whispered with a teasing glare. She half-turned away before I could catch a glimpse.

I rolled my eyes, focusing my gaze on the window instead. A lone raven flew up against the grayness of the sky, then swooped down to perch on the roof.

Weird… ravens aren't native to Idaho.

A sharp pain jabbed my shoulder.

I raised a brow, glancing at my arm. "Huh?"

Alex eyed me warily. "Dude, I finished five minutes ago."

"Sorry. I got distracted looking at birds."

She turned toward the window, then back to me. "What bird?"

When I glanced again, it was gone. "Never mind."

"You're so weird sometimes."

I chuckled. "I know. Now, can I see the picture?"

She slid my day planner back onto the desk. Drawn in the back, an anime-style woman in a dark, flowing dress smiled. Alex had sketched her with long, wavy black hair. An arrow pointed with "Lady Person!" written above it. I snickered, drawing a cat on the woman's shoulder. My arrow pointed, with "Kitty" written above. Alex laughed, reaching for my planner again when the door creaked open.

Mrs. Anders strutted into the room. Taking a second to catch her breath, she started in, "Today we're going to begin our study of *Romeo and Juliet*, which is often considered one of the greatest love stories of all time."

Alex barked with laughter. "Yep, a great romance, all right. Romeo's a dumbass and Juliet's whiny."

"Watch it, Alexis," Mrs. Anders glared. "We don't need your commentary."

That made Alex lift her chin, hitching up a shoulder in a nonchalant shrug. "Sorry, Mrs. A. I call 'em as I see 'em."

Mrs. Anders impatiently raked her fingers through her elaborately coiffed graying hair. "Miss Mordaw, be more respectful in my classroom or you'll find yourself in the principal's office faster than you can say 'Wherefore art thou.' Now, without any further interruptions, let's get started."

WHILE WE READ the classic tale, my mind wandered to the topic of my own non-existent love life. Though my existence spanned nearly four hundred years, I'd never truly fallen in love. I'd felt physical attraction before—my eyes still worked, after all, but after my first couple of lives, I quickly figured out the way my existence worked. Indulging in relationships would be pointless, with time so limited. During my original life, my mind often wandered into daydreams about a handsome prince bursting into my room, sweeping me away to some wonderful castle. Of course, he never came.

THE INSTANT THE bell rang, I shoved books, pencils, and binder into my bag.

Alex shuffled up next to me in the hall, her hair brushing against her shoulders, like mine never would. "Sorry about all the drama earlier," she apologized. "That play always pisses me off."

I'd learned that the hard way. When we were eight, I brought the DiCaprio version to a sleepover. Alex nearly threw me out of her house.

"What's your problem with it, anyway?"

"It's stupid. Romeo and Juliet aren't in love. They're in lust. And they get themselves killed over it. Love doesn't just happen in an instant."

My eyebrows waggled conspiratorially. "Says the girl who told her first boyfriend she loved him after a week."

She smacked my arm. "Shut up. Just because I criticize teenage infatuation doesn't mean I'm immune to it."

Suddenly, Alex squealed.

What caused the ruckus? A tall, pale boy with auburn dreadlocks holding Alex off the ground, spinning her.

Oh, it's Carl.

They'd been dating for a few weeks. I usually tried avoiding being around when Alex spent time with boys, so we'd never been properly introduced. The whole *third wheel* thing sucked.

"Put me down before I hurl," she squeaked through peals of laughter.

"Gross. Fine. Here ya go." With a snicker, he turned her loose.

"Don't you need to be out at the stadium?"

"They finished fixing the lights in room 204, so Mr. Thom gets to use it now."

Her face lit up. "Baby, that's great. Now, we can see each other this time every day!"

He kissed her forehead, smiling broadly. "This is gonna kick ass."

I spoke up, waving. "Hey, you must be Carl. I'm Heather."

He beamed, holding out his hand for me. "Yep, I am. Alex told me all about you. Nice to finally see the girl behind the stories."

"I hope they're good ones," I said, looking to Alex with a teasing grin.

"She talks about you like you're her sister."

Alex bounced on her toes, a smile lingering on her lips. "It's true."

I hooked my thumbs in the front pockets of my jeans. "Well, I need to go. Nice to meet you, Carl. I'm glad she's found someone to make her happy."

"Thanks. Nice meeting you, too."

I glanced one last time at the two of them and turned to leave, only then allowing the happy face I'd put on to crumple. I wanted to find someone to be happy with, too, unlikely as that seemed. It was a foolish wish, I knew that. That was why I had long since filed the notion away as a pipe dream. Even if I tried to have a relationship, it wouldn't last. That wasn't fair to anyone, especially the poor boy I'd leave behind.

ALEX FOUND ME sitting alone in a corner of the cafeteria at lunch. She plopped down next to me, two trays at her elbow, a slice of sausage pizza on each.

"Sausage, your favorite. Unless that's changed in the past five seconds." She grinned, sliding one of the trays in front of me.

"Oh, hey." I picked up a slice and took a bite. "Thanks, I owe you one. So, how's your grandma doing?"

"She's powering through." Alex said, between bites. "I visited her at the hospital yesterday,"

"Any news on a surgery yet? I mean, she was diagnosed a month ago…"

"They're not even sure how big the tumor is. Once they know, they can go from there."

I raised my milk carton in a defiant gesture. "I hope they annihilate the little bastard."

"Me too. Mom's a nervous wreck."

"Next time you see her, tell her I hope she gets better soon, 'kay?"

"Yeah." She bit her lip, hesitating. "So, this is way off-topic, but what do you think of Carl?"

I hiked up one of my shoulders. "He seems alright. Can't really get a good read on someone I just met, but he doesn't come across like a bad guy or anything. Where's he at, anyway?"

"He's in the library working on his math homework." She winked. "Seems he got too distracted last night to get it done…"

I gasped. Had Alex taken the ultimate step? It seemed so unlike her to just do something like that without thinking. "Did you…?"

She jerked back in shock, shaking her head. "No. Are you kidding? I'm not giving up the V-card after only three weeks. Plus, I'd totally tell you if it happened."

I hoped she would. We confided everything to each other. At least, everything I *could* confide.

Leaning forward, I tilted my head to the side, curiously. "Do you think you guys will soon?"

"Dunno. I mean, he's a sweet guy. But I want to be absolutely sure, ya know?" Her teeth came down on her lower lip.

It was a hard question to answer. I took a bite of my pizza. "Makes sense. It *is* a big decision."

She waved her free hand dismissively while she took a huge bite, talking with her mouth full. "Enough about my sex life, or lack thereof."

"You're doing better than I am."

"Maybe that'd change if you actually talked to someone at school who's, ya know, not me." Her nose wrinkled when she laughed.

"You're *so* nice to me." I said, sarcasm leaking from every syllable.

She grinned. "You know you love me."

Alex spent the rest of lunchtime gushing about a band I hadn't heard of yet. To appear less musically incompetent, I grunted occasionally in agreement.

"I'm still hungry," she grumbled, leering at her empty plate.

"What else is new?" I teased.

"I'm walking to the gas station for some potato chips. See ya." She gave me a quick, powerful side-hug before standing and dancing out of the cafeteria, up the stairs to the ground floor.

I REACHED INTO my pocket, spending a second scrolling through Facebook. Anything to keep the sudden loneliness at bay.

My world stopped when I noticed the date: January seventh. Isabel's birthday.

How did I forget? What is wrong *with me?*

My lungs ached. My throat swelled shut. I gasped for air.

My new Converse squeaked on the linoleum floor; the sound chased me down the hall. I ran to the restroom where I sat in a stall. Once the echoing voices of other girls dissipated, I put my face in my shaking hands. My fingertips went numb. Everything fell silent except for a loud banging sound I couldn't quite place. Was someone knocking at the door? Pressure was building up in my head—I was sure it would explode any moment. Tears cascaded down my cheeks. I wrapped my arms around my chest and rocked back and forth, quietly sobbing. The thunderous pounding sound grew even louder.

To compose myself, I forced the image of Isabel living a long, healthy life into my mind. Even though what became of her remained a mystery, despite my best efforts to find any sliver of information, that image gave me a small comfort. To at least hope I'd saved her. Eventually, my emotions settled into a numbed calm. The banging noise faded, leaving only the buzzing hum of fluorescent lights in its place. Only a dull ache in my chest reminded me of the pain.

I DODGED MY way to my next class. The halls seemed suddenly labyrinthine. I'd just managed to open the classroom door, when the two-minute warning bell rang.

Mr. Banisk, my drawing teacher, waved enthusiastically once he spotted me. "Hey, Heather."

Around us, most of the kids were just setting up and pulling supplies from the cubbyholes that lined the back wall.

"Hey, Mr. B. How's your new workout routine going?" I smirked. "Are you benching a thousand pounds yet?" Mr. B's arms could easily be mistaken for spaghetti noodles.

"Oh yeah." Imitating Arnold Schwarzenegger's Austrian accent, he continued, "I'm totally pumping iron, man." He laughed, flexing.

I chuckled, pulling my art portfolio out of its cubby. "Keep living the dream, Mr. B."

He saluted, adjusting his glasses with the other hand.

Shivering, I took my seat. For warmth, I rubbed my hands together, turning to glance at the boy next to me. "Hey, Tom. Are you cold, or is it just me?"

He shrugged, brushing his jagged orange bangs away from his eyes. "Eh, maybe a little bit. The heating system's is older than dirt."

"True." I rolled my eyes. "God, this school is run by cheapskates. It's bad enough that we get stuck in the Home Ec kitchen while the pottery class gets their own room."

"It sucks. But at least there's snacks sometimes if the home ec students cook enough."

"I guess that kind of makes it worthwhile."

Tom turned away, focusing on his drawing.

Well, guess I won't be getting any more out of him. Would have been nice to talk a little longer. I wish Alex could've taken drawing now instead of second period.

All problems fell away while I poured my feelings onto the page, absentmindedly doodling.

Mr. Banisk's reedy voice pulled me back to reality. "Okay." He called from the front of the room. "This next assignment needs to be a drawing representing who you are. It can be anything, just keep it school appropriate. Please incorporate the gradients shading technique I taught last week, too."

An excited murmur rumbled through class.

I let my pencil dance across the page. But, cycling through ideas, nothing promising emerged. Every art teacher I'd ever had, in all of my lives, told me I second-guessed myself too much creatively. They were right. But it wasn't because of typical youthful insecurity, like they assumed. Art was supposed to be a reflection of what lies inside its creator. It was a battle I faced every time I had to be creative for others: how does someone express their truth, when their whole truth can't be shared?

And then, a second question came—one cutting even deeper: *I've been so many people...is there even a cohesive 'me' to represent anymore?*

Someone turned on the radio—a female voice shrilly belted a generic pop song about believing in yourself. If there was some kind of higher being, they had to be loving the irony. Suddenly, inspiration sucker-punched me in the face. It almost took my breath away.

Yes! Of course!

Other students quietly murmured amongst themselves, bouncing ideas off each other. Some sang along as they drew. It was impossible to make anything out over the music. It became easier to focus.

Near the end of class, I brushed the eraser bits off the paper, and took it to Mr. Banisk's desk. "I think I've got the start of an idea for the assignment. Would you take a look?"

"Sure. Let me see it."

After appraising my work, he glanced up, his eyes wide.

My face scrunched with confusion. "What?" I asked.

He turned the drawing to face me. It was a pretty simplistic rough draft, mainly just line work, but it was enough to get the point across. A girl encased in shadow. She lacked a face, but her twisted body still fought against the darkness.

Mr. Banisk looked over it again. "You want *this* to symbolize who you are?"

"Yeah. Why? What's wrong with it?"

He shifted his weight. "Nothing. It's just, I don't know, a little darker than what you usually draw."

"I guess I've just felt a little depressed the past few days."

Wrinkling his brow, his eyes met mine. "Is everything okay? You can talk to me or the school counselor if you need to, you know."

"Yeah, I know. Thanks for your concern. But I'm fine, really. Just stressed out."

"Okay, then." A smile came up, but not one of his best.

A FLASH OF Alex's red hair shone in my peripheral vision as I tossed my things into the open locker.

Now what?

A sharp jab to my ribs answered my question. "Poke," she shouted with a grin.

I rubbed the assaulted area through my cotton sweater. "Ow."

She scoffed. "I didn't poke *that* hard."

"Says you," I grumbled.

"Who pissed in your Wheaties?"

A shiver coursed through me. It was like the hallway had just teleported to Antarctica. I grabbed my hoodie from the locker, slipping the faux-fur lined jacket on. "I'm just… freaking out about the dissection, is all."

"Why are you even taking a class with dissections when you break down every time you accidentally kill a bug? For God's sake, you didn't even go to your grandpa's funeral because you couldn't handle seeing the body."

Pausing for a moment, I considered this truth. "I don't know. I'm curious about science, I guess."

Learning new things during each lifetime made this whole curse a little easier to bear. In almost 400 years, humankind had gone from using leeches or smelling salts to cure almost every ailment, to mapping the human genome. I only wished my original family were still alive to experience it, too.

"If you can handle it, Heather, more power to ya."

Before I could respond, Carl came up behind Alex, leaning close to whisper something. The crowd stampeding through the hallway drowned out whatever she mumbled when she waved goodbye to me.

I don't think I want to know.

THE BELL RANG. Anxiety over the frog dissection became razor blades twisting in my stomach.

Pushing open the zoology room door, a stench of biblical proportions assaulted my nostrils. Within a few hesitant sniffs, the origin of the stink made itself known—a dead frog lying on its back on a metal slab. One each per Lab-team's station. Gagging, the acidic taste of vomit threatened my taste buds.

My lab partner, Collin, chuckled as he sat. "Got a weak stomach, huh?" His seat squeaked as he dragged it closer to the table.

Keeping my breathing even wasn't easy; my eyes locked on the animal posters lining the walls. *Why isn't he retching at the smell?*

Stumbling, Ms. Paulson dropped her tome of a binder on her desk, making me jump a foot in the air. "Whoops! Sorry. Today, we're going to dissect these. You'll work in pairs. One person will cut, while the other identifies the different organs using a labeled pin."

Nudging my shoulder, Collin kept me grounded. "I'll cut. You can identify. Sound good?"

Dizzy with relief, I managed a nod. Everyone else seemed so calm when I dared to glance around the room. It didn't make any sense. Why weren't they freaking out too?

He shot me a reassuring glance while we each slid our hands into latex gloves.

Approximating a smile, I gave a thumbs' up. Then, not wanting to see the horror, I clamped my eyes shut when he brought the scalpel close to the frog's chest.

Collin tapped my shoulder. "Um, okay. It's done."

Hesitating for a moment, I wished my eyes hadn't opened when my gaze fell upon the torso of the poor amphibian. Behind me, the sound of someone laughing quietly wafted through the air. An icy breeze, short and quick, brushed against my neck. I turned to check if anybody stood behind me, but no, nothing out of place.

Focus on the assignment. Be normal. Our desk is closest

to the door. Of course there's a breeze. You're just nervous.

Fighting the urge to heave, I appraised the little animal's corpse. The heart and lungs stuck out conspicuously. I took a deep breath, grabbed two pins, sliding them in. *Not good,* was all my mind could think.

The frog's eyes moved to meet mine, its heartbeat drummed into my ears.

Grabbing hold of Collin's arm helped in no way whatsoever. Around me, other students turned their heads because I'd jumped up, pushing back from the desk. "It's not dead… *It's not dead!* Did anybody see? Anybody?"

It got real silent even before Ms. Paulsen rushed over. The class stared at me like an insane asylum inmate. "Heather, what's all the fuss?"

"It looked at me. It's still alive. That frog looked at me!"

Ms. Paulson placed a hand on my shoulder. Gently. "Honey, it can't be alive. The frogs arrive at school already dead. Every one of them. We freeze them until it's time to dissect."

"But—"

"You look like you're about to collapse. Why don't you go to the nurse's office, hmm? Get some rest and see if your parents can come get you?"

Taking her up on that wasn't a problem. Nodding, I robotically grabbed a laminated pass off her desk.

THE HALLWAYS SPUN around me. Swaying, shakily I

clutched the doorknob to the nurse's office.

The last thing I heard was, "Can I hel—"

Everything went black.

"Are you all right?"

The worried expression across the nurse's brow greeted me when I found consciousness again. "You passed out for a minute there."

My voice croaked. "I still feel a little dizzy."

The nurse carefully took my vitals before declaring, "Everything seems normal. You came from zoology class?"

"Right."

"I thought so. Overstressed about dissection. It happens to someone every trimester. Go ahead and rest here for a minute."

My legs wobbled when I tried to stand, threatening to send me tumbling. I decided to appear composed, and held myself up by leaning against the filing cabinet. "I'm fine."

She clicked her tongue, not believing my act for a second. "You're pale. Let's call your parents."

Mr. and Mrs. Kütz. In my heart, they weren't my parents. I liked them, but *my* parents remained Jonathan and Caitlin Jerbins. The Kützes were supportive and kind, though a bit overprotective. But they weren't *mine*.

THIRTY MINUTES LATER, they'd signed me out in a hurry—we were sat in the car within seconds. This was so embarrassing. On top of that, I'd have homework to catch up on from the couple of classes I was going to miss. But it was hard to deny part of me was grateful I'd get to go home and rest. Before I could catch my breath and fasten my seatbelt, the interrogation began.

"Heather, is there more to this than what they told us? Are you eating enough?" Mrs. Kütz turned to Mr. Kütz, "Andrew, she's so skinny…"

"You're not pregnant or on drugs, are you?" He sternly added with a frown through the rear-view mirror, "We raised you better than that. You're lucky we don't make your curfew earlier than it is, young lady."

She shot a sideways glance at him. "Her curfew is fine the way it is."

He grunted, rubbing his temples. "Of course, dear."

The entire ride home felt like a scene from a bad courtroom movie. I answered their questions as honestly as possible, feeling my cheeks burn all the same.

They finally stopped when we got into the house.

Mr. Kütz placed his jacket in the closet by the front door. "Do you feel up to helping your mother with dinner?"

Neither of them were talking about going back to work.

I stood next to Mrs. Kütz, my back to the end of the kitchen that led to the dining room, where Italian vineyard-themed wallpaper with vibrant grapes lined the walls. "Want some help?"

"Sure. I'm making stew tonight. If you're feeling okay, can you cut the vegetables?" I nodded, following her into the kitchen. Always the pre-meal prepper, she gestured to a bowlful nearby. That was Mrs. Kütz; meticulous no matter what. Her floor tiles gleamed a brownish red, providing an almost Mediterranean feel.

The carrots crunched loudly when I took up the sharp knife to cut them.

Mrs. Kütz cut a large steak into smaller pieces. "You *would* tell us if something was wrong, wouldn't you?" her voice lowered.

I made a show of staring only at the wooden cupboards that covered every inch of the wall, save a little window over the sink. My teeth pressed down on my lip. I focused on the solid wood counters, which circled the room, the tops covered with faux marble.

I wish I could.

"Of course," I lied, looking at her over my shoulder with a pasted-on smile.

"I'm sorry about us giving you the third degree. We just worry about you. No matter how much you grow up, you'll always be our little girl."

I set the knife down, turned properly, and gave her a big hug. "I'm glad you guys worry. If you didn't, I don't think anyone else would."

She chuckled, kissing the top of my head. I looked past

her to the small table in the middle of the dining area with four backless chairs, which I always assumed took inspiration from Asian decor. She patted my hand, saying, "That's silly. You're such a sweet girl, you wouldn't have trouble finding people who care about you. I love you, Heather."

I closed my eyes, letting myself pretend for a moment she was really my mother. "You too."

Mrs. K turned back to the cubed steaks, sprinkling on some spices. She shook her head. "I still can't believe you're graduating this year. It seems like just yesterday you were a baby in my arms, my stone-faced little cuddle monkey."

On that, Mr. Kütz stepped in and opened the fridge to grab a beer.

She reminded him, "Remember how serious she was when she was little? She barely smiled at all."

Can't imagine why.

I tossed the chopped carrots into a pot.

AFTER A QUIET dinner, I went to my bedroom to doodle, not really paying attention to what I drew. The television hummed in the background—some trashy show about selfish people doing terrible things.

During a commercial break, I glanced down at the page. There, a portrait of a boy with short, shaggy hair confronted me. His chin was slightly upturned, giving him a cocky air. Steely eyes focused into a faraway gaze, his eyebrows knitted together in concentration.

His face seemed familiar, but I couldn't recall ever seeing anyone who looked like him.

Is he a character from a book I've read or a movie I've seen? A person from one of my past lives, maybe?

I'd seen so many faces it was impossible to remember them all. I shrugged it off, spending the rest of the evening darkening the shadows and adding more detail to his hair.

AFTER SLIPPING INTO flannel pajamas, I snuggled into my pillow with a tired groan. *Things may be going nuts, but at least I've got my favorite sheets.*

Sometime in the night, something woke me. I opened my eyes wide in the dimness, my skin crawling. Someone was watching. I peeked through my covers, searching the moonlit room. Was someone in my chair?

No, no. Just a dream.

CHAPTER THREE

RAYS OF SUN spilled through my bedroom curtains. Sweat drenched my pillow. Eager to shake off the disturbing nightmare, I crawled out of bed. As always at this time in the morning, the house was peacefully silent— Mr. and Mrs. Kütz were at work already. I dragged myself to the bathroom; a shower sounded heavenly.

Standing under the warm water, I felt my woes swirl down the drain. Then it happened again. While washing my hair, that feeling of being watched stabbed at my mind… like the night before.

Is that a shadow out there?

I peered from behind the shower curtain—just my imagination. After grabbing a towel, I shuffled to my bedroom, still-wet feet leaving damp spots on the carpet. Slipping into what Mrs. Kütz would call a *respectable outfit*—a striped T-shirt with a comfortable pair of jeans, I hurried back to the warmth of the steamed-up bathroom.

Dots of mist still lined the mirror when I reached for my hairbrush, trying to tame the beast on my head while I still could. Snatching a threadbare towel from the counter, I wiped the mirror clean and studied my pores. That's when the reflection behind me appeared. With a shriek, I spun, raising my brush to strike the intruder.

No one there.

What the hell is wrong with me?

Something about it seemed so familiar…

Just forget it. Get through the day. Be normal.

I finished getting ready and headed out, dismissing the sightings. Stress combined with lack of sleep caused people to see all sorts of things.

A FEW OF my classmates murmured when I took my seat in English, only this time a few words stood out—*freak, weirdo,* and most importantly, *frog.* My cheeks burned. Why the hell did my face have to betray me? I covered my eyes with my binder, hiding the redness and my shame.

I'm not going to hear the end of this until I die in this life.

Ducking my head, I tried in vain to tune out what people said around me.

Where's Alex? I wondered.

I kept my head down and worked at sketching a rose on a random notebook page.

Just blend in. Maybe they'll stop.

MORNING CLASSES PASSED. But by lunchtime, everyone's eyes burrowed into me. My hair proved less effective a shield than my binder, but desperate times called for desperate measures.

I wished I could joke with Alex. *Now would be a great time to gain invisibility powers.*

Of course, I would never be that lucky. Tiffany and her friend Jenna cornered me the second I entered the cafeteria. Their evil grins stretched from ear to ear.

"Look, Jen. It's Princess *Toadstool.*"

Jenna snickered, nudging Tiffany's arm.

In the lunch line, Tiffany shot a conspiratorial glance at Jenna before hissing, "So, Poodle, do you think they'll come and take you to the looney bin soon?"

A boy I didn't even know giggled at their gibe. I slunk to a table with a cookie and a steaming bowl of tomato soup, though I'd rather have flung it at them.

Alex suddenly appeared. "You holding up okay?" She frowned, hugging me from the side. "I heard what everyone's saying."

I gave a slight nod. "Yeah. I'm all right." And let out a deep sigh before taking a sip of my soup.

"Want me to kick some asses?" she offered, raising a fist and sliding in next to me.

That managed to get a half-hearted chuckle. I set my spoon down. "Nah. Thanks, though."

"Are you sure everything is all right? I mean, saying the frog you're dissecting's *alive* isn't really normal," she said, mouth full of chili.

Hunched over my cookie, my eyes fell. "Nothing's wrong." I avoided Alex's gaze.

"Bullshit. I've known you since first grade. You can't lie to me."

Slumping, I bit into the cookie and surrendered. "Fine. There *is* something going on. But I don't understand it. If I give you the wrong information, and you get hurt trying to help because of it, I'd never forgive myself. Once I've got all the facts, I'll tell you everything. I promise."

"If you say so..." Alex mumbled, not seeming appeased. After a quiet moment of chewing her chili, she let out a sigh, poking her roll with her spoon. "It's too bad we can't make those bitches pay without getting in trouble."

I leaned on the table, stirring my soup. "I know. If I could do anything, with no consequences, I'd shave their heads. Let's see them try to constantly brush something that's not there."

She threw her head back with a laugh. "That'd be the best thing *ever*."

"What should we talk about now?" Chewing on the last bite of sweet baked goodness, its sugary taste momentarily distracted me from my anxiety.

"Um, how about..." She paused, looking around for an idea. Finally, her eyes lit up. "This chili?" She picked up the bowl from her tray, inspecting it. "Looks like there's only *one* human toe in there this time."

I laughed in spite of myself. "Thanks, dude."

She rubbed my back, smiling. "Figured you needed a pick-me-up. What are friends for? Anyway, I've got to work on some homework that totally isn't due in five minutes. See ya."

"Bye."

Alex stood, and flew up the stairs. I watched her go with a wistful smirk, the red of her hair all I could make out in the blur of her haste.

Staying and being gawked at wasn't the best move, I knew, but still, I pulled out the drawing of the boy. The more I studied his face, the more it looked like the face I'd seen in the mirror.

What does all of this mean? My existence has been strange for 300 years, but this is a whole new level.

The bell's squeal brought my musings to a halt.

That was quick…

My teeth pressed down on my bottom lip. It was hard to comprehend why, but somehow I knew time was running out for me to discover the truth. My heart thudded with impatience, almost as if it were whispering *hur-ry, hur-ry, hur-ry.*

That's it. I'm getting some answers, consequences be damned.

I shoved the drawing into my backpack. The computer lab seemed the best place to look for answers, so I started there.

THE LAB SAT empty when I crept through the door. Rows of desks, with modern flat-panel monitors, spread across the room. Fluorescent lights crackled overhead.

What am I doing? This is stupid. I'm gonna get detention for skipping class.

Taking my pick of computers, I sat down and pressed the 'on' button. The computer took forever to boot. Our computer at home was much faster, but Mr. Kütz never let me use it alone. He or Mrs. K had to be in the room at all times. He was paranoid some predator would manipulate me and snatch me away.

"Hurry up," I quietly groaned, tapping the monitor. "I don't have time for this."

After an agonizing minute or two, I was finally able to log in. A search engine seemed the logical place to start. My chest tightened and my fingers trembled as I hurriedly began to type.

They'll see what I'm typing and lock me away. I'll have to spend the rest of this life in an asylum, catatonic from all the medications.

It took a few minutes and several deep breaths, but I eventually calmed down enough to resume my search. The first attempt, "reincarnation connection to mental illness," wasn't fruitful. "Reincarnation and hallucinations" didn't seem any better. Eventually I stumbled upon a forum for reincarnation believers. Nothing relevant there, either.

Even typing a vague account of my dilemma didn't turn up a single result.

Am I truly alone?

The light fixture let out a roaring thrum. Its flickering forced me to squint. As my fingers pressed the keys to describe the boy I'd drawn, the entire light fixture, fluorescent tubes and all, came crashing down on top of the monitor with a cacophonous boom.

Screaming, I threw myself out of its path. Shards of glass shattered all around, cutting my arms and face. Blood dripped onto the floor, speckling the white linoleum.

The door flew open. Mr. Hart, one of the biology teachers, rushed in. He knelt next to me after surveying the scene. "Are you all right?"

My eyes darted around the room, hyperaware of everything around me. The rancid musk of Mr. Hart's far-too-potent cologne, the rattling of the windows as the wind crashed against them. "I-I think so…" I trembled.

"The damned electricians need to work on those lights."

He gently helped me to my feet, leading me to the nurse's office. She used too many bandages on my wounds—I ended up looking like a mummy.

Mr. and Mrs. Kütz rushed in twenty minutes later. They filled out some legal documents, then took me home. Dread scratched at the back of my mind while I shuffled out of the car, lagging behind the Kützs.

I just want to do my homework, text Alex, eat dinner, and forget this insanity.

My house keys jangled from my fingers. Mr. and Mrs. Kütz had just barely stepped inside, when footsteps coming from behind startled me. A chill filled the air.

Without even thinking, I knew who I'd find behind me. I just *knew*. Turning around confirmed it.

"Good afternoon," he said with a bow, gracefully sweeping his golden hair away from his eyes as he straightened. He looked like any boy around my physical age, but something behind his flame-brown eyes gave it away: he was someone or some*thing* much older. He wore a crisp, clean black suit with a white undershirt and a blood red tie.

Like it would provide some kind of protection, my shaking hands pressed my backpack to my chest. "What do you want?"

"I need to discuss an important matter with you."

A thought had occurred to me before, at least, on some unconscious level. Now I stood with my heartbeat thrashing in my ears. "Me first." And I dove in, fear behind me now for some reason. "Why do I draw you all the time? How do you show up randomly, then vanish? Couldn't you have told me you wanted to see me, rather than following me home?" These questions all spilled from me in a torrent.

He whispered with a playful grin, "I am not one to warn people of my arrival. They tend to become upset when they know I am coming," as if letting me in on a secret.

I hadn't wanted to face the truth, but now the answer became clear. This innocent-looking boy was Death.

His lips curled into a knowing smirk. "You finally recognize me. I wondered if you ever would."

My knees buckled. "But, you don't look like…"

"Like my form at our first meeting?" He waved his hand, becoming the shadowy figure constantly haunting my memories. With another wave, he became the blond haired, brown-eyed boy again.

Words failed me. Taking a deep breath, I spun and desperately tried to open the door. It was a long shot, but I had to try. It proved useless, however, when I suddenly froze in place. My mind screamed at my arms and legs to try to move, but nothing worked. A panicked squeak passing my lips was the only result.

His expression softened. "I've distressed you unnecessarily. My apologies. At times I take my jokes a tad too far."

A tiny sob escaped, betraying me. "Please…just leave me alone. Haven't I suffered enough? What more could you possibly want from me?"

He looked at me with what I would've interpreted as sympathy, if this were anyone else. How could someone who let me suffer for hundreds of years be anything but a monster? "We must go."

"Go where?" I managed to ask.

No answer.

He grabbed my arm before I could protest.

Darkness overcame me. I floated on the breeze like smoke.

CHAPTER FOUR

AT FIRST, MY heart's thudding was all I could hear. I tried to move, but my limbs felt like they were made of stone. Fighting against my heavy lids, I managed to open my eyes.

Death leaned over me, his brow furrowed with concern. He spoke, but his voice sounded muffled.

Where am I?

Moonlight shone through the red-needled pine trees surrounding us. Every fiber of my being longed to scream, to smack him, *something*, but I remained there in the dark, incapacitated. Moments ticked by before the strange weight lifted.

My legs swayed under me as I pushed myself to my feet. "Where is this?"

"We've gone nowhere in the way you might mean, but further than you can imagine. Welcome to my domain— the Land of the Dead. I will be your guide."

My heart crashed to my stomach. "Am I…?"

"No, you are very much alive."

"Why am I here?"

He extended his hand, like a boy who'd escort you to the dance floor at some sixteenth century ball. "I will explain after you've adjusted."

I eyed him, appraising his impatient expression. Without further choice, my trembling hand slipped into his ice-cold grasp.

He led me to a strangely shaped dark mahogany carriage. At its reins were four living, skeletal horses, their manes and tails smoldering fire. For reasons I couldn't fathom at first, looking at the vehicle made anxiety swirl in my stomach. The horses seemed like an obvious answer, but somehow I knew they weren't the primary source of my unease. After a brief moment spent studying the carriage, it finally clicked—the carriage was shaped like a coffin. The urge to retch was powerful, but not impossible to overcome. The sweat building up on my palms, however, was another story.

I couldn't take my eyes off the contraption in front of me. One of the horses turned its head to gaze at us, and my jaw dropped. For some reason I thought it might blink, but it possessed only black holes in place of eyes. The beast stamped, snorting and edging toward me.

My pulse raced a marathon. At my wide-eyed expression, a throaty chuckle passed Death's lips. "What? Teleporting with another is a new experience for me. I cannot teleport you again so quickly, it could harm you. We must travel somehow, so it may as well be in style."

The horses whinnied when I stepped into the carriage.

A WINDING, NARROW path of coarse stone stretched out between the trees. With a cocky grin, Death snatched the reins and cracked them against the horse's rumps. They burst into a gallop. The force of their unbelievable speed knocked me back against the seat, holding me captive. We rushed through the trees, creating a red blur all around us. A shudder jolted through me as the image of blood ensnared itself in my mind and refused to leave. Closing my eyes for a moment helped enough for my heart to stop panicking. Once out of the woods, we passed endless blocks of identical two-story homes, all dark and silent. It wasn't easy to get a good look at them as we rushed past, but I managed to make out pristine white siding and onyx roofs. Staring at them as long as our speed allowed, I couldn't help but wonder who resided there. Before the question could pass my lips, the houses were far behind us. An empty grassy field lay before us for miles, with a large gray structure looming in the distance. As we drew closer to the building, my jaw fell open. A colossal, intricately built castle came into view.

Blood-red vines twisted up its towers, culminating in patches of freshly bloomed white roses at the highest points. They seemed to glow against night's sky. Gargoyles loomed over us, their stone eyes peering down. Unable to move, I viewed their frozen snarls; each changed to welcoming grins. Anxiety swelled in my gut, intensifying as I stared. Such odd statues. The idea of a gargoyle approaching its victims with a smile unnerved me. Eventually we skidded to a stop about twenty feet from the door.

"Follow me," Death called.

Sweat dampened my palms, causing me to lose my grip on the carriage handle when I exited. Regaining my balance, I took a deep breath to calm myself, but the night air smelled wrong—too floral, too sweet. The scent stirred memories of Mother's flowerbed. She'd spent hours cultivating the perfect garden. I shoved the memories aside.

I can't be distracted. I need to find a way out of this place. The enormous castle doors creaked, opening into a hall, and beyond that the most lavish sitting room I'd ever seen. To my left, fine dark leather couches trimmed in gold sat in front of a fireplace spanning the entire length of the far wall, faced all in smooth marble, which reflected everything in the room like huge mirrors. Golden statues of men in full suits of armor stood poised for battle, holding very large swords. Everything sparkled and shone.

The hallways stretching from this room proved to be equally elaborate once we walked through them.

I paused in front of a painting of a woman holding a white flower. "Wait a minute. I recognize this painting. I've seen it in books. Is this *Portrait of a Courtesan* by

Caravaggio?"

"Yes, it is."

"A fire destroyed it decades ago."

"Correct."

Dumbfounded, my eyes couldn't look away.

"If you're going to gape at every little thing, we are in for a long day." Death gestured toward rows of paintings lining the hall. "These," he said with a flourish, "are mere decorations."

Red chiffon curtains covered each window along the way. Running my fingers over them, they felt very smooth, probably brand new. Glittering chandeliers lit with vibrant flames hung everywhere.

I can't decide if this place is beautiful or ostentatious.

After a while, a thought began to nag at me. While we strolled through a ballroom where diamonds embedded in the walls, I couldn't help but ask. "In such a grand castle, shouldn't there be servants running all over the place?"

"I create servants whenever I need something, then they vanish when their task is done."

Death snapped his fingers. Out of nowhere, a looming figure appeared from a cloud of black smoke. The being's lifeless, wooden appearance reminded me of a store mannequin. Impeccably dressed in an expensive-looking black tuxedo, it gave a precise, stiff bow. With another snap from Death's fingers, the servant vanished.

After it vanished, my gaze turned to Death. His demeanor echoed the easy manner of an aristocrat at home in his country estate, but something in his eyes didn't match his behavior or relaxed body language. I'd seen the same pain in my own expression far too many times.

"See? Easy," he declared.

AFTER EXPLORING THE maze of elegantly decorated rooms together, each one more lavish than the last, we stopped in front of a pair of glass doors with white roses painted on them. They swung open to reveal a stone ramp spiraling down to the ground outdoors. Vines snaked up the wall. Massive trees towered above, their red berries dangling overhead.

I cautiously walked down the ramp, then stared ahead in wonder once I reached the bottom. A garden of unnaturally lush fruits and vegetables sprawled out before us. Brightly colored flowers of every imaginable shade shimmered vibrantly around the perimeter of the garden. A sudden chill shook me, making me rub my arms. Something felt…wrong. It took me a moment to figure it out, but it eventually fell into place. The garden sat in complete silence. The buzzing of insects and the trilling of birds were nowhere to be heard. Where were they? Did Death not make any?

Death watched me, expectantly. "Do you like it? I constructed this last night."

I balked. "This is all for *me*?"

He frowned in confusion. "Mortals require food, do they not?"

"It's a little much, don't you think?"

He shrugged. "I found it to be an entertaining diversion from my day-to-day responsibilities. Besides, what good is something if it cannot be taken to excess?"

I shuddered. "That sort of attitude brings people to you before their time."

"Everyone dies. Some sooner than others."

Unable to reply, I took a slow, shaky breath.

Glancing over his shoulder, Death brushed a speck of dust from his jacket. "I believe dinner is ready. Follow me."

WE SAT IN a room rivaling the size of the school gym, at a table so large it could sit an army. Mannequin-like servants shoved mammoth-sized helpings of vegetable stew and fruit salad in front of me. The heavenly aroma of the dishes caressed my nostrils. The food appeared absolutely perfect, but I couldn't bring myself to take a single bite.

I'm not falling for his tricks.

Arms folded, I hunched over the table, staring across at him. "Tell me why you've done all this."

He laced his fingers, shrugging. "Because I require

your assistance.”

“Why should I listen to a word you say?”

A condescending smirk. “I did you a favor long ago, if you remember. Is asking for one in return such an imposition?”

Leaning back in the chair, I let out a dark chuckle. “Do I really owe you anything after what you did for said ‘favor’? All I wanted was to help my sister, and what I got in exchange was centuries of misery.”

He picked up a glass, cocking his head to the side as he swirled his wine. “You think you have any choice but to at least listen to my request?”

“Okay, fine. What do you want?” I asked, shoving the food away.

“This is a complex issue, but I will try to explain. The spirits of mortals come here after they expire. Once they’ve accepted their fate, they *move on.* I do not know where they go, but at some point, every spirit *needs* to go elsewhere. It’s the natural order of things. The living are living, the dead are dead. They each have their own worlds, their own realities. These two realms do not, and *should* not, intermingle. There is a delicate balance between life and death. For every soul born, another dies. The numbers are always in perfect harmony. Unfortunately, a group of spirits desires to unravel that harmony.”

He leaned forward, raking his fingers through his hair with an irritable grunt. *These guys really have gotten under his skin.* "Some of them are longtime nuisances," Death admitted, "while others are new thorns in my side. If they continue much longer, I will be forced to resort to drastic measures. I would prefer not to. Despite what some may believe, I do not *wish* to be a tyrant. Violently dealing with this issue would further sully my already disastrous reputation. Which is why you are here." He gestured to me, casually reclining in his chair. *So that was the deal.* "You understand mortals—at least, I hope you do," he continued. "After all this time. I want you to convince this group to *move on*. Once they are persuaded, you may return from whence you came."

My eyebrow perked up. "Couldn't you just ask another spirit who's not part of the group to do it?"

"I've made attempts, but everyone I approached denied me. For whatever reason, they firmly place the blame with me for their demises. Therefore, they do not exactly hold me in high esteem."

"Imagine that." I let my voice do the damage I wanted to inflict.

Death slammed both hands on the table, snapping upright. "Do *not* mock me!"

A cold gust of air whooshed around our seats, making the candles in the chandelier above us flicker. The delicate china on the table shook. We sat in silence for a moment. My fingernails dug into the ornate wood carvings on my chair. My heart raced like hummingbird's wings.

Sitting again, Death's expression relaxed. "Now, where

were we? Ah, yes. You agreed to help me with my problem before those heathens throw the balance of life and death out of sync."

My palms went clammy at the veiled threat. "C-can't you just bring them back if they make it out?" I managed to stammer.

Pursing his lips, he considered this. "I suppose that I could, but unfortunately the damage would already be done." He produced a small black notebook. "Think of it as tearing a page out of a book." Opening the front cover, he callously ripped a page out and cast it aside. "While it is true that you can use an adhesive to hold it in its original position, it will never again sit perfectly where it was. A structural flaw will always exist."

"I suppose that makes sense…"

He stood, brushing dust from his pants. "Shall I show you to your room?"

Nodding, I slowly pushed away from the table.

WHEN WE REACHED my bedroom, it looked elegant beyond my wildest dreams. Against the far wall stood a bed worthy of a queen. Its red satin sheets and exquisite cherry wood frame pleaded for use. A golden vanity table sat in the far corner next to a window, its mirror reflecting my tense posture.

Anxiety tugged at my voice. "Another accommodation?"

"Yes. None of us require sleep. Though the

circumstances are not ideal, and your opinion of me is not high, I do want you to be comfortable here."

"Thanks," I mumbled.

"The closet, over there, is fully stocked." Death pointed to his left. "I hope everything fits."

"Right."

"I will leave you now. Other matters demand my attention." With a quick burst of cold air, he vanished.

The reality of the situation fully sank in. Homesickness stabbed at my heart.

Does anyone even know I'm missing? The Kützes are probably frantic. I need to get home. Fast. God, I wish Isabel or Alex were here. They'd keep me sane through this.

Sighing, I shuffled to the closet.

May as well dress for bed.

Row after row of gaudy gowns hung on either side—a frilly horror story. Sliding into an inoffensive lacy nightgown, I paced the room aiming to come up with a plan. When that proved futile, I climbed into bed, frustration weighing me down.

I tried pushing everything in my mind aside so sleep would come, but no such luck.

There's no choice but to go along with his scheme. Without Death, I'm stuck here.

The unfamiliar mattress, intended to offer comfort, did nothing but stab my spine. The cushy down pillow felt too soft, the silk covers too heavy. The irony of the situation wasn't lost on me as I tossed and turned for hours.

I'm the only one here who sleeps, and I can't. I'd laugh if I weren't so exhausted.

A painful twinge grated at my back when I pushed out from the covers and stood. Yet another thing I missed about my Idaho home—the luxurious comfort of my own bed. Tears stung my eyes—I refused to let them fall. He wouldn't get the satisfaction of seeing me weep.

Stumbling around in the shadowy room, I plopped down at the vanity table. Already, dark circles rimmed my eyes. Incriminating red splotches dotted my face. In the moonlight, my eyes glistened an unsettling silver. I cringed.

Fantastic. I look worse than I feel.

It felt stupid to fret over my looks, but my restless mind begged for some form of comforting normalcy. A sparkling, jewel-encrusted hairbrush seemed a good place to start. I began to rake it through the nest on my head. It only succeeded in making things worse.

I should've known better.

Without warning, a black shape appeared behind my reflection, the face obscured by a dark hood.

Before I could react, it reached out to grab me. Yelping, I attempted to struggle, knocking us both to the floor. The figure fell on top of me. My chest rattled with a strained grunt at the weight. The burden made breathing nearly impossible, so screaming for help wasn't going to happen. Trying to shove the assailant away proved useless;

their knees pressed down on my arms. My legs kicked while tears rolled down my cheeks.

The attacker lifted a bottle of thick purple liquid from a bag hanging over his shoulder. One free hand reached down to pinch my nose, successfully blocking my air. My head jerked back and forth trying to get free. Breath refused to stay contained any longer. Gasping for air, my mouth flew open. The liquid snaked its way down my throat.

My cries faded. A guilty pair of blue eyes stared into mine before the world fell away in a wave of blackness.

CHAPTER FIVE

T HE CRACKLE OF a fire woke me. Smoke stung my eyes. I attempted to rub them, but rope held my hands captive behind my back. It scratched at my wrists, holding me tight. Whispers buzzed around me. Was it a campfire? I couldn't tell through my blurred vision. A tree blocked my view of my surroundings. Closing my eyes again, I continued to feign unconsciousness so I could eavesdrop.

"This is stupid, Pete. We can't trust her. She's a Breather in the Land of the Dead, for one, and was in *his* castle, for two," a woman hissed.

A younger man responded. "She's a tool we can use to get to him. If we can get her on our side, maybe she can make him listen."

"He hasn't paid attention to us, so why the hell would he listen to her?"

"Look at her—she's breathing. I checked her pulse

earlier. She's got one. You saw his garden, Emily. Why would he build one when no one in this hellhole eats? If he went through the trouble of making that for her, then this girl must be important."

"She could compromise everything."

Ending the pretense, I moaned, struggling to sit up.

A boy who appeared about my physical age knelt in front of me. A thick mass of jet-black curls lay on his head, blended in with the shadows around us. The woman's auburn hair was slung into a ponytail. Her thin lips were pursed in agitation. Dimples imprinted the boy's rounded cheeks. A grey T-shirt firmly hugged his torso, highlighting his physical fitness. The switchblade in his hand shone in the campfire light. His blue eyes met mine.

My ears rang from fear. *The guy who kidnapped me!* Suddenly, a deep gash formed on his forehead. Blood trickled down his face. He tried to speak, but it was pointless—all he could manage was a gagging cough as water spilled from his mouth. Using my legs to push back, I scooted away. "Get away from me! What the hell are you?"

As quickly as they'd appeared, the wounds vanished. He set his blade on the ground, holding his hands in gesture of surrender, a reassuring smile on his face. "Relax. I'm not going to hurt you."

"How did you do that with your face? It was …"

He jerked back ever so slightly, brow raised. "Huh?" He shook off my comment, continuing. "Look, you're scared and in shock. I promise, you're safe here."

I don't feel like I'm in shock, but then again, would I even know if I was?

"Real cute, coming from the guy who force-fed me God knows what, dragging me to God knows where."

He flinched. "I'm really sorry, but I didn't think you'd come with me if I asked."

"You're right."

"Don't think you need to worry about the purple stuff I used. It's something we whipped up using various plants around here. Helps get us out of sticky situations. It's perfectly harmless once you're awake. Weren't sure if it would work the same on someone like you, but it seems like it does." He picked up the switchblade again, inching closer.

Frantic, I swung my legs to keep him away. "No! Somebody, help me," my voice yelled. Cracking.

"Shut her up. They're going to hear!" the woman, *Emily?* ordered in a serious voice.

"Please," he whispered, "quiet down." His eyes widened with his plea.

Legs still pumping, I struggled to escape. "Don't hurt me," I cried. "Please! I know martial arts. I'm warning you—if you try to hurt me..."

He grabbed my arm.

I shut my eyes tightly and prepared for the worst, but instead heard the sound of rope being cut. Hesitant, I let myself look. He closed the blade and slid it into the front pocket of his jeans. "See? I told you I wasn't going to hurt you. What's your name?"

"You've kidnapped me, scared the hell out of me, now you want my name?"

He rubbed his neck. "Yeah, probably not very smart of me. But I *do* want to know. You're the first living person to be brought here. We're curious, Death doesn't normally change things this drastically. Personally, I'd like to know the girl causing all the fuss."

Pursing my lips, I paused before answering. "My name's Heather. Heather Kütz."

"Pete Bronx. This lovely ray of sunshine is Emily." He gestured to a twig of a woman nearby. A glare soured her face. She stomped away without a word.

Pete watched her disappear into the shadows of the surrounding trees, then turned back. His pinched expression softened. "Don't mind her. Emily isn't really a fan of strangers."

Rising, I assessed my surroundings. A campfire burned in the center of a circle of modest two-person tents. The now-familiar red pine woods engulfed us. In the darkness beyond the fire's glow, I swore several pairs of eyes watched the two of us.

I nodded toward the tents, a brow raised. "Nobody here needs sleep. What's with the tents?"

"Nights get cold. Wouldn't *you* want somewhere warm to relax after a long day?"

"Why not use the houses I saw, instead?"

A dark intensity burned in his eyes. His hand tightened into a fist. "And just be little sheep, blindly doing what *he* wants? No thanks," he grumbled.

"Not a fan of Mr. Head Honcho?"

He gave a droll chuckle. "Guess it's pretty obvious."

"I'm not really his biggest fan either." *That's putting it mildly.*

Pete turned, looking over his shoulder. He called, "She's all right, come on out, guys."

"Are you sure? Emily said that'd give away our numbers," a deep voice responded.

"It's fine," Pete replied. "I'm sure Death already has some idea of how many we've got, so it won't matter if she tells him."

Nearly a dozen people crept out from behind trees.

Uncomfortable with the sudden crowd, I lowered my head. "Um… hi."

With a quick glance to my side, a tiny girl with flowing blonde locks peeked out from behind one of the adults. A large, clear jewel hung around her neck on a silver chain. "You aren't with the bad man, are you?" she asked, approaching carefully.

Kneeling to her level, I held out both hands. "No, I'm not."

A grin spread across her face. "Good. My name's Lily."

"I'm Heather."

Splotchy bruises began to grow all over Lily's body. They started on her arms, working their way up to her chest. A mark in the shape of a handprint emerged on her cheek. Her tiny eyes began to swell shut.

My stomach turned in horror. All I could do was gasp. Before I could ask who had hurt her, the markings of some unfathomable cruelty vanished. A middle-aged woman in a vibrant tie-dyed shirt shifted in front of Lily, pushing her from my line of sight. "Stay away from her."

I knelt for the longest moment, unable to do anything but stare at the woman. Why wasn't anyone else saying something about what had happened to Lily? Rising, I said, "*I'm* not about to hurt anybody."

Emily interjected, folding her arms across her chest. "Please. For all we know you're just biding your time until Death comes for you." Her ponytail smacked her shoulders as she shook her head in disapproval. A murmur of agreement spread throughout the group, while the woman carefully pushed Lily into a tent.

This Emily seems to be stirring the rest of them up. My fingernails bit into my palms. "If you're so wary of me, why did you bring me here?"

A pudgy man with thinning red hair spoke up, jabbing a finger accusingly in Pete's direction. "It wasn't our idea. Pete thought of it."

Pete snapped, "Oh, can it, Jack. When I brought it up before, you liked the idea."

Kicking a loose piece of bark, I interrupted their exchange. "Look, I don't even want to be in this crazy place. I just want to go back to the living world, where I belong."

Pete's attention turned to me. "We're after the same thing. All of us feel cheated. We want a second chance. Some of us haven't been dead that long; we can resume our old lives if given the chance. Others have been dead longer, so they'd just find a new home and live out the years they would've had. If we can prove it's possible, hopefully others who feel the same way will want to do it too."

An elderly man, dressed in attire taken straight from *The Three Musketeers*, threw up a fist in agreement. "Hear, hear."

Perhaps foolishly, I found myself nodding. There were worse things to believe in.

Pete shifted his weight. "I don't think it's too much to ask, but Death disagrees. So many spirits have tried to talk to him about it over the years, but it never works. He says it'd throw off an important balance or something."

"Well, wouldn't it?" My voice rose with curiosity.

"Who knows? He won't fully explain it to anyone. Once he goes through his spiel, he says 'that should be enough to understand the situation' and leaves it at that. But if the rumors are true, he's full of it."

"What rumors?"

There was a hum of voices, then Emily sneered. "It's just a stupid fairytale."

Pete ran his fingers through his hair. "You're *here*. Are you telling me you still don't believe in unexplainable things?"

"No, I don't. Not this bullshit story."

"Whatever, Emily." Pete's eyes met mine. "There's this legend that's been around so long no one remembers where it started anymore. It's about a girl who somehow outsmarted Death. To reward her for her cleverness, he bestowed a gift: she'll never truly die. Whenever her time comes, she's just born into a new life."

That's not how it happened. The urge to tell the truth scraped at my throat, but I pushed that down. *Don't trust them.*

I kept my eyes down. "She's right. Sounds like a load of bull."

Pete shrugged. "Maybe it is, but isn't it still worth looking into?"

"I think it would be more worthwhile searching for real clues, rather than chasing rumors," I said.

"What else is there? We haven't exactly got many leads."

"Do you have *anything* to go on?"

He rubbed his forehead with a grunt. "Scraps of information. Rumors. Coals stop us on every intel hunt we go on, which doesn't help."

My head tilted at this. "Coals?"

"Our nickname for Mr. High and Mighty's armored soldiers. Their armor is black, so we call them Coals."

Ah. Despite myself, a chuckle rumbled my chest. "How clever."

"You think so?"

"Rolls off the tongue easier than *creepy armored dudes.*"

Pete's raven curls shook when he snickered. "Yeah, it does."

"What do you mean by 'intel'? Are you this world's FBI or something?"

He snickered. "Nothing like that. We go out and find out what we can. Ask trusted spirits what they've heard. Where Coals are patrolling, anything they've been overheard saying, whether Death's been seen outside his castle and why. That kind of stuff."

"Oh. Makes sense, I guess. So… what now?"

"Well, you can't be comfortable standing around in a nightgown. We've got clothes if you want to change into something else. If anything fits, you're welcome to it."

"Where'd you get them?"

He flinched, "Our group was a lot larger once…" The pain of some memory rippled across his face and the others surrounding me.

"What happened?"

"Coals got 'em, mostly."

My eyebrows squished together. "But you're all dead. How can you die again?"

"Don't know. If one of us gets injured badly enough, they disappear."

I reached to touch his shoulder, but thought better of it, drawing my hand back. "I'm sorry."

"It's not your fault. They gave it everything, but Coals are relentless."

"Remind me to never mess with one." At the thought of it, coldness plunged into my stomach.

"If you get that close, it's too late."

Anxiety made the nape of my neck itch. "How comforting."

"Just giving you the facts. War isn't pretty."

"I know." The horrors of two World Wars flashed through my mind.

Pete coughed, staring at the ground. "The clothes tent is over there." Without glancing in my direction, he gestured to the far edge of the circle.

Nodding, aware of the entire group watching every step, that's where I headed. As I sifted through the piles, I found most of the items were men's, and would fit my minuscule frame like old elephant skin on an ant. Eventually, I donned a tank top, flannel shirt, jeans, and boots close to my size.

Much better.

Outside, many of their stares remained fixed on me. Slinking to an isolated spot about fifteen feet from the campfire, I plopped onto the ground. Alone, I gazed at the fire until it was reduced to embers. In the near darkness, Lily crept to my place, a blanket in her outstretched arms.

"Are you cold?" she asked, her tiny voice a whisper.

"A little."

"Here, we've got plenty of blankets."

All I had for her in return was a grateful smile, which I doubted she could see. Her blanket instantly warmed me when slipped around my shoulders. "Thank you."

"You're welcome."

Before I could speak again, the woman in the tied-dyed shirt's voice shouted, "Lily, you get back here!"

"Is she your mom?" I asked.

"No, that's Tina. But she takes care of me." She turned toward Tina's voice, then skipped back to her tent.

I smiled at her thoughtfulness. Maybe I'd made one friend.

Moments later, Pete approached from across the circle of tents, stretching his arms above his head. "Lily's a handful, isn't she?" he said, warm fondness in his voice.

A smirk threatened to break through. "She's a cute kid." Suddenly, the unwelcome image of her being cornered by a Coal popped into my head. My smile vanished. "I'm not sure how logical it is to keep her around all this, though."

"You're right. We found her and Tina together a while ago. I told Tina she should take Lily to the houses, let someone else take care of her, but she wouldn't do it."

There's no telling what's out there... My gaze swept over the campground, the shadowed forest surrounding us. "Is she really safe here?"

"Each of us does our best keeping her out of harm's way. So far, it looks like the Coals don't even know about her."

"Good. Keep it that way."

"Why so protective?" he asked. "You've just met her,"

My heart clenched. "She…reminds me of someone I lost."

"Your sister?"

I froze. *Am I that transparent?* "How'd you know?"

With a shrug he said, "You look a bit young to be a mother to someone Lily's age."

A smile came, but fell quickly. "True. I had a sister. She died a long time ago." Tears stung. I blinked to keep them from falling.

Pete took a deep, pained breath, closing his eyes. "I'm sorry. Have you tried looking for her here?"

The thought had crossed my mind, but I knew it was futile. "No. She's probably *moved on* already."

"How awful."

"Is *moving on* a bad thing?"

He leaned against a tree with a weary sigh. "Nobody knows. It might be a wonderful paradise with harps and everything. Or a horrific dimension where your nightmares come to life. Or it could simply be non-existence."

I couldn't help but shake my head, wistful. "Even post-mortem we don't get all the answers? How funny."

Humorlessly, he pointed out, "In a way, it kind of is. Anyway, are you hungry? I'm about to raid the castle to get food for you."

"Are you daft?"

"You need to eat. Most of the group may be suspicious of you still, but I'm not going to let you starve."

I shook my head. "I don't understand. Why take such a huge chance?"

He smiled. "We aren't soulless, like Death." A glint of playfulness lit in his eyes. "Emily, maybe, but the rest of us care."

My hand shot over my mouth to hide my smile. "You really think you can get food for me?"

Nonchalant, Pete shrugged. "I ran track in school. Those stupid Coals can't even touch me."

"Sports isn't a friend of mine. I'm not *entirely* uncoordinated, but I wouldn't exactly call myself *graceful*."

In faux disappointment, came a frown. "Damn. Well, there goes the obstacle course we'd planned."

I threw my head back; out flew a laughing bray. The tension I'd been holding in for the past day or so was finally beginning to seep out of me. "I'd actually pay to see me try."

"It'd be better than a sitcom, I bet." He grinned and I pushed my hair out of my face.

"Oh, it would. Trust me." Wrapping the flannel blanket tighter, I continued. "Thanks for the laugh. I needed it," I hesitated for a moment before adding, "I really appreciate the risk you're taking here."

"No worries. Rest up and I'll be back soon."

With that, he walked back across the campsite and ducked into his tent.

I stayed put, keeping my head down to shield myself from the stares of the others in the group. *If I wanted to be stared at, I could've gone to school. At least then Alex would be with me…*

I hoped Pete returned early. But only darkness loomed in the shadowed pine trees, whose shapes shot up like arrows towards the sky.

CHAPTER SIX

THANKFULLY, PETE DID return to camp unharmed, carrying a woven basket filled with food. Lily came barreling towards him as he set the basket down by his tent. I couldn't help but smile at the scene as he caught her up and spun her high. These weren't the dangerous heathens Death made them out to be. They were only spirits who wanted to reshuffle the deck. I could relate.

Hoping to ease the tension, I tentatively approached the campfire.

Emily stopped sharpening her machete. The hateful gaze she shot me could've easily melted any Alaskan glacier. When I didn't turn away, she blew out a gruff breath, then marched to her tent, plopping on the dirt in front to resume her work, mumbling obscenities all the while.

Turning to the group, I asked loudly, "Is she normally so rude, or am I just special?"

Everyone except Pete and Lily ignored me.

I raised an eyebrow, sniffing myself. "Do I offend?" Lily's giggling echoed through the trees.

Pete cracked a grin, but soon his expression grew serious. "You need to understand the big risk it is, bringing you here."

"If I'm too much trouble, send me back."

He dragged a long, flat stone across the space, positioning it over the edge of the fire—a makeshift skillet. "If problems come up, we'll take care of them."

When the stone burned hot, he sprinkled a handful of minced vegetables onto it, pushing them though the heat. Everyone else watched in silence, their expressions curious, yet still wary. Being stared at wasn't a new thing, but the intensity of their interest was becoming a little much. Trying to make myself look as small as possible, I slumped my shoulders. *It always worked in school…*

He scooped this concoction into a wicker bowl and held it out to me. "Here you go. Pete's vague memory of Food Network recipes à la king."

Graciously accepting the bowl, I took a bite once the food was cool enough to eat with my hands.

Pete leaned forward, watching me with fascination, and, as I noticed, so did everyone else. Edging to the other side of the log, awkwardness flamed at my cheeks. "Yeah, this isn't creepy at all…"

Pete coughed, turning away for a moment. "Sorry. Between not needing to eat and there not being any real food here until now, we barely remember what food tastes like. Living vicariously, I guess."

"It's still a little weird, but I think I understand. Do you want to try some?"

He gazed down at the food, staring at it like it was a precious jewel. "Sure."

I held out the bowl. "Here you go."

"Thanks." He graciously took a couple carrots and popped them in his mouth. After a few seconds of chewing, he grimaced with a shudder and spat them out. "Eugh…tastes like ash." Quiet mummers of disappointment rolled through the crowd. A deep sigh rumbled from Pete's chest. His eyes watered ever-so-slightly. "I really liked carrots…"

"I'm sorry."

He held up his hands to pacify me. "Don't worry about it. It's not your fault. It sucks, sure, but it just gives me more reason to want to go back."

"That's a good way to look at it, I guess," I said while Pete lowered his gaze to the fire, then I asked, "So, what happens now?"

"Whatever you want. Just stay close to the camp."

My mouth tightened into a straight line. "Am I a prisoner?"

"Not in the slightest," He balked. "Staying close is just for safety, that's all. Coals patrol these woods. I doubt you want to run into them. We don't know what they'll do if they spot you. Death could've decided you aren't useful anymore and commanded them to kill you on sight. And this is the longest we've ever stayed in one place without getting spotted. I'd like to keep that going as long as I can."

"I'm stuck here forever?"

Waving a dismissive hand, he tossed a stick into the fire. "Nah. Nobody's forcing you to do anything." He scratched his head. "But…"

"But?"

"I know we've just met, and you probably still think I'm an ass," at this his eyebrows knitted together. "But do you think you could do us all a favor?"

My heartbeat picked up speed. "What?"

"After you've calmed down from the…er… kidnapping, would you be willing to hear our side of this? Maybe you can convince Death to help us go back to the living world."

My throat clamped shut. "I don't think he'll listen to me."

"I won't ask you to decide right now, but you might be the only one who can get through to him." Pete asked, "Would you consider it, at least?"

My teeth clamped on the inside of my cheek. This wasn't a decision I wanted to make. While I wasn't a member of Death's fan club by any means, he held the key to *my* return to the living world. Betray him, and my chances of going home would vanish. He'd consider it crossing a line I could never uncross. After that display he made during dinner, angering Death hardly sounded appealing. On the other hand, I couldn't help but feel sympathy for these people. Most of them were so young. I'd sacrificed everything for someone else a long time ago—would I do it again? Should I?

Raking my fingers through my knotted hair, I told him, "I'll think about it, but don't rush me. Okay?"

"Of course. Take your time." Pete looked over at the others still watching me eat. "We're gonna do a recon of the castle while it's still dark. You're welcome to join, or you can stay here."

I rubbed at my sore wrists. "Think I've reached my excitement quota for today. I might try to sleep."

"All right. Just try to keep an ear out for trouble, if you can. We aren't going far, so getting here fast won't be hard."

I frowned at Pete. How could I stay alert while sleeping? "Okay. I'll try."

Pete stood and moved to join Emily, Jack, and the elderly man, now gathering several yards away—roughly a third of the camp. With a barked command they moved out, disappearing into the darkness.

Slumping, I sighed. Alone again. Undergrowth snapped with every step to my tent. I crawled inside. A pile of quilted blankets and pillows covered the canvas floor. After zipping up the tent flap, I collapsed on the bedding. Consciousness fell away.

I WOKE THE next morning drenched in sweat with a pillow clamped between my arms and my heart hammering under it.

Fantastic…my nightmares are getting worse.

For the briefest moment, I forgot where I was and considered calling Mrs. Kütz for comfort, but then I remembered: she wasn't there. I was in a world of strangers, unsure who to trust.

Before I was fully alert, my tent shook. A violent cacophony of shouts and howls seemed to surround me. Cowering under my blankets, I screamed.

The horrendous sounds transformed into peals of laughter. Wringing my hands, I cautiously eased my way out of the tent. The sky was still black, although a faint line of sunlight crept up the horizon.

Outside my tent stood a pair of fully-grown dark-skinned identical twins and a young Asian boy, who looked about fifteen. The twins were laughing their asses off until they noticed my furious scowl.

"Time to bail," one twin said to the other. "Have fun, Jeremy," he shouted over his shoulder in a deep baritone. The twins disappeared into the shadows, snickering.

"MaghwI'," the remaining boy muttered to himself before facing me. *Was that Klingon?* "So, um, hi. I'm Jeremy."

He held out his hand, so I shook it while trying to smooth my unruly hair at the same time. "Heather, but you probably already knew."

Jeremy pushed at his thick glasses, which covered most of his face. "Yeah. Sorry for scaring you. I was shanghaied. It was the twins' idea. Wouldn't have gone along with it if they weren't so…" he bit his lip.

Waving dismissively, I smiled. "Hey, no blood, no foul. I'm used to being messed with. It's no big deal."

"Thanks." His eyes shifted while he stuffed his hands into his pockets. "For once it would be nice to be on the *other* side of one of their jokes. Thought bullying would stop when I died, but apparently not," he grumbled.

After he'd left, I zipped the tent flap closed and moved to the smoldering fire in the center of the campsite, I took a seat. Whomever had cut these logs hadn't done it carefully—one of the edges jutted outwards, while the other curved in. It was the furthest thing from comfortable I could possibly think of, too. No one had smoothed it to make it bearable to sit on. A loose piece of bark kept jabbing me in the hip, so I twisted it free and threw it onto the fire. A couple I recognized from the night before glanced in my direction, sitting on the log furthest from mine. They kept their distance, watching my every movement.

What am I, some vicious animal about to pounce?

"For God's sake," I snapped. "I'm not an alien, or monster, and I'm certainly not a leper. Stop acting like I am." They flinched, scooting closer to each other.

The boy, a hulking brute with a brown buzz cut shifted uncomfortably, rubbing the arm of his letterman jacket. "To be honest, you scare the hell out of us. You're alive. It makes no sense for you to be here. And it's obvious you were in *his* castle for a reason."

My hand squeezed into a fist. "I don't want anything to do with Death."

The girl, a tall, lanky thing, awkwardly twisted the ends of her dirty blonde hair. "How do we know you aren't lying? You could, like, be a *spy*."

"You don't, but do I really look like some sort of evil mastermind?" I chuckled, hoping it might calm them.

She pondered this for a moment. "Well, no. But looks can be deceiving."

"She's right." He nodded.

I sighed. "Why not get to know me? *Then* make judgments about my character? I'll start. My name is Heather Kütz. What's yours?"

"I'm Nathan," he mumbled, suspicion lingering in his eyes.

Warily, a reluctant, "I'm Kate," came from her.

My lips curled—a friendly smile. "See? Easy. You don't *have* to like me, but I'd rather be defined by my actions. Not by my pulse."

Nathan shrugged. "That's fair. But don't expect us to change in a snap."

"Fine with me. It would be creepy if you did."

Kate coughed. Her gaze shifted around the area, looking for an escape. "So, um, we've got some things to do."

Nathan stood, taking her hand. "You're right. We need to go."

Wanting to end things on a positive note, I half-heartedly waved. Soon after the couple disappeared, Pete arrived. His brow furrowed as he spotted me. "Are you okay? You're pale as a sheet."

A shiver charged through me. Rubbing my arms didn't help at all. "Yeah. Bad dream, then I got pranked. Not to mention all the staring."

Pete illuminated, "The pranksters are probably Shaun and Greg. Sorry about them. I swear to God…" He shook his head disapprovingly. "It's like they're twelve-year-olds in twenty-year-old bodies."

"Thanks, but why do you care if I'm upset? For all you know I could blow the whistle any minute and Death will be here to wipe all you guys out."

He nodded, looking me in the eye. "True, but that doesn't instantly change me into an uncaring ass."

I chuckled, tucking some hair behind my ears. "I appreciate it. Honestly."

"I'd feel pretty shitty if I did anything less."

I let my eyes wander to the ground. In all my years I'd seen far too many heartless people ignoring the cries of those in need. From the Dickensian-like urchins of old, to the homeless veterans of the Iraq War who I saw almost every day by the Wal-Mart back in Idaho Falls. "I don't know many who'd say the same."

"I'm not *many people*."

"You definitely aren't. It's refreshing," I turned to face him again, looking him up and down. My cheeks burned.

He kicked a rock. Quiet rumbling echoed in the distance—an approaching storm? "Ahem. So, our mission wasn't a great success last night. We didn't discover much information."

I offered a frown. "That sucks."

"Yeah, but what're you going to do? Sometimes you win, sometimes you don't."

Pushing stones around with my feet, I assured him, "Believe me, Pete. I know."

He raked a hand over his face. "We'll find something soon. It's bound to happen eventually."

"What if there isn't a way back? What if your only choice is to *move on*?"

"If there's only one option, why's Death being so persistent?"

Leaning on my knees, I thought on that. "I don't know. It's not like he's upfront about his reasons. For *anything*." The strange pounding sound grew louder, drawing nearer. My gaze turned upward, to the bright, sunshine-filled sky above us. "I didn't think there'd be days and nights here. Bit of a mind-screw when I woke up."

Shaking his head, he chuckled ever so slightly. "That's *him* trying to make us 'more comfortable,' so maybe we'll be too complacent to cause trouble, and hopefully *move on* faster."

A deep sigh escaped from my chest. "Always an ulterior motive."

Suddenly, the sound was close enough that I could recognize it. That was no storm. Thunderous hoof beats shook the ground. The color drained from Pete's face. "They found us."

Four imposing figures, astride their fearsome mounts dressed in matching midnight suits of armor that seemed to extinguish the light around them, charged into camp. Their helmets were long and sharp. Six jagged points jutted from atop each head, like hideous crowns. The way their eye and nose holes slanted brought to my mind a skull. My breath puffed out colder, as their approach brought a scent of dread to the space around us.

Spikes, in rows of three, curved out wickedly; covering their broad shoulders. Simply looking at them made me feel the sharpness of their cut across my torso. I shivered.

Pete and a few of the others raised their weapons, taking aim.

The Coal at the head of the cluster, presumably their leader, bellowed in a gruff voice and held up a hand, "Give us the girl, and you will be spared."

Pete stared the armored figures down, a dark expression on his face. "You freaks will just stab us in the back once she's gone."

"We give our word. There will be no betrayal."

"I'm having a hard time believing that," Pete scoffed.

Both sides readied their weapons, save the two Coals

holding torches.

Stepping between the two groups, beads of sweat rolled down my neck. "Don't fight. I'm here. I'll go willingly. Just leave these people alone."

Pete's face froze. "What are you doing?"

My knees trembled. I paid them no heed. "I'm keeping you all from being slaughtered."

Across the fire I saw Emily glance at Pete for a moment, before returning her gaze to the Coals, her lips curling in a self-assured smirk. "See, I told you." She called, "She's running back to Death at the first opportunity. Shoot her."

"Hold your fire," Pete responded, holding his arm out in front of her. "You know we can't take on that many Coals at once. Not without losing people."

Hanging my head, I climbed on a horse, sitting behind a Coal, cringing when he let out a *harrumph* of satisfaction. I took one last apologetic look at the people before the riders left. In their eyes, all I read was that I'd just betrayed them.

The Coal who sat in front of me gestured to the camp behind us, commanding, "Burn it."

"*No!*" Holding my hand out like I could stop what was coming, a primal scream escaped me.

The other Coals turned. "Yes, sir."

In synchronized formation, the horses galloped back to the camp at full speed. Soon the tents were ablaze. The rapidly spreading flame lit the woods.

Trying to slide off the horse was useless. The Coal grabbed me midair, shoving me back behind him while kicking his mount into a gallop. As we sped away, my cries fell on deaf ears.

CHAPTER SEVEN

AFTER AT LEAST two hours and God knows how many miles of hard riding, we reached the castle. I'd long since given up on struggling. A Coal slung me over his shoulder and carried me inside without a word. Once we'd reached the main foyer, it tossed me at Death's feet.

He knelt by my side. Was that relief in his eyes? "You weren't easy to find. My soldiers scoured the woods from the moment you vanished. I will say this of those rabble-rousers… they certainly understand how to be covert. Remaining almost silent at night, constantly relocating their camp, staying in places my soldiers would not think to check." He offered his hand to help me up. "Are you well? If they molested you in any way…"

Ignoring his assistance, I pushed myself to my feet. "No, they haven't harmed me. I'm fine. Now, if you'll excuse me, I want to be alone."

He sighed, pinching the bridge of his nose. "As you

wish."

The Coals stood at attention, saluting their master before marching down a hallway and out of sight. Death took one last glance before allowing me to walk up to the second floor.

Wandering through the castle, I tried to clear my mind. Not looking back at Death.

My sense of time disappeared for a while, but once I'd calmed down, something odd caught my eye. Everything about the castle remained inhumanly beautiful, but nothing appeared immaculately tidy like before. The walls didn't glisten as brightly; smudges of dirt blemished them in various places. The statues seemed less polished—my reflection in them cloudy, rather than gleaming. Specks of dust lined shelves and painting frames.

Why did he neglect his cleaning like this? How'd it get so dirty in only a few hours? Was he...actually worried about me? No, it must be something else.

My aimless meandering eventually brought me to two immense wooden doors with an intricate forest scene carved into them. On the artwork, two wolves rested on a cliff high above a waterfall, a thick forest of trees below them. A disturbing shudder rattled my bones. Their lifeless wooden eyes stared at me. Curiosity outweighing my trepidation, I opened the door.

It was the most expansive library I'd ever seen. Hundreds of bookshelves stretched higher than I could crane my neck to see, filled to capacity.

Does he own a copy of every book ever published?

Scouring the texts, my hunger for knowledge roared. Darting from one shelf to another, I thrilled at every supposedly 'lost' text hidden within the shelves. Novels that historians would kill to get their hands on. Books of poetry, historical biographies, even modern fare could be found. A snicker came out despite my best efforts as I spotted the familiar covers of a popular vampire romance series. Death hardly seemed the type to be a fan of that genre, but he didn't exactly disclose much about himself. I skidded to a stop in front of a leather-bound book with gold detailing. The urge to own it scraped and clawed at my mind. I snatched the book from the shelf, and opened it where I stood. The handwritten words were half gibberish, at least to me.

It's been so long since I've taken a Latin course…

My longing to possess it hadn't abated. It was like a voice was screaming in my head non-stop that I needed to have that book. That it belonged to me, was a *part* of me. Nails scraping on a chalkboard. Gritting my teeth, I tossed the book back on the shelf.

This thing is bad news. No thanks.

My legs wandered aimlessly as I perused, until I eventually found myself at that shelf again.

What the hell?

I TRIED TO leave the book three more times. Each time I ended up right back where I started.

After thirty minutes of this torture, I couldn't take it anymore. I fled from the library, clutching the book to my chest for dear life.

Can't let anyone catch me with this. Who knows what he'd do to me if he saw?

Managing to find my way to my bedroom, I stuffed it into a drawer in the vanity table. Groaning, I sank into a nearby armchair.

Now I can add thief to my generous supply of desirable traits.

THE LIGHT IN the windows faded to black.

One of the servants appeared in the room. "Dinner… is… served." Its voice was strangled, as if speaking were difficult.

I followed him through the winding halls to a dining room. Death looked up from reading, a hint of a smile curling his lips. "Ah. There you are."

Grinding my teeth, I didn't resist the urge to confront him. "Why'd you do it?"

He set the book aside at his elbow, his brow furrowed. "I am afraid I do not follow. Do what?"

"Burn down their camp! The Co—" I shook my head, stopping myself. "Your *soldiers* gave their word they wouldn't harm them."

"They were not shot, stabbed, or maimed, were they?

That qualifies as 'no harm' to me. In any case, these spirits must be stopped. Every step they take is a step toward catastrophe."

Folding my arms, I countered, "And that gives you free reign to treat them like garbage?"

His tone became grave. "They are dangerous. I could expound, for hours, on their assaults. On my palace, their injury of innocent bystanders. And their slander," he replied, jamming his finger on the table with every supposed sin they'd committed.

"An eye for an eye makes the whole world blind."

"How cliché." Death scoffed. "Do not judge me before you know the facts," he paused before continuing, "and before you have heard my offer."

"Offer?"

A devilish grin spread across his face then. "I can give to you something I know you yearn for: knowledge of Isabel and your parents' fates."

A swell of dizziness overcame me. "You know what happened to them?"

He nodded. "I do indeed. I will disclose that information if, and *only* if, you convince these naïve ignoramuses to abandon their foolish crusade."

A cold hand of dread punched me in the stomach.

"I will give you time to decide. But do not keep me waiting long." He picked up his book and stood, reading it as he walked away.

Conflicted, I collapsed into one of the dining chairs.

Death's servants shoved overflowing plates of food in front of me. I shoved them all away. It had only been a few hours since I'd last eaten, and my stomach was too knotted, even if I had wanted to eat. Literally weighed down by the burden of this decision on my shoulders. I leaned on the table with face in my hands.

Forcing myself to move, I shuffled back to the dark, lonely bedroom, and fell onto the mattress. Ridiculous as it seemed, the bed of blankets in my tent back at the camp provided more comfort. And neither bed compared to my bed in Idaho Falls. A melancholic quiver shook my heart. Staring at the ceiling, I lay motionless all night. Mrs. Kütz always brought me a warm glass of milk on nights I couldn't sleep. Now I wasn't sure if I'd ever see her, or any of those I loved back home, again. Tears began to pool in my eyes. This situation had to end. Being the rope in a far-too-intense game of Tug-Of-War had gotten old already. God, was this really my life? How could I make the decision whom to betray?

RAYS OF SUNLIGHT shone through the open curtains, making my eyes itch. I'd barely had a chance to brush my hair when a servant appeared beside me. The scream I let out was not a quiet one.

It bowed. "Your… presence… is requested."

"Right. Thanks."

"We've... drawn... a bath, and...... selected... a gown... for you."

"I appreciate that."

The being led me a short distance down the hall to a golden bathroom, ten times larger than any I'd seen. Too worn out to truly appreciate its grandeur, all I could manage was a yawn. The water felt perfectly warm when my toes slipped into the Olympic-sized marble tub.

What seemed like an hour later was only ten minutes. I hesitated at the edge of the bath, biting my lip, before accepting that I needed to face the situation at hand. Wrapped in a luxuriously soft red towel, hoping to avoid being spotted, I flew back to my room. To my horror, I wasn't alone. Three servants stood waiting for me.

Shrieking, I pulled the towel tighter around myself. "Christ! Does privacy not exist in this damned castle?"

They kowtowed, speaking in unison. "We... shall... help you dress."

I took a step back, as if they'd wanted to yank my heart out. "I can dress myself! Thanks."

"We... have orders. We... must."

"I don't give a rat's ass! You're *not* dressing me!"

"We... must... follow... orders."

Conceding, I hung my head with a resigned grunt. They gave me the courtesy of letting me do some of the work myself, but all too soon they'd shoved a lace-trimmed slip, petticoat, and wire skirt frame over my head, pulling and straightening as they worked. Once my arms were through the straps of the slip, they forced me into a corset fastened so tightly I could scarcely blink, let alone breathe. Finally, came a black dress. With long sleeves and red ribbons over those underpinnings. The way the ribbons wove through the slim ruffles on the skirt mystified me. It could've been a dress Anne Boleyn wore.

I opened my mouth to ask if they'd finished, when I was dragged over to the golden vanity and they sat me down, my back to the mirror. Makeup brushes poked and prodded at my face. They tugged my hair into a ponytail, lacing matching red ribbons through it. Icy hands slipped ruby earrings into my lobes and clasped a matching necklace around my neck.

After meticulously painting my lips, the servants drew back, motionless for a moment. "Done."

A sigh of relief crossed my lips. *Well, I guess I'll take a peek.* I turned to face the mirror.

My mouth fell open.

The girl in the reflection *couldn't* be me. The dark eye shadow made her grey eyes a vibrant silver—almost luminescent. The dramatic blush and crimson lipstick sharpened her features too much. The jewels she wore added another dimension to the overall effect. Elegant. Powerful. Graceful.

Beautiful.

Everything I wasn't. My shaking hand rose to touch my face. The stranger in the mirror did the same.

This has to be some sort of trick.

"Follow… us… to his chambers."

IT SEEMED, IN that dress, a longer walk through the corridors of the castle, but we eventually arrived at a massive room. Death sat in its center on a large golden throne; garnets and other shimmering jewels embedded its frame.

His eyes widened momentarily, before he adjusted his expression to something more aloof. "You look lovely. My servants do impressive work, do they not? It must make a wonderful change from filthy boots and secondhand rags."

I swallowed in an attempt to wet my mouth, suddenly dry. "Thank you."

"A spirit wishes to meet with me for a request of some sort. Once that is done, the day is yours."

For some reason, the idea of being alone with Death brought anxiety bubbling to the surface rather than fear. To combat this, I fidgeted, twisting the jewels of my necklace. "Um, okay."

"Oh, before I forget—you misplaced your bag when we arrived in my land. My soldiers located it on their hunt for you. I will have it delivered to your room."

"I didn't leave it behind at my house?"

"Apparently not."

The apprehension certainly wasn't easing. Scratching at my shoulder helped a little. "Thanks for finding it, I guess."

Clomping echoed down the hall. The door opened again, revealing a tall, bony man. Knees shaking, this dark-skinned fellow slowly approached Death. "Are you the one who can help me?"

Death sniffed haughtily, raising his chin. "This could be."

His eyes lit up. "Wonderful!"

"What is your need?"

Gesturing broadly, the man explained. "A famine has come to my home in the living world. If it isn't stopped, my friends and family will die. I've seen your great power, so I beg you—please help them." His voice broke—he cleared his throat, wiping his eyes.

Death let out a harsh, barking laugh. "Why would I assist you? Such catastrophes lead to more spirits entering my domain, maintaining the balance. Who do you think *created* the pestilence of which you speak?"

Tears stained the man's cheeks. "My wife is expecting a child."

"You should be grateful. Soon you shall be reunited with your loved ones." Death waved a dismissive hand. "Now, away with you." Two Coals entered, dragging the hysterically screaming man from the room.

My stomach heaved.

Death looked to me, a peaceful smile wreathing his face. "I do enjoy it when meetings are short. My attention is now yours."

I jabbed a finger in the door's direction. "Why treat him so cruelly? You could've done *something*!"

Death brushed a speck of dust from the arm of his throne, his voice cold. "I have heard such protestations every day since the dawn of humanity. If I assisted every creature who marched into my castle, this realm would be empty. There would be no spirits in the Land of the Dead to maintain the balance, and it would break. You must see that calamity would befall all creation. Eventually the very concept of existence would collapse upon itself and there would simply be nothingness."

My mouth drew tight, into a straight line. "You still should've treated him with some respect."

"To quote Machiavelli: 'It is better to be feared than loved.'"

Scorn wasn't mistakable in my words. "I'm sure fear brings you many friends."

He looked away for a moment, hearing it. His eyebrows knitting together. "I do not need friends."

"Right. You just create servants for shits and giggles."

He glared. "Enough of this."

I held up my hands in defeat. "Fine, I'll drop it."

After a tense, silent moment, Death stood. "What would you like to do now? I *did* promise the day was yours."

Brushing lint off my skirt, I replied, "I'd really like to go riding on one of those impressive horses." A scheme had formed in my head.

Death chuckled warmly, folding his arms. "You admire them, eh?"

Swallowing bile at the memory of dreadful monsters, under my paint, I forced a grin. "Oh, yes. They're beautiful."

"Then we shall go on a short jaunt."

"I want to grab my bag first, if you don't mind. Just in case I need anything while we're out."

He cocked an eyebrow. "What could you possibly need that I cannot bring into existence?"

Gingerly biting my lip, I weighed my options. Suddenly, inspiration whapped me upside the head. Shifting uncomfortably and casting my eyes downward, I prayed my act would fool him. "Well…there are," I coughed "certain things that happen to a lady every month, and I didn't really want to put either of us through the humiliation of me having to ask for, er, the necessary supplies, should I need more of them."

He grimaced, waving his hand dismissively. "Very well. Please be swift."

I ran to the bedroom and grabbed for my bag, stuffing into it the clothes I'd found at the campsite and the book from Death's library.

He smiled when I returned, diplomatically not mentioning the mismatch of gown and bag. "Follow me."

We walked down the ramp to the garden, taking a sharp left, and eventually coming to a large, grey brick structure. Inside stood at least thirty skeletal horses in cramped stalls. Bucking and stomping, they were obviously agitated at Death's presence. Or mine.

Death eyeballed the angry horses, an amused twinkle in his eye. "Looks like they are happy to see us."

Emptiness writhed in my stomach. "Yeah, overjoyed."

Advancing toward the stall containing the calmest-seeming horse, my heart quickened when the beast approached me, and swatted its flaming tail back and forth.

Death leaned on the door to the stall. "This is Hazel. A bit of a disappointment. Her temperament is so mild, yet she's one of the physically strongest of them." He sighed. "Such a waste."

Hazel nuzzled against my hand while I patted her skull. I giggled at the odd sensation. "She's charming."

"Charm and gentility do not a guarantee a good war horse."

Hazel turned her rump to me. Careful to avoid the flames, I stroked her spine. "Perhaps she isn't meant to be a war horse."

"There is no other choice for her in my stable. My soldiers need these beasts to travel."

"Why not create another horse and let Hazel be herself?"

He shrugged, watching the two of us. "If that would make you happy, so be it."

"I'd like to ride her."

"Very well. I trust you know how to ride side-saddle?"

"Yes, I do. Did you forget that my first life was on a farm?"

He grabbed the proper gear and led her from her stall. Hazel stomped and snorted, clearly excited.

I accepted hesitantly when Death offered a hand to help me onto the horse. Gently nudging Hazel's ribs with my feet, she took a few steps forward. When I kicked a little harder, it sent her into a gallop out of the stable. Looking over my shoulder as we sped away, Death stood gaping with momentary shock before he settled into his normal calm. He'd anticipated my move. Had I just done exactly what he'd wanted?

EVENTUALLY, THE CASTLE faded in the distance behind me. A tug on the reins brought Hazel to a skid near a bubbling stream. I leapt from her back, tying her to a tree before kneeling in front of my reflection in the water, wary of the beautiful stranger they'd made me into. Cupping icy water in shaking hands, I splashed my face, scrubbing until I looked like myself again.

Hurriedly, I slipped out of the dress, changing into the clothes I'd brought. The jewelry made a satisfactory *plunk* when tossed in the water. I left the dress on the bank, and mounted Hazel once more, tugging the ribbons from my hair. This time I rode astride, the way I'd always preferred.

CHAPTER EIGHT

D AYS PASSED. SEARCHES for food hadn't yielded much. My stomach ached with hunger. Attempts to sleep on the rough, cold ground proved futile. My only blessing was that I didn't need to worry about tending to Hazel. She didn't eat, drink, or sleep, just like everyone else in the Land of the Dead. Except for me.

As we raced across the terrain, I clutched Hazel's neck for dear life while the world whizzed past me. Eventually, a blurry figure came into view. My shaking arms weakly managed to pull Hazel to a stop. I slipped from her saddle.

A young woman with flaming orange hair and a face splattered with freckles stood frozen before me. As I came closer, she looked over her shoulder, shouting in a high voice, "I found something."

From a short distance away, Pete's voice called. "What is it?" Investigating, his eyes widened when he saw me. "Holy shit. Heather! What happened? Did *he* do this to you?"

My legs wobbled, nearly giving way. "…ran away from the castle… looking for you for three days."

He offered an arm and held me up, shaking of his head in a show of disbelief. My appearance must have been horrific going by the strain in his voice. "You're full of surprises."

The redhead giggled. "I'd say. She nearly gave me a heart attack."

I chuckled. "Sorry."

"No worries." She offered a hand. "I'm Megan."

I shook it, smiling but forcing myself not to shiver at her cold touch. "Nice to meet you. I'm—"

Her gentle smile interrupted me. "I know who you are. Pete's been in a frenzy since the Coals took you. Hasn't shut up. 'Do you think Heather's safe? He'd better not hurt her. Should we send a team? We gotta get Heather.'" She shot Pete a teasing glance.

He ducked his head, embarrassed. "Stop exaggerating."

I asked, "Was anyone hurt in the attack?"

"No, everyone managed to escape." Pete's cool arm soothed my aching muscles, adding to my overall relief. Everyone was safe. *Thank God, no one was hurt because of me.* "We've set up a new camp nearby."

My stomach roared. "Please tell me the food survived."

"Yes, we managed to save some." Megan tipped her

head Pete's way, "He was hell-bent on making sure we did, in case you came back."

Pete rolled his eyes at Megan. "Shut up." Turning my way, he ordered, "Let's get you something before you keel over."

My stomach growled. "Suits me fine."

Megan took Hazel's reins. Pete and I walked behind her.

Before long, we arrived at a campsite mirroring the previous one. An audible gasp permeated through the group when they spotted me.

Lily waved, grinning from ear to ear.

Emily charged at us, fury written all over her face. "Pete, you seriously brought this little Breather bitch back here after all the damage she caused? And you let her bring a Coal's horse with her? That thing could give away our location."

He puffed out his chest. "If Heather and the horse cause problems, I'll deal with it. I can bring whomever I want into this camp, just like everyone else."

She stomped her foot. "Not people who lead the Coals straight to us and get our camp burned down!"

"You can't really believe she planned that."

Emily stared at me, a frosty glare, before turning her attention back to Pete. "The hell I don't!"

"She broke out of his castle and spent three days trying to find us." He gestured to me, exclaiming, "Look at her— she's starving."

"It could be an act."

"Give it a rest, Emily. She's staying." His arm wrapped around mine. "You can just suck it up." Pete led me to the fire.

Megan shook her head, securing Hazel to a tree. "Emily could make the Wicked Witch look like a saint."

Pete raised an eyebrow when Megan shuffled away. Shrugging, he got to work building another makeshift grill. "So, what'll it be, mademoiselle?"

"The 'Pete's vague memory of Food Network recipes' special, please." I let out a weak, coughing laugh. Forgetting my manners in favor of avoiding starvation, I inhaled the food the second he handed me a bowl.

He stared at the now empty dish, eyes wide. "Damn, you *were* hungry. Do you need more?" I nodded, still chewing. The next course lasted even shorter than the first. Nathan and Kate sat near us, dumbstruck expressions on their faces.

"You really spent three days trying to find us?" Nathan asked.

Still shaky, I managed a nod. "Yes, I did. Didn't eat or sleep the entire time."

Kate blinked in disbelief. "Why?"

"I wanted to be here. I needed to make sure you all survived."

"You're more forgiving than me," Kate muttered, guilt written on her face. "I wouldn't come back after what we did. How we treated you."

"Don't worry. I've been treated worse."

"Still, I'm, like, *so* sorry that we didn't listen to you. We judged you before knowing you."

"Water under the bridge." I handed the bowl to Pete, my eyelids drooping. "Okay, I'm having trouble chewing now. Takes too much energy."

Pete grinned, pointing to a tent on the furthest edge of the circle. "That one's yours. Jason and Megan managed to sew us some tents using blankets that survived the fire. Lucky for us she always has a sewing kit in her pocket."

I stumbled to it, collapsing once inside. Voices argued behind me, but I shut them out, letting sleep claim me.

IN THE CRISP morning air, a peaceful quiet drifted through the camp. Things seemed deserted except for Megan at the campfire.

She glanced over her shoulder at me with a smile while she added kindling to the pile of ashes and surrounded it with larger logs. "Good morning!"

My head was heavy, but I felt rested for the first time in weeks. No nightmares or weirdness… a normal night's sleep. But in this new world, that word, *normal*, seemed foreign. "Morning." I yawned, stretching my arms above my head. "Hey, I have a question. Probably a dumb one."

"I could have an answer."

I gestured to the small fire just starting to bloom.

"What's with the fire? Dead people don't need to keep warm the last time I checked."

She pulled her light pink shrug-style sweater tighter around herself. "We don't really *need* to keep warm, but it still feels nice. Besides, it helps us keep an eye out for Coals at night. Their armor's surprisingly reflective."

"Fair enough." I turned my head, suddenly noticing the silence. "Where is everyone?"

She gestured to the east. "Fight practice. Nasty stuff, if you ask me. I prefer to keep the camp tidy and watch Lily while Tina's with the others."

That's weird, I thought. My brow shot up. "If you hate fighting, why are you part of this group?"

"I want to go back, escape this place, just like everyone else." Her tone of voice made the statement seem like the most logical thing in the world.

"Fair enough, but aren't you willing to fight for that?"

Vehemently, she shook her head. "No. I'm not going to let my desire to live again or fear of *moving on* change who I am."

I nodded, impressed. "Cool."

Blinking in confusion, she turned to glance at the fire she'd kindled, hands over the small flames now licking the new logs, she shook her head. "It feels warm to me…"

"I meant it's good you don't compromise your beliefs. 'Cool' has a new meaning now."

She hung her head and laughed, her shoulders shaking. "Pete uses that all the time. I assumed his sense of temperature was off!"

"It sounds like you've been here a while."

"The year was 1945 when I passed."

I blinked in surprise. "Wow. You must've been a sheltered one. But, yeah, the living world's changed so much since then."

"So I've heard. Hopefully I'll be able to adjust once we make it back."

I smiled, a reassuring smile. "I'm sure you will. Who knows? Maybe I'll help if things work out."

"That'd be swell, er, cool!"

Patting her back, I gave her a warm grin. "See?"

She beamed. "There's hope for the old girl yet."

SOON, THE CLANG of metal-on-metal pierced the silence of the camp. Heading closer to the noise, a small, circular meadow opened up. Everyone had lined up, and stood in pairs, locked in the heat of faux battle. Arrows fired at targets painted on trees at the edge of the area made *thunk* sounds. Others fenced with real gear like in the movies.

Pete was in the middle of a sword fight, to my right, with one of the burly twins that had shaken my tent on the first night I arrived. He noticed my presence, pausing to wave. His training partner lunged and sliced Pete's arm.

"Ow, Dammit, Greg! Didn't you see I stopped?"

Greg chuckled, a deep, booming sound. He smacked Pete on the shoulder with the flat of his blade. "Don't blame me. That's all you and the chick, man. You get distracted when you're supposed to be a big ol' badass," he tutted. "Sorry, though."

I approached, leaning forward to take a look at the wound. A deep slice marked his bicep, but no blood flowed. "Are you okay, Pete?"

He rubbed his arm. "Yeah, I'm fine. For us, non-fatal wounds heal fast. But it still hurts."

"I'm glad it's not too bad." I tucked some strands of my hair behind my ears, anxiety taking over my otherwise calm demeanor. "So, I thought about it, and decided I want to learn how to fight."

"What happened to 'I know martial arts'?" he snickered, imitating my voice perfectly.

"I took a class." I coughed, mumbling, "Once. Ten years ago."

"Humph, I thought it might be something like that."

"But seriously, I'm tired of being snatched. Three times in as many days is more than enough. Easy prey…no offense."

"None taken. You're right. You deserve a chance to defend yourself, no matter whose side you're on."

In the practice session next to us, Emily'd pinned Tina to the ground, holding a sword to her throat before backing away, sneering at me. "More like the chance to rip us to shreds."

Pete sheathed his sword with a huff. "Ignore her." He led me to a basic firing range to our far left, offering me a pistol. "She needs to learn respect for other people's decisions."

I took the weapon, turning it over in my clammy hands. "I've never used a gun before. Besides, won't Coals hear the noise?"

"I can tell. Relax. It's not going to bite. And Coals don't really come out much during the day. Here, let me show you first." He grabbed an extra pistol from the cluster of non-personal weapons in the corner of the clearing. "First, make sure the safety is off, otherwise it won't shoot." He turned a knob on the gun's side. "Then, you put the hammer down," he continued, pushing it with his thumb until he let out a faint click. "After that, all you need to do is aim and pull the trigger." With one eye closed, he furrowed his brow in concentration before finally firing.

I plugged my ears, expecting to hear a cacophonous boom. Instead, all I heard was the faintest *click*. "Huh? Where's the bullet?"

"They aren't easy to come by. Only way to get more is find someone who died with a gun. So, we hold on to 'em as much as we can. We can let you use a couple, though, since it's your first practice." He turned to me with a grin before popping two bullets in the chamber. "Now it's your turn."

I raised the gun slowly with both hands, my wrists shaking.

With a light chuckle, shaking his head, he waved a hand. "Stop. The safety's on. And your stance is horrible."

Then he touched me, adjusting my posture. A strange warmth flooded my cheeks. "Thanks."

"Now, squeeze just the trigger."

I squinted, focusing on the target, easing pressure on the trigger. A loud bang startled me. The gun flew from my hands, smacking me square in the face. I landed flat on my ass. *What a kick!*

Pete reached out, helping me up, the hitching of his voice making me blush more. "That was… something. You aren't hurt, are you?"

Stabbing pain ripped through my nose. I checked, patting at it, gritting my teeth with a hiss. "Think I might've busted my nose."

"You weren't kidding about being a klutz. I thought shit like that only happened in Looney Tunes."

Great. Now I look like a moron. "Yeah, yeah. Laugh it up." Ignoring the radiating pain behind my eyes, I snatched up a bow and some arrows.

"Everybody, step back! She's trying archery now!" Greg hollered, inciting bursts of loud guffaws.

Pete stepped next to me, grabbing his own bow. "Ease up, guys. It's her first training. Okay. You hold it like this, see?" He spread his legs into a firm stance, gripping the front of the bow with his left hand. "Then you hold your arrow this way." He put the arrow between his right index and middle finger, slowly drawing it back. "And then…let 'er go."

The arrow darted across the clearing, striking the

bull's-eye of the target painted on the tree ahead of us.

Hunger Games and Lord of the Rings marathons, don't fail me now.

Carefully, I held the bow in place exactly as Pete had, took aim, and pulled the string back. The part that held the string in place snapped, smacking the top of my head. I yelped in pain. The arrow dropped pathetically to the ground.

That did it. The others roared with hysterics. I threw the broken bow on the ground, storming away into the trees, hoping to find the main campsite.

Pete chased me. "Heather, stop! I'm sorry!"

Despite my anger, I did stop, but kicked rocks and pieces of bark in random directions, not particularly caring what I hit. Pete walked up. A boom of thunder crashed in the sky, shaking the ground. "God, I can't do *anything* right," I bellowed.

He lifted his eyes skyward for a moment, then focused on me in astonishment. "It's okay. You're just starting out. Everyone's awful at first. I know I was."

"I'm just so sick of being a joke."

"You're not a joke to me. I mean, the way you *flailed* was pretty funny, but it doesn't mean I see *you* like an idiot or anything."

"Thanks." My shoulders heaved with a heavy sigh. "I'd just get you guys killed. Well, re-killed. Whatever."

"Not necessarily, if you train enough."

"Maybe." I bit my lip. "Pete, can I ask you something?"

"Sure."

"What's it like to… die?" My palms began sweating merely saying the word.

He flinched, then stared at a tree ahead of us. His eyes grew distant, going back to another time and place. "Everything felt so cold…then a bright light surrounded me. The next thing I knew, I woke up in one of those houses near the castle."

"It's probably none of my business, but how did it happen?"

"My little brother, Spencer, and I were swimming in the canal." Pete's shoulders slumped. "By our house. He'd only learned to swim a few months before, but I thought, 'I'm Mr. Bigshot, the track star. I'll keep him safe.'" He let out a long sigh. "God, I was stupid. He went out too far… I'd told him a million times to stay where I could see him…"

He paused, voice breaking, before continuing, "He got swept up in the current. I dove in after him. The water was freezing. By the time I got to him, his leg was caught in some weeds. I tried pulling him out, but a rock must've dislodged; it hit me hard, on the head. Everything went black. Then it was all over."

"Did he live?"

He looked to me. "No. We woke up lying next to each other. For a while, we just messed around, waited for our parents. If this was Heaven, we wanted to enjoy it. Then one day Hugh, the original leader of this ragtag group, found us in the woods while Spencer was playing Robin Hood. Spencer's the one that wanted to join. He wanted to be a hero, see Mom and Dad again."

He nudged a rock with his foot, smiling ruefully. "Those were good times. We made some friends, learned to be pretty decent fighters. Until Coals raided our camp one day. Death led the attack, which should've been a sign—he usually never involves himself. Hugh held them back for a while, but they took him out. Spencer—brave, stupid little Spence—ran at 'em like a bat out of hell. He loved Hugh like a second dad. Wanted revenge."

Tears pooled in Pete's eyes, his words occasionally hitching. "He didn't stand a chance. They grabbed him within seconds. I charged them, but a Coal got his hands on me, holding me still no matter how hard I fought. Those assholes are strong. A couple of 'em pinned Spencer down. He cried, screamed my name, struggled with all his might. He was so scared…"

"Then, *he* gave the signal." Pete's hands clenched. "They slit Spencer's throat. Right in front of me. My brother just vanished into thin air. His clothes were the only thing left of him. He was ten. *Ten*, for God's sake!"

My jaw dropped. "I'm so sorry."

"They retreated after that. Guess they thought they'd broken our morale enough." Pete wiped his eyes, giving a slight smile. "It's not your fault, but thanks."

I shook my head. "I've seen him be cruel, but killing kids?"

His face soured into a scowl. "He's a vicious, evil monster. That's why we keep such a close eye on Lily. Why I hesitated to bring her here in the first place." His tone grew lighter. "I'm glad she's around, though. You can't help but love that li'l angel. Looking at her, it's almost like Spencer's still here."

I shoved my hands in my pockets, meeting his eyes. The agony in them before was nearly gone. "Do you think you'll ever see him again?"

He folded his arms, looking up at the sky again. "I hope so, but I want to get back, live until I'm old in Earth years first. Live a full life—for the both of us."

"Then you'll, *move on*?"

His gaze shifted back to me. "I don't want to live forever, I just want to *live*. Can you imagine what it's like to die at eighteen, unable to experience the rest of what life's got to offer?"

His words stabbed my heart. *I can relate more than you know.* The urge to tell the truth gnashed at my throat again. "Pete, there's something I need to—"

Megan skipped over to us, appearing from the direction of the campsite, humming a chipper tune. "Hello, you two."

Pete nodded with a cough. "Shouldn't you be watching Lily?"

"Tina's done with practice, so she's taking care of her now. I decided to check on Heather's first training session, but I think that shiner says it all." She giggled, offering my shoulder a sympathetic pat.

Pete adjusted his scabbard. "You'll get better. Don't worry." He rubbed his chin with a puzzled expression. "You know what's weird, though? Usually the bows hold up better, even for first-timers. Don't you usually make them, Megan?"

"Not the newest set. I only sharpened the arrows this time."

"Do you know who made them?"

"No, I'm sorry." She shook her head, apology written on her face. "I wouldn't get too riled up over it. A less sturdy bow could've been mixed in with the others by mistake. Or maybe the twins are up to their usual shenanigans."

Pete scratched his head. "You could be right. I'm not sure about the prank theory, though. Tampering with the weapons doesn't seem like a stunt the twins would pull. I'll keep an eye on the new bows during practice, just to be safe."

THE THREE OF us returned to the main campsite while everyone else was returning from the practice area.

Pete leaned over, whispering, "Did *you* mess with the bow, as some sort of sympathy play?"

I frowned, taken aback. "Of course not. I don't even know how weapons work, why would I ruin one on purpose?"

"I figured. Sorry for suggesting—"

"I get it. I'd be worried if you *weren't* a little suspicious."

"Anyway, what were you about to say earlier, before Megan showed up?" he asked, gesturing as she ran ahead of us.

"Oh, I just wanted to thank you for helping me so much." *What the hell? Where did* that *lie come from?*

"No problem. I'm gonna talk to the others about this problem with the bows. Want to join me?"

I shook my head. "Not really. They'd just accuse me. It'd be a huge mess."

He considered for a moment, regret in his eyes. "Good point. I'll see you later, okay?" He patted my arm—the touch sent a cold jolt of electricity surging through me.

"Um… okay."

I leaned against a tree, unable to move. My stomach did somersaults, my head reeled, my face burned.

What is wrong with me?

Everyone else had gone to the far side of the campsite, out of sight beyond the tents. I stood by the tree until whatever was going on with my body subsided. I walked the rest of the way into the camp and sat down by the fire, hypnotized by the flames. I watched them twist and writhe, adding more wood whenever it got low.

CHAPTER NINE

I EXITED MY tent, hoisting my bag over my shoulder. Everyone's eyes were fixed on me. Usually, it wouldn't have struck me as odd, but the expressions gave me pause. At the sight of me some dropped the new bows they'd worked on. A clattering went up around the campsite. Impossible to ignore. Tina grabbed Lily and held her tight. They looked confused. Frightened, even.

Even Pete looked startled. "Your nose…"

Humiliated, I raised a hand to it. "It's worse? Everyone's looking like I've got twenty arms."

"Your nose is fine."

"Then what's going on?"

"Don't you get it? Your nose is *fine*. It's like you didn't break it yesterday." Pete drew his sword, carefully holding it near my face. "See for yourself."

Peering at my reflection in the blade, I saw he was right. I looked perfectly normal. "What the hell? This can't be right. Unless…… am I dead?" My blood ran cold.

He grabbed my wrist, checking my pulse. "Nope. Still alive. It doesn't make sense."

"Maybe it's just something this place does to the living."

"That might explain a few things, but I don't know if it accounts for the thunder."

"Thunder?"

"When you got angry yesterday, thunder and lightning. Out of nowhere. You heard it happen. The sky's usually nothing but clear and sunny in this place."

"*He* could've done that!"

"Maybe, but I'm still going to look into it during the next intel run."

Fishing the book I'd taken from Death's library from my bag, I offered it to him.

Pete stood frozen for a moment. "Where'd you get that?"

"The library in the castle. I don't know why, but I *had* to have it. It's like the book called me. Here's the thing, though—it's in Latin."

He stroked his chin. "Jason can read some Latin, I think."

"The old guy, looks like a Medieval Times employee?"

"That'd be him."

"If this is a cookbook or something, I'll look so stupid."

Pete let out a gut-busting laugh.

WHEN WE FOUND Jason, we sat with him in front of his tent. His wrinkled face was stretched into a congenial grin as he whistled to himself, sharpening a dagger.

"How now, Sir Peter?" He glanced at me. "Lady Heather, 'tis good to see your abrasion has healed nicely, though the rapid pace of its recovery is quite disconcerting."

"That's actually part of why we're here."

Face alight with curiosity, Jason set the dagger aside. "Oh, indeed?"

Giving him the book, I tucked some hair behind my ears. "I found this book in the castle library. It's in Latin. I think. I can't read it but Pete says you can. Would you be willing to translate?"

Jason thumbed through the pages, a '*humm*' rose. "Certainly. It does not seem any more difficult than the texts I would read as a boy. But a quality translation must not be done in haste. I fear this will take time."

Pete winked, patting Jason's shoulder. "That's understandable."

"I shall try my hand and send word of my progress, were anything substantial to catch my attention."

I sighed with relief. "Thank you so much."

He bowed his head, and retrieved his dagger. "No trouble at all, m'lady."

WANDERING OVER TO where Hazel was tied made me smile; she perked up at seeing me. "Hey, girl," I said at her whinny. The afternoon sunlight gleamed on her bones, making them look even more ghostly white.

Lily ran to us when she heard Hazel's happy nicker. "A pony," she squealed.

I couldn't help but grin. "Yep."

Lily stepped back, her face tightening in a grimace as she appraised the animal. "It's kinda creepy lookin'."

"She is a little scary, but she's really a big ol' marshmallow. Come see, if you want."

Lily approached slowly, giggling when Hazel craned her neck to sniff Lily's face. "That tickles!"

"Want to ride her?"

She bit her bottom lip, hesitating. "Mommy said riding horses is dangerous. She never let me ride one. I even asked nicely."

"Where *is* your mommy, anyway?"

"I think she's alive, like you."

Tina barreled toward us, snatching the child up. "Dammit, how many times have I told you not to wander off?"

A frown soured Lily's tiny face. She whined as Tina carried her away. "Aww, but I want to pet the pony."

Unbidden, the memory of teaching Isabel to ride Mother's pony came to mind. At first, she'd feared the beast, and even wept. But she'd never asked to stop the lessons. Such a brave little thing…

Seconds later Pete's familiar snicker came from behind. "I swear, if Tina was alive, Lily would've given her three heart attacks by now."

A smile threatened at his presence, but I shifted into neutrality. "I know why she does it, but I think she's keeping Lily on too tight a leash. She should be allowed a *little* fun."

Pete pursed his lips, thoughtful. "Maybe we could play some games with her one of these days."

"She'd like that, I think."

"Ya know, I'm amazed." He shook his head and grinned. "Jason doesn't do things for just anyone."

"I'm just glad there was no crucifix, or calling me a witch."

He let out a short, quick laugh. "Why would he do that?"

"I'm the only one here with a heartbeat? There's also the issue of my overnight healing?"

"Good points. You certainly are a mystery."

"Should I be flattered or insulted by that?"

I glanced over my shoulder to see why he'd grown so quiet. He stood completely still.

Glancing around, everyone else in the camp was petrified too, Hazel included.

I turned to Pete, shaking his arm. "Pete? Are you okay?"

From my right, a soft voice chilled me. "He cannot hear you. None of them can."

Not Lily! No! I spun to face Death. "Please tell me you haven't hurt them."

He leaned against a nearby tree, "Fear not, they are unharmed. Merely immobilized for a short time so we may speak freely." It was startling to see Death dressed in a bright blue pair of jeans. Those were topped with a black suit jacket, a white undershirt and a blood red tie. I nearly missed the dress shoes as I sighed, fighting to keep my irritation in control.

"What do you want?"

Death folded his arms. "Did you truly believe your thievery would be ignored?"

Panic swirled within my stomach. *Will he hurt me?*

I took a careful step backward. "Thievery? I didn't steal anything from you."

He jerked his right hand in the direction of the campground. "These buffoons may be deceived by your lies, but you cannot fool me."

The anxiety bubbling up grew, but I managed to keep an outward appearance of calm. "I'm not lying to anyone."

"Oh no?" He snapped his fingers with a dark chuckle. From a cloud of white mist came a ghostly version of myself. It opened its mouth, spouting with relish every lie I'd told since arriving in the Land of the Dead. After those, it began to utter lies from my current life, in Idaho Falls, mostly things to hide my secret.

I clamped my hands on my ears. "Stop!"

The transparent apparition fell away with a second

snap from Death. "I must say, your talent for spinning falsehoods *is* extraordinary."

After taking a few slow breaths, my attention refocused. "I'll tell everyone the truth when the time is right."

At that new lie Death let out a mocking bark, "Are you so foolish to think they will accept you once you admit your dishonesty?"

"They might be upset, but I think they'll forgive me."

He brushed a wayward lock of hair from his eye. "What is the phrase? 'Do not count your chickens before they hatch'?"

"And you made fun of me for being cliché," I muttered. "Look, unfreeze them. Leave me alone."

"After my book is returned to its proper place. I will give you this opportunity to give it back. You may keep the beast, she's useless as she is."

I steeled myself, folding my arms. "I'm not giving it back."

"Why ever not?"

"It might hold answers to—what I am—how I can undo this cycle."

He pushed off the tree, coming nearer. Slowly. "You wish to know?"

My heart did a somersault. "Yes."

"Well..." He paused, drawing out the moment. His lips curled into a smirk. "Unfortunately, I will not divulge that."

My eyes narrowed. I clenched my fist, anger surging. *I should've seen that coming.*

"I don't need you to tell me." I spat, "I can figure it out myself,"

"Oh yes. Of course. You've certainly done an impeccable job of it these past centuries."

I held my voice from shaking. "Stop it."

"What? You can hurl insults and mockery at me, but doing the same is unfair?"

"Just get out of here," I barked.

Death shook his head with a strange, almost rueful smile. "You *are* fascinating. I have existed since the dawn of time, met every mortal—ever. I was certain nothing they'd do or say would surprise me. And yet, on a regular basis, the exact opposite is true of you."

My cheeks burned hearing that. Death reached a hand to brush something off my shirt What was I *doing*?

His hand fell limp at his side. I'd recoiled.

"Am I *that* unbearable?" He sighed.

"They told me about the things you've done."

"You've only heard their side."

"How can there be any other side to what you did to Spencer?"

Death's gaze fell to the ground for a moment. Was his face pinched with sadness? "Ah, yes. The boy. That simply—got out of hand. My intent was to handle the situation diplomatically, but overreactions took place. What happened was regrettable, but I had hoped it would send a message. End this pitiful conflict."

"You only made them angrier than they already were."

"I realize this now." His shoulders slumped slightly. "My previous methods have not resulted in the conclusion to this war, but hope lives on that this can end peaceably."

"Well, a good place to start would be to not kill kids."

"I explained my reasoning for that." Death ran his fingers through his golden tresses with an air of irritation. "You may keep the book for now, but do not think you can steal from me without consequences." He vanished in a flash of white light.

The camp burst into motion. Laughter and conversation echoed through the woods. Pete chortled behind me. "Maybe both."

No one had noticed. Nothing was harmed. "I… need to go now," I mumbled before running into my tent.

CHAPTER TEN

MEGAN PLOPPED DOWN on the log next to mine as I ate breakfast—an apple. "Pete said you got all riled up. Something he said yesterday?"

I flinched at the memory of the previous night's conversation with Death. "No, it wasn't anything he did or said. I was just in a weird mood."

"Oh. Well, Pete thinks you're cross with him."

"Not at all," I said through laborious chews.

"I'd steer clear for a while then. He's pretty steamed."

I blinked in surprise. "Really? Over *that*? Seems a little much to get angry about."

All Megan did in response was shrug.

TRAINING KICKED MY ass that morning. Sword fighting and using guns were unmitigated disasters. The bright side was I'd managed to successfully shoot an arrow—though it struck the ground rather than the target. I approached Pete afterward while he polished his weapons. *Better nip this drama in the bud.*

"Hey, you got a minute?" I asked, wiping sweat from my brow.

He propped his sword against a tree with a grunt. "Sure, what is it?"

"I wanted to apologize for going off suddenly yesterday. Nothing to do with you. I just had a lot on my mind."

He shrugged. "It's all right. You're dealing with some crazy shit right now."

"No argument there." I brushed some hair from my eyes, what else could I add? "So, you aren't angry? Megan said you were really upset."

"What?" He frowned. "No. I got a little worried *I'd* said something stupid, but that's it."

I tilted my head, curious. "Did you talk to Megan about us?"

"I mentioned something to Greg and Shaun. Maybe she overheard, misunderstood?"

"That makes sense."

He folded his arms after sliding his sword into its scabbard. "But I'm not mad at you, okay?"

Suddenly fraught with nerves, I bit my lip. "Okay."

MEGAN FOUND ME an hour or two later sitting on the ground by Hazel's hooves, apology written on every line of her face. "I'm so sorry about what I said this morning. Pete explained the whole thing to me. I can be such a busybody…"

I waved a hand. "Don't worry about it, you just wanted to help. It's nice to know my status as a pariah is starting to change."

"Not everyone is singing your praises yet, but mentions of wanting to abandon you in the woods have lessened."

The color drained from my face momentarily. "They want to leave me stranded somewhere?"

"It's Emily, mostly. Though, Jack liked the idea, too."

I groaned, leaning back against Hazel's hock. "I'm not surprised."

"Don't take it personally. She's just a very spiteful person."

"What's her problem?"

Megan hunched her shoulders in a shrug. "No one knows. Anyone who's tried asking about it gets a nice kick in the teeth."

I winced. "Ouch."

"The first lesson most new recruits learn is to generally stay away from her."

Suddenly a rock flew, smacking Megan in the cheekbone. Emily spat, "Stop gossiping about me, you blabbermouth bitch."

Glowering at Emily as she crawled inside her tent, I turned. "Are you okay?"

Megan rubbed where she'd been struck, which wasn't bleeding. *Not sure I'll ever get used to that.* "Yeah, I'll be fine. This isn't the first time she's thrown something at me."

"Why don't you stand up to her?"

"She'd get angry. She'd attack me, win, and our numbers would be smaller."

"Fair enough."

She stood, brushing dirt off her jeans. "I think I'll go read awhile before the sun sets."

Did she steal from Death too? "You've got books?"

"Of course. A shelf in one of those houses was filled with them. It looked abandoned, so I helped myself to some books and blankets." She put her hands up at my shocked expression. "Don't worry, I'll return them if I see someone in that house."

I nodded. "I think I understand. It's not really fair of me to judge someone when I'm doing my best to not be judged."

"Have a nice evening," she smiled. "Oh, if Lily comes out of her tent, let me know. I'll round her up and put her back." Megan meandered away, humming a tune I recognized as one from the thirties.

A short time later, I sat in front of my tent, soaking up what sunlight I could through the trees.

Lily came near, shyly sitting beside me. Her floral

dress swished with every move. "Hi!"

I gave her a light noogie. "Tina's going to be upset you've wandered off again."

"Tina's looking for something with Petey and the others. Megan's watching me," she smiled, gesturing toward Megan's tent. "Well, listening, I guess."

"So why are you here with Tina?" *Kids shouldn't be soldiers.*

She grimaced, fidgeting with her necklace. "Uncle Bobby got mad at me while Mommy and Daddy were out. He gave me lots of ouchies."

The contents of my stomach threatened to make an appearance. It took a full minute of strained silence before I could speak without acid burning my throat. "I—I meant why are you here, with the fighters?"

"I miss my Mommy and Daddy," she said matter-of-factly.

"Wouldn't it be easier to wait for them in the houses? In town?"

Tears pooled in her eyes. "I hate it here. I want my old house, my old room, my kitty, my life…"

My heart swelled. I held open my arms. "Come 'ere."

She flew into my embrace, sobs shaking her little body.

Closing my eyes, my mind drifted to another time and place. For a moment, I returned to my first life, comforting Isabel after our dog, Daniel, ran off. Both our hearts broke that day. From that afternoon on, I'd sing her favorite hymn whenever she needed comfort. I sang it shortly before Death came and changed my world forever. Though the lyrics had long been forgotten, the melody'd never left me.

Humming it for Lily, I rocked her slowly. Eventually her weeping subsided, I brushed a few stray golden hairs away from her still-damp face.

She sniffled, smiling up at me. "Thank you. I feel better now," she mumbled, wiping at her eyes.

I wished I could alleviate her pain. "You're welcome. I'm so sorry you have to deal with all this grown-up stuff, Lily."

"It'll be okay. Petey says we'll all go home, and things will be good again."

I ruffled her hair. "I hope he's right." I pulled her closer for only a moment, then let her go. "You should probably head back to your tent now."

She groaned. "Do I *have* to? I get bored sitting in that smelly tent all the time."

"No, but do you want to get into trouble?"

"Nuh-uh. But I wanna play," she whined.

"I actually talked to Pete about this. You might get some more freedom around here."

Her eyes lit up. "Really?"

Her smile was contagious. It was impossible to not return it. "Yep! But for now, you need to be a good girl. Listen to Tina and Megan."

She let out a huff. "Okay." She left my lap, walking slowly back to her tent, head hanging in mock despair.

I waved, chuckling. *Such a silly girl.*

AFTER ANOTHER TRAINING session the following day, pain radiated through my shoulder. I'd actually managed to hold the gun steady and successfully fire a shot. The bullet hadn't hit the target, but pride still surged all the way to my bones. Progress, even if at a lesser degree of failure, was still progress.

Jason approached, sheathing his sword, as I carefully placed my own blade with the others and gingerly set my gun down. "Good day, Lady Heather. I bring happy tidings of my advancement with the text you bestowed upon me."

Wearily, I smiled. "Great! Let's hear it."

He sat, knees snapping and popping at his descent. "I believe it involves the maiden of legend who bested Sir Death."

My head swam. At his words I needed to sit to steady myself. "What does it—say about her?"

Fishing the book from the satchel that was slung over his shoulder, he patted its front cover. "If this book is accurate, this maiden holds great power."

"S-she does?"

He nodded, speaking enthusiastically. "Yes. The ability to view the circumstances that led to one's perishing. Possibly, she can raise the recently dead. For a moment or two. The author hypothesizes, were she to come into this realm, she'd be almost as powerful as Sir Death while here."

"Who's the author?"

Jason opened the book, tapping a name on the first page. "Mr. Richard Mortisa. Does this name hold any significance for you?"

"No. Does it for you?"

His mouth turned downward while he stroked his beard. "I fear it does not, m'lady."

"Any other pertinent information?"

"There is mention of a way to reverse the maiden's condition and return her to the state of an ordinary mortal. But the language is quite vague from what I've read thus far."

Struggling, I somehow managed to maintain a calm expression. "Keep up the fantastic work, and thank you so much, Jason. For everything."

"My pleasure." He rose amid more creaks and pops. With a bow, he moved back to the camp.

My legs managed to take me about five or ten feet from the training ground before I swayed, clutching a tree for support. Could it be true? Was there a cure for my curse? Did I actually have power while in this strange place? Could I use it to get home?

THE SUN HAD begun its crawl toward the horizon by the time Pete's voice, calling in the distance, caught my attention. "Heather? Are you out here?"

I dragged myself from my reverie. "Over here."

Pete appeared through the trees, letting out a deep sigh of relief. "Thank God you're okay. When you didn't come back from practice, I started to worry Coals took you again. Emily was absolutely sure you'd run back to Death and had betrayed us all."

He worried about me? Heat rose to my cheeks. "I'm sorry I scared you."

"No big deal. It's just…" He fidgeted, not meeting my eyes. "I've started to kind of like having you around."

"I feel the same way," *Why am I feeling so reluctant to admit that?*

He coughed, scratching his arm. "So, uh, I saw you with Jason. He learned anything from that book yet?" he seemed eager to change subjects.

"He thinks it's got something to do with the girl from your legend."

Pete snapped his fingers, a huge grin spreading across his face. "This is fantastic! Physical proof she might exist."

"Listen… I'm—" I began, I took a step toward him, but my legs protested at having been tucked under me for so long while I'd been sitting, and I pitched forward as a thrum of pins and needles shot through them.

He managed to sidestep in time to catch me.

Our eyes met. Everything else vanished. My heart crashed erratically against my ribcage. I felt I'd drown in the matching set of sky-blue pools.

Pete gazed down at me with an intensity I couldn't define burning in those eyes.

Just as my spinning mind begun to decipher where this situation was heading, footsteps sounded behind us. In my periphery, I recognized Greg and Shaun.

Greg panted, "Coals. Only a few miles from here."

Shaun added, voice tense, "They're armed to the gills."

The color drained from Pete's face. He helped me stand. "Tell everyone it's time to move. Do it quietly. Do it quickly. Code Black."

CHAPTER ELEVEN

THE CAMP HAD been thrown into a whirl of frantic activity. Everyone was running in different directions. It was impossible to keep track of who was doing what while people were frantically hissing commands at one another. Tents were collapsed, weapons tucked into satchels and bags. The fire pit, demolished. Within minutes, there was barely evidence we'd ever been there. I seized Hazel's reigns.

After dashing off to help the others, Pete returned with Tina, clutching Lily's hand. "Heather, Tina, get Lily out of here. We have a new site for our camp picked out, about thirty miles west. Tina knows the way. You'll know you've made it when you see a red bandanna tied to a tree."

I blanched. "But, Pete…"

He gave me his best reassuring smile. "We'll meet you there."

Tears rolled down my cheeks. *What if I never see him again?* "Please be careful," I whispered to Pete.

He put a gentle hand on my cheek, wiping my eyes. "It'll be fine. I promise. Lily, we'll be at the new camp by sunrise."

I hoisted myself onto Hazel. "You'd better be."

Grabbing Lily, Tina nodded and gingerly set her onto Hazel's back before she climbed on herself. She held Lily in a vise-like grip.

He smiled grimly. "That's the spirit. Now go!"

Taking one last look around, I kicked the horse into a gallop.

IT WAS A tight squeeze, but the three of us managed to fit on Hazel's back. She took it like a champ, not even letting out a grunt of complaint. With Tina's help, finding the new camp was relatively easy. The sunset's regal golds and blues were almost gone when we finally found the tree with the red bandanna. A few stars began to pop into view.

After coming to a stop, Tina slid off Hazel's back. "Okay Lily, ready to get down?"

She nodded emphatically. "Yes, please."

Her hands slipped under Lily's arms, carefully setting her on the ground. Once she was safe, I climbed off Hazel's back, collapsing to my knees with relief and no small amount of exhaustion.

"Mommy's gonna be so mad when she finds out I rode a pony."

Facing me, Tina's voice quivered. "Thank you so much for helping me to keep her safe."

"Of course."

She tenderly kissed the top of Lily's head. "Your face is filthy, sweetheart. Let's get you cleaned up."

SECONDS PASSED LIKE hours, which made the actual hours feel like years. Eventually, Pete, Jason, and Megan appeared, running through the trees.

Dizzy with relief, I ran to Pete, throwing my arms around him. His chest vibrated with a chuckle when he returned my hug. "See? Told you I'd be okay."

Megan coughed. "Ahem, we're here too. Are we unimportant?"

"Indeed," Jason harrumphed with a playful smirk.

My cheeks burned as I pulled myself from Pete. "Of course, I'm happy to see you're all okay. Where's everybody else?"

Pete said something, but a despaired howling drowned out his words.

All four of us gasped. The five remaining spirits had restrained Greg, dragging him closer to the new campsite.

Using all of his strength, Greg fought them, bellowing through choking sobs, "No! *No!* Let me go! I'll crush those sons of bitches into scrap metal. We were almost here…just a few more miles…"

"We can't." Jack dragged Greg forward, saying in a barely-even tone, "You'd be ghosted in seconds."

"I don't care." Greg continued to struggle, every inch of his body shaking with the effort. "They're going to pay for this!"

"Shut the hell up," Emily snapped, struggling to hold one of his arms. She gritted her teeth, never pausing her efforts to pull him. "I know it's hard, but they'll find us if you keep up this racket. It was hard enough losing 'em in the trees in the first place."

"Let 'em find us," he shouted. "I'll tear them apart. Then I'll find whoever messed with his bow and make them regret the day they died!"

"Dude, stop," Nathan plead.

Pete approached the weeping man. I could now see the dark circles under his eyes. "Greg, would Shaun really want you to put us all in danger?"

That's all it took. Greg hung his head and ceased his struggle. With a wavering sigh, he whispered, "No."

"I'm sorry," Pete continued, "I know how you feel. When they got Spencer—it's unimaginable." He paused, placing a comforting hand on Greg's shoulder. "We *will* find who sabotaged the bows. They'll pay. But now isn't the time."

"You're right." He sniffed sadly.

"When the camp's set up, we'll hold a memorial, then plan our next move."

Greg's shoulder seemed a bit straighter, like he was

ending his struggle.

We exchanged glances as they let him go and he passed me. My heart caught in my throat looking into those brown eyes, now lifeless and dull. Though I'd barely known Shaun, the grief that came from losing a sibling was all too familiar.

We worked at a slower pace than before, heavy from despair. A melancholic fog hung over the woods, shrouding us while we constructed tents and a fire pit was dug in silence.

The sky was jet black when we solemnly gathered to sit around the new fire.

Pete, weary, rose slowly. "This morning we lost not only a great soldier, but also a great brother and friend. Whenever you needed a sparring partner, a good laugh, or just someone to talk to, Shaun was there. True, his direction-following skills could've used a little work, but he never ignored or abandoned those who needed him. He was a valued member among our ranks, and," Pete's voice trembled, "I'm really going to miss him." He collapsed onto the log, his face in his hands.

Greg stood next. "When Shaun and I were shot in a riot in sixty-four, we thought we'd wound up in some sort of hellish purgatory. Stuck in a big empty house, no one we knew around, woods stretching out forever, every day the same—we were miserable. We tried to stay positive, but it wasn't easy."

He gave a small, sad smile, his eyes sweeping over the group. "Then we found you guys. You accepted us, never looked down on us. You're the best group of friends a man could ask for, a-and if Shaun were here, he'd say the same thing. Because of you, I believe there can be heaven in hell." Tears streamed down his face as he took his seat. Pete patted his shoulder.

Then Jack stood, pulling his shirt down over his ample stomach. "When Greg and Shaun joined us, I was a little nervous. In my small town in Utah—well, there weren't many non-whites around. So, at first, I avoided them."

A warm, almost sad smile tugged at his mouth. "Until the day Shaun came to borrow some arrows. I got to know these kind, generous boys." He sighed, glancing at Greg. "It's a shame we didn't meet sooner. I'm sorry for your loss, Greg."

After Jack, everyone took turns sharing their memories. Silently creeping to my tent after the memorial was over, my ears rang and my head pounded. Clutching a pillow, I desperately wished for some form of comfort to lighten the gloom. Memories came of Isabel and myself spending whole afternoons listening to the birds sing during the spring and summer.

I sure could use a chipper birdsong right about now.

A joyous, trilling melody filled the air.

Darting from my tent, my mouth fell slack as dozens

of birds, every imaginable shape and color, sang from the treetops. *Did I do that?*

Others crawled from their tents to see the commotion. A crowd formed. Their cacophony and the chirping seemed to reverberate through the woods.

"Birds? What the hell?"

"I've never seen a bird here before."

"This is weird."

"They're beautiful."

"They'll bring the Coals right to us!"

An arrow flew from behind us, landing in the ground a few feet from the tree line, scattering most of the birds.

"There. Now the noisy little shits are gone," Emily declared coldly.

"Well, that's one way to get rid of them," I mumbled.

Standing next to me, Pete shook his head. He watched the others disperse, then faced me. "Did you do this?"

"I don't know…maybe?"

"First the thunder, then your nose, now this. No way is all that together a coincidence."

I hated thinking it, but I said, "I'm starting to believe so, too."

WANDERLUST THRUMMED THROUGH my veins, so I took Hazel for a short jaunt around the campsite's perimeter. She wanted the exercise; I needed the distraction. It must've worked, because my muscles actually felt less tense when I hobbled her to her tree again.

Pete waited at the edge of camp, rubbing the back of his neck. "I thought about it; maybe we should test this out … this *thing* you can do. See the extent of it."

I'd been pondering the same thing. "That makes a lot of sense, actually. Sure, let's do it."

He rubbed his chin, observing the surrounding trees. "Probably be best if we go somewhere secluded, though, just in case."

"M'kay."

We found a clearing away from the camp but I could still make out the colors of the tents from where we stood.

"So, how did you do the thing with the birds?" His wide-eyed expression made him seem like a kid asking about the 'coin behind the ear' trick.

"Dunno. I was thinking how birdsong cheers me up when I'm upset, then there they were."

He made a face while considering. "Okay, so it has to do with your thoughts and feelings."

I shrugged. "Seems like a solid theory."

"Let's test it. Try to imagine a butterfly."

I closed my eyes, envisioning a vibrantly orange Monarch butterfly resting on my hand, daintily fluttering its wings.

An odd tickling, crawling sensation ran up my index finger.

"Whoa!" Pete gasped. "Heather!"

I nearly crawled up Pete's back. On my finger stood the Monarch butterfly I'd imagined, down to the double set of white dots on its wings' edge. "Oh my God."

My movement must've frightened the tiny creature; it shot off into the air, flying up against the sun till we both lost its path.

"Amazing!" Pete stared, his jaw agape. "It just appeared out of thin air."

I stammered incoherently. The words I needed to describe what happened just didn't exist.

"Let's try something a little less complicated this time," Pete suggested. "A flower?"

I closed my eyes once more.

While I tried to produce the image, my focus drifted to the beautiful garden at Death's palace. "Okay, I think I've got it." The bright colors, the decadent aromas…

"Shit. Heather," Pete whispered frantically, "*Heather!*" Shaking my shoulders. "Open your eyes—stop!"

A sharp pain throbbed near my temples. The blood in my veins felt like ice once my vision adjusted to our surroundings.

We stood in the center of a flowerbed—in Death's garden.

CHAPTER TWELVE

THE GROUND SHOOK with the rhythm of Coals marching, the pounding noise growing louder and closer every moment we lingered. Though we couldn't see them yet, it wouldn't be long before they found us.

Pete drew his gun, his posture rigid. "Do you think you can take us back?"

"I can try." My knees shook.

I squeezed my eyes shut, throwing all my concentration into imagining the meadow, the tents' colors peeking through trees, being safe with the others.

A cold gust of wind circled us. When I opened my eyes, we stood in the exact place we'd been before we'd popped into Death's garden.

My relief was cut short—horrific pain tore at my skull. Gripping my head, I screamed, pitching forward onto the grassy earth. Hot blood oozed from my nose. I jerked, surprised to find my fingers covered in crimson.

Pete knelt by my side, his face pale. "Dammit, this was a bad idea."

"I'm okay now, I think." The pain in my head faded as quickly as it'd arrived.

"Do you need something for your nosebleed?"

I pushed onto my knees, then stood. "No, it's over."

"I'm sorry. I pushed you too hard." Reaching into his pocket, he pulled out a square of cloth which looked as though it had been torn from an old shirt, and offered it to me. "I put us both at risk. Here, use this to clean up."

Wiping the blood from my face helped settle my stomach. "Thanks. No need to apologize. You didn't do it on purpose."

My words didn't do much to ease the guilt in Pete's eyes. "No, but I pushed too hard. It's a bad habit I need to break."

One of the birds I'd created after Shaun's memorial darted from one tree to another. "Well, now we know to ease into this. We'll start simple, I'll work my way up to things like transporting people and the gushing blood bit will subside, right?"

"That's a solid plan, but for now, go get some rest. You've earned it."

I SAT ALONE, my knees curled to my chest. The clanging of metal merged with the cracking booms of gunfire in the distance, but I paid it no heed. Training just didn't sound appealing this morning.

Footsteps crunched nearby. Pete. He took a seat next to me. "Hardly anyone's at practice today. Everyone's off investigating some noises we heard last night. I've been neglecting my archery. Can't let myself get lazy." He scratched at the nape of his neck. "Anyway, training by myself's less fun than watching grass grow. Figured I'd come see you. I could sure use a smile."

I wasn't feeling it. I kept my gaze locked on the ground. "Sorry for not joining you. I'm just still rattled over yesterday." But then, desperate for reassurance, I let my eyes meet his. "What do these powers make me? Am I even human?"

He almost patted my shoulder, but stopped his hand mid-air, then drew it back to rest on his knee. "Of course you are. You're one of the most human girls I've ever met."

I squeezed my knees tighter to myself. "You've only known me, what, a couple of weeks, maybe? It's so hard to know how much time is passing… Anyway, how can you be so sure I'm not some psycho monster under all that?"

"A 'psycho monster' wouldn't risk her life to try getting back to us, to camp. She wouldn't be so protective of Lily. Wouldn't cry in her sleep, begging for forgiveness."

I scooted away from him.

He snickered, waving his hands. "No, no. I don't watch you sleep; that'd be weird. Your tent's right next to mine, if you haven't noticed."

Relaxing my tensed muscles, I scooted back. "Oh. That's right."

"Only spot there with enough space."

"I still talk in my sleep?" I muttered, mostly to myself. My parents in several of my lives had complained about my wailing and making a ruckus nightly.

I thought I'd stopped that many lives ago.

"Yeah," Pete was saying, "Not loud. I haven't paid enough attention to transcribe it or anything. But you beg someone named Isabel for forgiveness."

A pain in my chest rattled at the mention of her. I grimaced. "That's my sister."

Pete set his hand on mine. "What would she need to forgive you for?"

"I abandoned her." It just came out. I hung my head. "I'd promised to always be by her side. It ended up being for the best; I accepted that a long time ago, but it still hurts sometimes."

"I know what you mean. I still beat myself up over Spencer every once in a while, but it doesn't erase the guilt. Or the thought that maybe I could've done more."

"You can't always know what path your choices will lead you down. All you can do is make decisions and deal with consequences when they happen. And hope your call's the right one."

He offered a slight smile. "If you ever feel like this again about your sister, think about what you just said. It could help."

I nodded, wiping my nose on my left sleeve. "I'll remember that."

Megan, followed more slowly by the rest of the group, came back from their latest mission. They were carrying something huge. "Pete, Heather!" she called, beaming, obviously excited. "You need to see this!"

They let it fall to the ground when we approached. It rattled when it landed. An empty suit of Coal armor.

Short of breath, Jack said, "Megan helped us take down a Coal. It was amazing."

Pete and I shot to our feet. I looked to Megan. "You said you didn't want to fight."

"I don't. Just came up with the idea that worked, is all. Didn't even lift a finger."

Pete stood frozen for a moment, staring wide-eyed at the armor, before looking to Megan. "What'd you do?"

"Well, I noticed they're hardly around in the daytime, so I guessed sunlight weakens them."

"Megan told us her theory," Greg explained flatly, his deep voice a lifeless monotone. "We tested it last night. Caught one patrolling alone, pissed it off, dodged it 'til sunrise, then started a fight."

"The bastard went down in a couple of hours," Emily stuck out her chin with a glow of pride. "If that. Black smoke blew everywhere when we finally killed it."

The smile on Pete's face was so bright it rivaled the sun. "This is amazing! Why didn't any of us come up with this before?"

"Maybe fear kept you from thinking properly," Megan offered.

His brow shot up. "You aren't afraid of them?"

"You bet I am. Just not in quite the same way as the rest of you. I don't have to worry about fighting them."

Emily muttered a comment so crude Megan grew pale.

Pete narrowed his eyes at her before continuing. "They *can* be destroyed. We have a fighting chance. We can win!"

Overcome, I joined in the rousing cheer that rang out from the crowd.

THE FIRE SNAPPED and hissed while everyone laughed. I sat, humming along to the songs they sang, watching them around the fire taking turns dancing. Patting their legs and logs to create a rhythm.

Pete grinned, running to me. "No wallflowering. There aren't even any walls around here." He grabbed my hands, hoping to pull me up, but I shook my head. "I'm an awful dancer."

"It's not a contest. C'mon, have a little fun." He jutted out his lower lip in an adorable pout. "Please?"

I rolled my eyes with a chuckle. *I swear this boy could convince someone with ophiophobia to pet a snake.* "Ugh, fine."

He pulled me close. In an instant, every inch of my body tingled. I swayed back and forth with him.

"See, you're doing fine," he noted.

"You won't be saying that when I crush your foot."

His chest vibrated as he chuckled. "Don't think that'll hurt me much." He exhaled a deep, contented sigh. "God, it feels great to know this isn't a suicide mission. Won't be easy, but at least we know it's possible to destroy them now."

"I can imagine."

"It's a lot of pressure, keeping everyone safe."

How does he keep sane? So many people count on him. "I can believe it. How did you become a leader of this whole thing, anyway?"

He spun me around, and weirdly I followed him effortlessly. "It's a long story."

My mouth curved into a smirk. "I've got time."

After another spin, he met my eyes. "After we lost Hugh, everyone expected me to take his place. I was his right-hand man, y'see. But I said no. Didn't want the responsibility. We had wiser, *better* people than me, I said. *They* deserved the position more. Bernard Alvarez got the job. Big Mexican dude who'd been here nearly two hundred years.

"Bernard was a hot-head. Always at Hugh's throat. Hugh was a pacifist. Thought we could use diplomacy, only fighting when necessary. Bernard, he was a warmonger. He'd fought at the Alamo, never really got over being killed, I guess. Think he saw winning this war as a chance to redeem himself." We'd slowed a bit, no dips or twists now.

Pete shuddered, disturbed by the memory. "Bernard's time as leader was brutal. He'd take squads out to provoke Coals, determined we'd beat 'em." I could feel his hand gripping mine as he spoke. "More people left than came back. Always. Made us train constantly without breaks. Since we don't need sleep, physically, we were fine. But morale was so in the dirt that it didn't matter how much we trained. We had one hundred members when Bernard became leader. Around a month later, only twenty-five of us were left. Now, there's only twelve. Including you."

I wondered if we should stop dancing. I contemplated his story. Emotions swirled through me like a tornado—disgust at Bernard's cruelty, shock at how Pete's fear caused so much damage. Sympathy for how much he'd been through.

"For what it's worth, I think you're doing a wonderful job. If you start going mad with power, I'll slap some sense into you," I cracked a smile.

"Thank you."

"No problem."

"I try my best to be a leader these guys deserve, even though I think I screw up more often than not."

"That's all anyone can ask of someone in your position," I said.

Continuing our swaying dance, an awestruck smile

tugged at Pete's lips. "How'd you get so wise?"

I evaded his eyes, focusing on the other dancers. "I've had a lot of spare time, thinking about such things."

"You don't hear most people our age having conversations like this."

I shrugged a single shoulder. "Well, most teenagers aren't in a situation like ours."

"True."

"It's weird. I've never fit in anywhere. God knows I *tried* to be like everyone else. But no matter what I did, I was always a reject. Here, though, I am not a *total* outcast. For the first time in who knows how long. Sure, not everyone likes me, but I finally feel like I belong somewhere. Funny... it took leaving the world I knew to find my place."

"Don't you miss your home? Friends? Your family?"

I nodded. "Of course. But home's been on my mind less as time's gone by."

His hand tightened on the small of my back for a moment. "That's how it is with most of the spirits here. They fall in love with this world. Eventually forget the one they came from. They get lost in the endless string of warm, sunny days. Some don't even remember being alive in the first place by the time they *move on*."

"It's not this world making me miss home less—" I began, but stopped. The sight of Greg sitting alone, staring at the ground, face in his hands, caught my attention. "Excuse me for a second."

Pete followed my gaze, he hesitated but eventually let me go. I sat down next to Greg. "Not much fun sitting all by yourself."

He lowered his hands, looking through bloodshot eyes. "I just wish Shaun was here. This would've been the best day of his afterlife, finding out those monsters can be brought down." He wiped his nose on his sleeve. "He should be here celebrating too, but he'll never celebrate again…"

"Maybe he's celebrating now, wherever he is."

"Don't give me that bullshit to try to make me feel better," he growled.

"You don't think there's anything after *moving on?*"

Greg snorted, "Hell no. I think it's a lie. Placating people into willing themselves into non-existence."

"So we just cease to exist?" *Should we even be discussing this?*

"We're lucky to get *one* afterlife." He let out a biting chuckle. "I'm supposed to believe we get *two?*" His expression soured even more. "Get the hell out of my face, Breather."

I rose, holding my hands out, placating.

Pete raised a brow when I returned. "What was that about?"

Tossing a stick into the fire, I watched it burn. "I tried to cheer him up. He flipped out on me."

"Did the same thing when I tried to talk to him."

"Guess we'll leave him be, then." I raked my fingers

through my knotted hair, taking a hitched breath. "That was a total disaster."

He frowned, warming his hands by the fire. "He's just grieving. Don't take it personally." He rubbed my back, leaving a trail of goose bumps down my spine. "Now, may I have this dance?" he asked, moving his arms into position to pick up where we'd left off, spinning me around.

I nodded, letting out the girliest giggle I'd ever heard. *God, I'm a dork.*

A few times I swore a pair of unfriendly eyes were glaring at my back, but I paid no attention. *It's probably just Greg or Emily.*

Talking and laughing, we danced all night.

CHAPTER THIRTEEN

T HINGS RETURNED TO business as usual the next day. Breakfast, then practice. During training, I managed to hit the target. True, it was hardly a bull's-eye, but I still considered that solid *thunk* a victory. The pride I felt overshadowed the throbbing soreness in my arms.

As Pete and I left the training ground, Tina ran up. "Pete, Heather, Jason found something at the old camp when he went to check if we'd left anything behind. It's big."

We all went running. Grabbing Hazel on the way, I rode as they followed on foot.

As we approached a couple of hours later, Jason stood, his posture tense, gaze transfixed. "Good day," he whispered.

Tiptoeing closer, I couldn't help but ask, "What's going on?"

"We are not alone." He pointed. "A small gathering.

Two gentlemen and two ladies were rooting through some of our weapons that were discarded in the chaos of changing locations, and now seem to be setting up camp here," he replied without turning his head.

Pete grimaced, squeezing his hand into a fist. "I can't believe we left stuff behind." He grunted, shaking his head. "Are they friendly?" he queried, shifting into commander mode as he lowered his tone.

"I am uncertain if they are friend or foe."

"I'll go investigate. You three, stay on my flank in case things get dicey."

Weapons drawn in precaution, we trailed Pete silently through the woods as he circled around to come at them from behind. Eventually, we positioned ourselves into a half-circle right behind the group of four spirits.

Pete crept to the treeline before standing and taking aim with his shotgun, calling, "Hands up!"

Three of them cried out, raising their arms. The last one—a young man with spiked green hair—calmly pushed himself to his feet. "Oi, was this your gear?" he drawled in a thick English accent.

"Never mind whose stuff it is," Pete answered, cocking his gun. "Who are you? What are you doing?"

The man took a step back, holding his hands up in surrender. "Steady on. I'm Ollie. These are my mates: Mindi, Kay, and that one's Wes." He gestured to the others. "We were mucking about, looking for a new campsite when we found all this. If it's yours, I'm sorry.

We don't mean trouble."

"Why would you need weapons?"

Ollie raised a brow, looking at Pete like he was stupid. "To help if we tangle with those nasty blokes in armor, mate."

"They've been giving you trouble?"

Ollie adjusted his spiked leather jacket with a cocky air. "Nah, we've kept things quiet, stayed out of sight. Tryin' to get back to the living world with Death miffed with us doesn't sound enticing. Weapons do come in handy, though."

Pete holstered his weapon. "We aren't the only one's trying to get back?"

Ollie shook his head. "You're the third group we've bumped into since we got here in eighty-five. Far as I know, we're all that's left. Rest of 'em had nasty run-ins with the armored gents."

"That's happened to a lot of our people, too."

Ollie put a hand over his heart, sympathy in his eyes. "My condolences."

"Do you need a place to stay? We've got a camp, you're welcome to join us."

Ollie grinned, revealing glistening white teeth, a gold crown covering one of his canines. "That'd be brilliant, actually. It'd be better being part of a group."

OLLIE AND THE others were met with a lukewarm response. Everyone kept their distance when we arrived, eyeing the newcomers with the same suspicious looks I often received. Emily, her usual welcoming self, stared them down.

"Charming bird, that one." Jerking his thumb over his shoulder, Ollie quipped, once she'd marched off to sit by her tent.

I stifled a laugh, but couldn't control it. "Emily's kind of moody. I'd just leave her be, for your sake."

"I think she's lovely," one of the women with Ollie countered.

"Right. I won't be pestering her. She'd whop me before I'd blink."

The mental image of Emily fighting Ollie crept into my mind—it wasn't a pretty sight. "Yes, she would." I paused for a moment. "What's your story?"

He clicked his tongue, scratching his chest. "Same as everyone else's, I assume. The whole 'second chance' bit. Plus, I miss booze. Gonna do a lot of drinking when I get back."

"There's no alcohol here?"

"Not a drop. Doubt it'd work, anyway," he grumbled.

Anxiously, I rubbed my neck. "Don't know if I'd want to drink after being given another chance at life. It'd kind of feel like wasting a gift."

He folded his arms, eyeing me judgmentally. "Bloody hell, we've got a prohibitionist on our hands."

I puffed out my chest. "No, I'm just saying, tempting fate after coming back from the dead doesn't sound smart."

Ollie beamed, a twinkle in his eye. "No one's ever called me a wise man."

Throwing my hands up in defeat, I let out a chuckle. "Well then, there you go. I'm not telling you what to do—feel free to ignore me. Just giving a suggestion."

He nodded, pursing his lips. He almost looked impressed. "You've got moxie, I'll give ya that. Fair enough, love."

The woman who'd been standing by us before—young with russet-colored skin and grungy, stringy brown hair, wearing a tattered black shirt with a British flag on it, had approached Emily. Her chestnut eyes were blazing, steely, as she stood to acknowledge Mindi.

"Aw, Mindi… you're gonna get your arse handed to ya," Ollie mumbled to himself, following my gaze.

Mindi whispered something in Emily's ear. As prophesied, she promptly got a smack square in the face. Mindi crumpled into a heap. "She broke my jaw!"

Ollie doubled over, squawking with laughter.

Mindi pushed herself to her feet, wandering over, grabbing her jaw to snap it back into place.

Wincing, my stomach churned.

Ollie ran his fingers through his hair. "Hope that taught you not to chase every girl y'see, Mindi."

Mindi grinned, looking back at Emily's tent. "I'll

give 'er space."

"Probably a good idea to back off. Emily would break every bone in your body," I added, shaking my head.

She tapped her chest in the spot where her heart once beat. "Lucky for me, I'm dead. She could do whatever she wanted, long as she doesn't lop my head off or somethin'."

Glancing to Ollie, I asked, "Is she blindly determined, or just stupidly bull-headed?"

"She's a stubborn ol' git, that's for sure."

Mindi defiantly raised two fingers, shoving them toward him. "Love you too, Ollie, ya numpty."

Ollie laughed, a sound like a car backfiring. "Steady on, I didn't mean nothin' by it."

Mindi charged toward Ollie, tackling him with a thud. The pair smacked, hit, and wrestled with each other, laughing all the while.

The other two guests, Kay and Wes, sat behind us with her in his lap.

"Any bets on the winner, kitten?" I heard him ask before noisily kissing her neck.

"Two blossoms says Ollie wins, he always does. God, they're so immature," she breathed, twirling her fingers through her hair, bleached so blonde it looked drier than wheat.

Mindi and Ollie's wrestling continued until Greg came out of nowhere, grabbing the two by the scruff of their necks. "Knock this shit off—*now*," he barked.

"Let us down," Ollie whined as he struggled.

"We was only foolin'," Mindi protested.

"I don't care," Greg snarled through his teeth, throwing them down. "If you want to be childish little twits and get ghosted by Coals, be my guest. But don't do it out in the field, or you'll answer to me."

The two of them stood, a bit wobbly, cursing under their breath while rubbing their sore spots.

Greg jabbed a finger at them. "If I need to shut you up again, I promise you I'll be less polite."

"We'll be absolute angels," Ollie replied, crossing himself.

"You'd better be, for your sake. Limey dumbasses," Greg muttered to himself before skulking into his tent.

Once Greg was out of earshot, Ollie glanced my way. "What crawled up his arse?"

"Coals got his brother not too long ago," I explained.

He flinched. "Nasty business, that. Condolences."

"I'll let him know."

"C'mon, you lovable bastards," Ollie called to his counterparts. "Let's go pack."

I watched them vanish among the trees, a sense of foreboding creeping up my spine.

CHAPTER FOURTEEN

L ILY AND MEGAN sat outside Megan's tent, singing a bright, cheerful song in perfect harmony. Their high voices complemented each other beautifully. Before too long, a few others returning from training joined in as they sat around the fire, sharpening and polishing their weapons. I closed my eyes, enjoying the moment.

A simple cough disturbed the peace. The warmth fled my body when I saw him.

Death.

In a flash, everyone drew their weapons.

Death gave a polite, flourishing bow. "Please, do not stop the festivities on my account."

"How the hell did you find us?" Pete barked, his shotgun aimed directly at Death from the opposite end of the fire, nostrils flared.

"A little birdie told me," Death replied with a knowing smirk.

"You aren't welcome here. Leave."

"I merely come with a message for the young lady amongst you. We have business. I grow impatient waiting for you to take part in our bargain. Do not forget what you shall receive should you succeed, and the consequences should you fail."

Gathering every inch of courage I could, I stood, looking at him square in the eye. "I won't be helping you. Leave. Now."

Death folded his arms, seeming almost amused. "So you are casting your lot with terrorists?"

"They are *not* terrorists." I kept my tone firm, my resolve solid.

"Oh, they are not?" He tilted his head. "I am sure the spirits whose homes were destroyed in your confrontations with my soldiers would disagree."

"Shut your mouth, you bastard!" Pete bellowed, firing at Death. The bullet smashed into Death's chest, leaving a hole in its wake.

With a huff, Death waved his hand. The hole healed. His white dress shirt stitched itself back together. He roughly adjusted his jacket and tie, seething at Pete. "You desire conflict? So be it," he hissed, snapping his fingers. "But it shall be on *my* terms."

Black clouds appeared, twisting and contorting until they took the shape of five man-sized ravens. They looked to Death as if awaiting instruction.

He waved dismissively in our direction, his voice

emotionless. "Destroy them. Spare the live one."

The beasts charged, with screeches that shook the ground.

Bullets and arrows filled the air, but the fierce creatures were undeterred. Dodging the assault, they tore with their beaks and talons at whomever they could reach.

Screams came from every direction.

I spun helplessly, witnessing a raven knock Jeremy off his feet and pin him to the ground with its talons. The impact of his head hitting the ground cracked his glasses. The monstrous thing gripped Jeremy's left arm and began to pull. He howled in terror and pain as he tried to wrench his hand out of the beast's maw; his cries only momentarily paused by his choking sobs. Running to help ended up being futile—before we were halfway to him, the bird ripped Jeremy's arm off with a final, harsh tug.

Tina cried, "No!" firing an arrow at the animal's head. The shot missed, but successfully drew its attack to her.

It hissed, pouncing. She managed to pry an arm free, but it still held her down. Drawing a hunting knife, she plunged it into the raven's breast. It threw its head back with a pained wail before disintegrating into dust.

I rushed to help her up. She gave me a nod of thanks before we knelt in front of Jeremy.

"You all right, kid?" Tina asked, her face drawn with concern.

He nodded, gritting his teeth. His left arm was completely gone. Torn at the shoulder. "Hurts pretty bad, but I think I'll be okay."

For the briefest moment, I considered asking Tina if she had anything to stop the bleeding, until I realized—there wasn't any blood. A gruesome reminder that these weren't living beings.

"Lily's hiding by a log about a hundred feet away," Tina whispered. "Find her. Keep her safe until someone comes for you," she commanded, setting him on his feet.

With a salute, Jeremy dashed away lopsidedly.

Relentless clicking suddenly came from our left. "Help me! Oh, God," Jack yowled. Two ravens had cornered him in a tight cluster of trees. He desperately kept firing his gun at them, despite the fact he'd long since run out of bullets.

Tina gathered her bow and reached for another arrow, but it was useless. One of the ravens had already raked its talons across Jack's throat. He fell to his knees and vanished, leaving only empty clothes behind.

I stepped back to catch my breath. One of the abominations leapt into the air and snapped at Pete, knocking him down.

Instantly, my gun was in my hands. I screamed in defiance, firing a shot at the bird's head.

The bullet hit its wing. The bird crashed to the ground with a squawk. As it struggled to stand, I holstered my gun, drawing my sword. The ground swayed underneath my feet, but somehow I managed to trudge toward the flailing beast.

Gasping, holding my blade high, I stood above the huge mutation. It tried looking in my direction. I snapped my eyes shut. With a sickening crunch, the raven's cries ceased.

My weapon dropped to the ground. I stared at my sweaty palms, which had left the dust thick and gooey. Almost as if my hands were covered with the blood of the thing I'd just killed.

The thing I just killed. I'm a killer.

Pete called something, but I couldn't comprehend words.

Emily shot at the nearest monstrosity, piercing its neck. Crashing to the ground, it cried in pain. Emily leapt in the air with her machete drawn. Black dust sprayed everywhere as she screamed at the top of her lungs, hacking even after it was gone.

The remaining two birds, the ones who'd got Jack, moved on the ground toward Megan. She frantically backed away from them with her hands up.

Frightened tears cascaded down her cheeks. "Please don't... I didn't do anything," she whimpered. Pete charged at them with a shout of pure rage. Jason followed, yelling, "Have at you, brutes!"

The birds took flight, swooping at the pair with a growl.

Jason took a heavy slice at one of them with his blade, cutting off its wing. The bird fell to the ground. I fired a shot—the bullet lodged itself in its left eye, blinding it. It craned its neck to bite Jason, but he struck it again. Its head tumbled, landing at his feet before disintegrating into dust.

The final creature tackled me, pinning me with its immense claws. My gun flew from my hands, clattering a few feet away. The creature's weight crushed my chest. My lungs screamed for air, but all I could manage was a shallow cough. Its dark, beady eyes locked onto mine before it let out a ferocious screech. Kicking and thrashing, I tried to scream, to reach for a weapon of some kind, *anything*, but it was no use.

Jason and Pete rushed to my aid, but a powerful swipe from the last raven's wing threw them back.

No!

Sharp talons digging into my hips, the beast slowly lifted off the ground. Before long, I was about twenty feet up.

"Dammit, I'm *not* getting kidnapped again," I shrieked.

If only I had my gun. Wait a minute!

Eyes snapped shut, I imagined my gun appearing in my hand, visualized the weight and feel of it. When I opened them again, there it was, just like I'd wanted.

After twisting my arm free of the creature's talon, I pressed the pistol's barrel roughly to the monster's gullet once its head was low enough. "Not this time," I growled, pulling the trigger.

The reaction was immediate.

The bird fell limp.

Black dust rained down on me.

The ground blurred as I plunged toward it at breakneck speed.

I landed with a sickening crack. Pain radiated through every inch of my arm. A scream ripped through my lungs when I tried to move.

Struggling to my feet, I saw Pete pinning Death to a tree, his dagger firmly held against Death's throat. "Still think you're hot shit, you son of a bitch?" Pete snarled through gritted teeth.

My entire body tensed with a panic I couldn't define.

Death's face remained calm and smooth. "You honestly are attempting to physically threaten one who cannot be harmed?"

"The gun didn't work, but maybe this will. Why don't we find out together?"

Pete made a quick strike at him, but it was too late. Death was already gone. As the smoke cleared, four figures rushed in our direction. In a flash, I raised my gun, cocking it. "Come back to finish the slaughter?"

But it wasn't the Coals. One dropped whatever he was holding, jetting up his hands in surrender. "Hold your fire, love."

My knees shook with relief. "Ollie?"

He slowly came closer. "In the flesh." Wariness in his eyes. Cautious.

I slid my gun into its holster. "Sorry. Things went

down the toilet. *He* came... tore us apart," I muttered, trying—and failing—to keep my voice steady.

A palpable jolt of shock passed through the quartet.

Ollie collapsed on the bundle he'd tossed to the ground, guilt staining his teal eyes. "I'm so sorry. We should've waited to get our junk. Maybe we could've done something."

Pete limped to my side, a sigh lingering on his lips. "It's too late now. Let's get moving. Time to relocate again. And let's try and be a little more covert this time. Can't have Death making another lucky guess."

ROBOTICALLY, I HELPED to move the campsite to yet another location, about a mile from the previous one. Despite the sling they'd made for me using an old pillowcase, my arm still throbbed with a deep ache. It didn't matter. They needed my help, so I grit my teeth and ignored the pain as much as possible. I couldn't speak, couldn't think, couldn't *feel*. Pete insisted I ate, so I half-heartedly downed some food once the fire was ready. My senses were too fried to even taste it. After everything was fully set up, I finally collapsed outside of my tent.

A strange, keening sound pierced the air.

It was only when Pete knelt at my side, scooping me into his arms that I realized those noises were coming from me. "Shh. It's all right, Heather. It's over now."

"N-no, it's not," I stammered through sobs. "It will *never* be over. Even if we make it out of here, today will haunt my nightmares for the rest of my existence."

He pulled me closer, careful to avoid touching my arm. "I'm so sorry for getting you caught up in all this."

"It's not your fault."

"Yes, it is. If I hadn't lost my temper…" He looked down, shaking his head.

"Someone else would've. Wherever *he* goes, pain follows."

"Maybe you're right, but I still hate that it happened. Jeremy lost his arm, you're traumatized, and Jack's…gone."

I choked. "It was awful. How do you do it?"

"Do what?"

"Get used to all the violence, all the killing." The memory of what I'd done to the ravens flashed in my mind. I squeezed my eyes shut for a moment in hopes of wishing it away.

When I opened them again, Pete's own eyes were weary. "You'd think it would get easier after a while, but it never does. I'm guessing you're feeling guilty over killing the birds?"

"I feel sick."

He rubbed my back gently. "Those things were monsters, Heather. They were literally ripping us to shreds. You saved me and who knows how many of the others."

Mercifully, my tears slowed. "Does that make it right?"

"Sometimes there isn't any other choice."

"Why do things have to be this way?" I whispered, my voice breaking.

"I wish I knew. Right now, all I know is we've got another memorial to get through, and I need to teach Jeremy how to fight with one arm." Deep sadness filled his words.

My body shook. He squeezed me tighter, helping me to my feet. "Go get some rest. Wish I could. It'd be nice to forget this shit for a little while."

"It couldn't hurt to try, I guess," I mumbled, though my hopes weren't high.

All night, till dawn, my dreams were plagued with screams and rivers of blood.

CHAPTER FIFTEEN

I STAYED ALONE for most of the next day, desperately trying not to think of the horrors I'd seen. Eventually, however, the time for hiding like a child came to an end. Pushing myself up to leave the tent, I couldn't help but notice my arm didn't hurt anymore.

Jeremy sat alone by the fire. The late afternoon light glinted off his cracked glasses.

For all I know he could hate me for what happened.

I gradually lowered myself to sit beside him. "How're you feeling?"

He nodded in greeting, then stared at the stub that'd once been his left arm. "It's just so weird. At least the pain's gone. Every time I look, it's like the first time I'm realizing it isn't there."

I leaned forward, my face in my hands. "I'm so sorry. If I'd—"

"Don't, Heather," he interrupted. "It's not your fault.

You did what you could. I'm just lucky I'm right-handed."

"And at least you've got some war stories to impress girls with when you get back."

He flinched, shaking his head. "Um…not really into girls."

My cheeks flamed. "Oh. I'm sorry. I just assumed…"

He gave a lopsided grin, but the smile faded. "It's fine. Not the first time, probably won't be the last. But really, what guy would believe me if I said I'd seen a real battle?"

"Not very popular at school, huh?"

"Korean, nerdy, *and* gay. I won the outcast lottery."

Gingerly, I patted him on the shoulder. "At least we've found some kindred spirits in the Land of the Lost."

"These guys are the best pals I could've ever hoped for." Slivers of tears pooled at the edges of his brown eyes. "My parents pretty much ignored me once they found out…I didn't have any friends. Do you think they'll stick around once we're back home? I've already lost Shaun and Jack… I couldn't bear being alone again…"

"Of course they'll stick around, Jeremy. It'll be different, for sure, but things like this bond people forever."

"I'm just so scared," his voice cracked.

I wrapped my arm around him in a side hug. "You won't be alone. I promise."

"Thanks, Heather." He jumped when a voice in the distance called his name. "That's probably Greg. He and Pete are going to teach me how to fight one-armed." He stood, adjusting his glasses before running toward the call.

Another voice caught my attention once Jeremy left.

Emily loomed over Pete a few feet away, shoving a finger in my direction, even from here I heard it all, "How many more people are we gonna lose before you admit the Breather needs to go?"

"Emily—" Pete began.

I charged over. *Enough of this shit.* "Emily, I've *had* it with your petty jabs, your dirty looks, and your baseless accusations. This 'Breather' killed two of those ravens, not to mention helped Jason take down a third," I shouted, placing my hands on my hips. "I've risked my life time and time again for this group. *And* I pissed off a being with godlike powers to stand up for you guys. Despite all this, you can only bitch about how I'm *the problem.* That I need to leave. Well, you know what, Emily? I'm not going anywhere. So stick that in your sour, bitter-as-hell pipe and smoke it."

Once the words left my mouth, Emily's fist came flying at my face, smacking me right in the cheekbone. Of course, I fell to the ground. "No one asked for your opinion, little whore," she snarled.

Pete shoved her, knocking Emily back a few steps. "Get your ass into your tent and cool off, or so help me God, dying will feel like a day at the spa compared to what I'll do to you."

She flicked up her middle finger at the two of us and stormed into her tent.

"Someone's wearing their ovaries on the outside today," Pete joked, helping me up.

Rubbing my cheek, I glared at Emily's tent. "I'm in no mood for her trash."

"I've got somewhere we can go if you wanna relax for a bit."

"Sounds fantastic."

"Then let's go."

MY LEGS ACHED by the time we came to a stop. A soft whooshing sounded in the distance.

Cold hands slid over my eyes, blinding me. "Hey!" I yelped.

"We're almost there. Don't want to spoil the surprise," he whispered.

We lumbered along for a minute or two before he lifted his hands. My breath caught in my throat once my eyes acclimated to the light. A small waterfall dove from a towering clump of boulders, crashing into a river flowing ahead of us. Red flowers littered the grass, complementing the red pines.

Pete took a deep, calming breath. "This is my favorite spot in this whole place. I call it my oasis."

"It's beautiful," I gasped, crouching to sniff one of the flowers. The scent was sweet, intoxicating.

"Isn't it? Found it shortly after Spencer and I died. We seemed to be the only ones who knew about it. We spent hours swimming in this river, skipping rocks. Spencer said he saw a fish in the water once, but he always had a talent for tall tales." Pete shook his head, smiling, though his eyes were downcast.

I glanced around us, taking in the scenery.

"Whenever I'm going through a rough time, and need to tune everything out for a while, like now, I come here. Seemed like you might need that, too."

"How thoughtful of you." A soft blush warmed my cheeks. "Thanks."

He stuffed his hands in his pockets, letting out a cough. "I also wanted a chance to talk to you in private."

"About?"

He wrung his hands. "Um, well, you almost got killed. I nearly got snuffed out myself. Made me realize a few things. When that thing grabbed you—all I could think was how important—" He looked up at me, his eyes filling with tears. "How painful it'd be if you were gone. I don't want to lose you."

I walked even closer to him, my breath slow, but hitching. "I don't want to lose you, either, Pete. It was terrifying when you got pinned."

He reached out for me and I stared down at how his hand was holding mine. "Heather, you're one of the best things to happen to me since I died. Spending time with you is the highlight of my day. Lame, I know. When we're together the anxiety, the sadness—all the war crap—it all goes away."

"It's the same for me. When I'm with you, I feel like a

normal girl instead of a circus freak," I muttered, unable to meet his gaze for a moment.

"You're not." His eyes sparked with mischief. "A little odd, maybe."

I pulled my hand away, hitting him with a playful smack. "Wow, you sure know how to woo a girl."

He grinned. "Just kidding." His expression grew serious as he brushed some hair from my eyes. "But, really, you're not freakish or weird. You're beautiful. Your nose wrinkles when you laugh. You get that cute little frustrated scowl when someone pisses you off. Your eyes shine silver in the moonlight, did you know that? You care about everyone's problems, when you're dealing with worse. You speak up, even if it's unpopular. You're amazing. Inside and out."

My gaze fell. "That's the first time someone's called me beautiful." I mumbled, burning heat flooding my cheeks. "Without it feeling like a joke or a lie."

He placed a finger underneath my chin, carefully lifting it so I'd look at him. "Wouldn't say it unless I meant it."

"It's one of the sweetest things anyone's ever said. But I've gotta be honest, it was a little high on the sappy meter," I noted, holding my fingers a couple of inches apart.

We bumped against each other while we laughed. *When did we move so close?* I froze. "Is this the part where we kiss?" I squeaked.

"You tell me," he whispered, leaning forward, touching his cool lips to mine.

My veins ignited. My hands wandered all over him, along his firm arms, his smooth face. His icy flesh felt almost warm, for once. My fingers snaked through his hair, tangling in his feathery curls. My heart sped so fast that a small, still-logical part of my brain worried it might burst.

He broke the kiss all too soon, gasping for breath. "Wow."

"You can say that again," I panted.

"What does this make us?"

I leaned my head on his chest. "Was about to ask you the same thing."

He looked away, considering the question. "I say we just let whatever happens, happen." His focus shifted back to me. "Let's just be us. The rest can come on its own."

Pursing my lips, I nodded, impressed. "Not bad. And you said you weren't good at this."

He bowed his head, embarrassed. "Honestly, I'm not. I dated a few girls before...well, you know...but the relationships didn't last long. Didn't have a clue what I was doing."

"A lot better than my track record. Big fat goose egg."

"That's not true anymore," he answered, pressing his lips against my cheek.

I gasped at the realization. "You're right," I responded, leaning forward to kiss him again.

EVERY PORE OF my body sang with joy. How had things gone from so bleak to so beautiful in a few short minutes? We walked back to camp hand in hand. The problems I faced weren't gone, but for the first time they at least seemed conquerable.

Pete looked to the group gathering by the edge of the fire. "Hmm. I'm supposed to be going on a recon mission right about now, but I'm tempted to blow it off. I'd rather spend the day with you," he murmured, wrapping his arms snugly around me, kissing my neck.

"Hey!" I gasped, giggling with shock at his affection. "No shirking responsibilities because of me."

"I'd be distracted thinking of what I'm missing here." He paused, his brow furrowing with concentration. "Wait a minute, why don't you come with us? I'm not sure why I didn't think of it sooner."

I took a step back, my stomach twisting. "Wouldn't I be a liability?"

He gave me a reassuring smile. "If this was your first day here, maybe. But you handled yourself pretty well with the ravens. Practices have been better, too. You've still got a long way to go, but I think you can handle this."

"Really?"

He nodded, grinning. "Yeah. I'm proud of you."

"Thanks." I dipped my head, tucking my hair behind my ears. "What do you even do on recon missions, anyway?"

"Talk to other spirits, see if they've heard anything of use. Sometimes we sneak into the castle and raid the library for anything relevant-looking."

"Sounds risky."

"It can be, but most of the time it goes smoothly. Finding anything useful is rare, but we keep trying."

My eyebrow quirked. "Some people might say that's insane."

"Far as I'm concerned, 'normal' is just a setting on a washer." His mouth curved into a lopsided smirk. The way his dimples poked into his cheeks made my heart do strange flips I didn't know it was capable of.

"Do you think the others will be okay with me being there?"

"It'll be fine."

"HELL NO!" EMILY snapped before Pete could even open his mouth. "This rude little Breather is *not* coming with us. She'll slow us down."

Pete ignored that. Instead, he focused on the others. "All right," he ordered, "The plan is to check with our usual informants and get back here before dark."

"Cross Bob off the list," Tina announced. "He doesn't want us coming around anymore. Coals won't leave him alone."

Jason revealed, "I must report my comrade, Reginald, has mysteriously vanished," gazing downward, his voice trembling slightly.

Pete's shoulders slumped. "That only leaves April and Geoffrey."

Tina groaned. "Do we *have* to talk to those two Carnheads?"

"Carnheads?" I asked.

Pete shot me a quick glance. "Remember those red flowers by the river?"

"Yeah."

"If you eat one, or squeeze it and drink its juice, legend says your heart will start beating again for a little while."

Emily added, "From what I've seen, it's a load of bull. Just seems like a potent, highly addictive hallucinogen. We call spirits hooked on them 'Carnheads'."

Tina shook her head. "They're the worst junkies you can imagine. They'd rip out their teeth in exchange for the location of a Carnadia patch."

"That's the Carnadia blossom?" I gagged. "Disgusting!"

Pete shook himself. "April and Geoffrey are our only allies right now, regardless of what they abuse."

"How do you even secure loyalty from people like that?" I couldn't help asking.

Emily grinned. "We give 'em Carnadia blossoms, of course."

CHAPTER SIXTEEN

MY STOMACH CHURNED. "You're drug dealers?"

Pete winced at my words. "We don't—it's the only way. We tried everything to get any information out of them. But they only respond to those flowers."

I wanted to vomit. How could he? "It's still wrong."

"Of course it is, but what choice is there? They're valuable informants. Their regular dealers see and hear *everything* in this place. Sometimes they tell April and Geoffrey things."

"Why not talk to the dealers, then?"

A shudder rattled Pete's shoulders. "Would *you* want to ask a drug dealer for something?"

I mulled this over then shook my head.

"Exactly. Besides, we don't go to them very often. Most importantly, we don't ask for teeth in return."

Arms folded, I grumbled, "I still don't like it."

Tina chimed in, flicking a blade of grass off her shirt.

"Believe me, none of us do."

This was wrong on so many levels. "Then stop." Sweat trickled down my neck.

Adjusting his belt, Jason grunted, "But then we would have no one to aid us."

"You can't find anyone else?" Desperate to lead them away from the moral quicksand they'd landed themselves in, I couldn't help asking.

Pete glanced over, eyes alight with determination. "We'll try, but for now this is all we've got."

WHEN WE FINALLY arrived, it was like stepping into a whole different world. Plain-looking houses with white siding and onyx metal roofs in seemingly endless identical rows. The siding shone so brightly as sunlight hit it I needed to squint. We searched for the right house number until we finally came across the correct one—546.

After a few loud knocks, a woman's voice spoke from the other side. "Who is it?" came the wheezy call.

"It's Pete," he answered.

"Come on in," the rough voice beckoned.

The door swung open.

The house's interior was the most horrific scene of garbage I'd ever come across. Paint peeled off the walls. A stench like something'd crawled into a pile of excrement and died befouled the air. None of us could move without stepping in some revolting glob. In the back corner of the room lurked a set of stairs leading to a grime-soaked door.

If the living room is this bad, I don't want to see the rest of the house.

The hag-like woman, who I assumed was April, didn't look much better. She smiled as we walked in, revealing the few yellow, crooked teeth remaining in her mouth. "What can I do for ya, Pete?"

Her hair was a matted blonde knot. Stains littered her tattered clothes. Pete forced his mouth into a grin, his eyes barely hiding his disgust. "We need any information you've heard in the past few days."

April sat down on a ripped, dirt-covered mattress, raising her chin haughtily at Pete. "Of course you do. You know the price, Bronx. Two C-Buds, then I'll talk." Her foot jerked where she'd crossed and dangled it on her knee. The shredded scraps barely concealing her feet hardly looked like if they could've once been shoes.

Producing two of the red flowers from his duffel, Pete tossed them to her.

She caught them, bowing her head. "Thanks. Champ said he saw a couple of those armored soldiers looking for this skirt that's giving them hell. This girl won't cooperate with Big Man, and he's not happy about it."

"Did they say who she is?" I asked.

"No idea. Champ said the soldiers mentioned birds. 'Bird this, bird that,' he said."

The ravens.

"Anything else?" Pete queried.

"Ah, man." April hacked and coughed. "Big Man's got

most his soldiers hunting for ya. If I were you, I'd lay low."

Pete looked around the room, then back to April. "Where's Geoffrey?"

She glowered over her shoulder, sullen, at the door at the bottom of the stairs. "Downstairs. Budding."

Jason, Emily, and Tina stood next to the door, rigidly doing their best to remain standing on the one tiny clean patch of the carpet.

"Champ came today?" Emily inquired.

"No. Geoffrey hid some C-Buds for himself, the bastard." April sniffed, glaring at the stairs. "If he weren't already dead, I'd kill him."

Pete pinched the bridge of his nose, breathing slowly; I saw he wanted to keep himself calm. "Focus, April. Did Champ tell you anything else?"

"Something about a book of Big Man's. Someone stole it." She picked at a cuticle, ripping at it with her teeth. "It's made a mess of things."

"Why's this book important?" I asked, my voice rising.

That must have caught April's attention. She looked right at me and deigned to say, "Champ didn't know."

"How helpful," Emily grumbled, kicking a piece of something that then scooted away on its own.

"Thank you for your assistance," Pete said with a polite nod.

Shutting the front door behind her with a slam, Tina shook her head, "What a gigantic waste of time."

"Not entirely," A smile in Pete's voice. "We're on the

right track."

I nodded. "Why else would he be getting more aggressive? He wasn't on the offensive this much before, was he?"

"No. We're pissing Death off, for sure." Pete looked at the sky, dyed magenta by the setting sun.

WE'D TRAVELED A mile or more, entering the forest again, when we heard the clatter of horses' hooves in the distance, growing steadily closer.

"Take cover," Pete whispered, ducking behind a tree.

We followed his lead. I crouched behind a boulder, drawing my pistol just in case. The pounding noise grew louder until it was right on top of us.

"Halt," boomed the familiar voice of the Coal leader. "I heard something."

There was a rattling thud as a Coal leapt off his horse. Twigs and branches snapped under the powerful stomp of his feet. Daring a peek, I saw five soldiers on his flank follow suit, searching the area.

"Over here," one of them beckoned, moving to the tree Emily hid behind.

I gripped my gun tighter, my knuckles white. Snapping my eyes shut, I pictured a wolf a short distance from the Coals. Within seconds, a deep growl rumbled nearby. I snuck a glance but wished I hadn't.

The wolf's eyes bulged, set too far apart. Its nose was deformed, twisted in a sickening way. It had only three legs, each of various size, a worthless stump hanging from where its fourth belonged. Its tongue drooped from its mouth, a mouth ringed with foam.

Oh, God... what've I done?

The animal threw its head back with a warbling howl. All six Coals spun to scowl at it. The wolf lumbered toward them, baring its teeth. The Coals drew their swords, which caused the beast to flee. Leaping onto their horses, the Coals gave chase.

Once they'd galloped out of sight, the five of us gathered on the road.

"What the hell was that disgusting thing?" Emily said.

"I made it," I mumbled, not looking up. A dull ache pinched at my head.

"What do you mean, 'you made it'?" she accused. She spun to face me, fists clenched. "You can create things like *he* does?"

I nodded, gritting my teeth against the intensifying pain in my skull.

Emily let out a barking laugh of self-satisfaction, eyes meeting all the others, and nodding. "I *knew* you were a freak!" Her rage now focused on Pete, "There's no way The Wicked Bitch of the West is staying with us now."

"Emily, stop," Pete barked. "She just saved our asses."

"She's a—" Emily froze, looking like Pete'd sworn the sky was chartreuse. "Wait—what?"

"I made the wolf lead the Coals away."

She turned, still suspicious. "You… helped?"

"Yes."

"Why?" she whispered, eyebrows knitted together.

I looked her in the eye, standing as straight as the pain would allow. "I may not like you much, but I don't want you ghosted. This group needs you, now more than ever. I've seen you training. You're one of the best."

Emily stared at me for the longest time before spinning on her heel, marching southeast toward our campsite.

Tina guffawed, "You've done the impossible—shut Emily up."

"Quite a difficult task indeed," Jason added a throaty laugh.

"At least she didn't punch me in the face this time."

Pete nudged me as we reached the bottom of a large hill. "Thanks for saving me." He brushed some hair from his eyes with an airy chuckle and kissed my head. "Again. I hope this doesn't become a trend."

"No problem. I feel awful for that wolf though." I sighed, wincing at the remembered image of the poor creature. "I don't know what went wrong."

"At least it helped us."

"Do you think it's suffering?" I asked, all but wringing my hands.

THE SUN HAD set by the time we reached the campsite. A fire already burned in the center. Lily played patty-cake with Megan by a tent. Jason smiled at the two of them, walking to his, sitting in front of it to read by the glow of the blaze.

Lily's blue eyes lit up when she spotted us. Tina knelt in front of her, wrapping her arms around her in a snug embrace. "Hey, jitterbug. Did you have fun with Megan?"

She nodded enthusiastically. "Uh-huh."

"Good. Grab your doll. You can tell me all about it."

The two of them walked off toward the training ground, Lily's squeaky voice chattering a mile a minute.

Megan stood up with a stretch. "You guys were gone a while."

"Coals tried sniffing us out," Pete explained with a proud smile, "But Heather got them away from us."

My cheeks flamed. "It wasn't anything special."

"Don't be modest. No way we would've made it back if you hadn't helped. I was stupid, telling everyone to go light on weapons. Thought we'd be back before sunset."

My face grew hotter.

Megan shook her head with a playful smirk. "C'mon, Pete. Let's get some firewood before *she* sets the camp ablaze."

Pete shot me a final, tender look before following Megan through the trees.

Trying to shake off my embarrassment, I took a deep breath as I knelt in front of my tent to put my things away.

I'd finally calmed down when Emily tapped me on the shoulder.

CHAPTER SEVENTEEN

"**T**HANK YOU FOR helping us today," Emily mumbled.

"Uh, I didn't do it for gratitude, but you're welcome." Swallowing hard, I quickly tied my tent shut and turned to face her.

"Honestly, I thought you'd let them get us to save your own hide."

I fidgeted, biting my lip. "Can I ask you something?"

She tightened her ponytail, hitching up a shoulder. "Depends."

I looked up at her, tucking some hair behind my ears. "Why do you hate everyone so much, especially me?"

"Hate might be a little strong." She sighed. "I mean, no one here's on my list of favorite people. The truth is," she paused, biting her lip, seeming reluctant to continue. "I'm jealous."

I blinked, unable to believe what I'd just heard.

Emily sat down next to me, pulling her knees toward her chest. "The others have things to look forward to if we make it back. I don't." She hung her head.

"What happened?" I flinched as soon as the words left my mouth, preparing for the smackdown that was sure to come.

She saw my flinch and smiled a little. "Relax, I won't hurt you. Maybe talking about this will help me. I don't know." She took a deep breath, her eyes shining. "I grew up in a small Massachusetts town. My parents weren't rich, but they made sure I was taken care of. We were happy and normal in every way that mattered.

"I had a few boyfriends in my teenage years, but they didn't really mean much to me. I wouldn't say I didn't care at *all*, but I wasn't as invested in my relationships as I should've been. Love just seemed like a waste of time. A roadblock on my path to becoming an English teacher."

She absentmindedly fidgeted with the sizable diamond ring sitting on her left ring finger. "That all changed the day I met Travis Kane. I'd just started graduate school. We had a class together. I can't remember which one anymore, but it doesn't matter. The moment I saw him, my world stopped. He sat next to me on the first day of class, asking if he could share my textbook because he'd forgotten his, and the rest was history.

"It wasn't long before I'd fallen head over heels for him. He was very charming, and we had so much in common. We'd been together two years when he proposed. I said yes, of course."

She confided, "Three days before our wedding, I was leaving the bridal shop after my final dress fitting. There was this restaurant across the street, an Italian place. I was starving, so I went in for a bite. What did I see in there? Travis…" She gritted her teeth, sucking in a harsh breath before continuing. "Travis sitting in a booth with some blonde, holding her hand. Kissing her."

Her hands curled into fists. She squeezed them so tight I'd worried they would bleed. "It hurt so much… how could he do that to me? For a moment, I considered canceling the wedding. Considered leaving him to his whore. Then it occurred to me—there wasn't a point in wasting the money we'd spent. The best way to make Travis pay was to go through with the wedding. Force him to spend the rest of his days with a wife who despised him."

I sat on the grass, unease creeping up my spine when she paused.

Emily shook her head, looking up at the sky. "Even though my wedding day was supposed to be the happiest day of my life, I felt miserable. I was fixing my smudged makeup when someone came into the bridal chamber. I thought it was my father, coming to walk me down the aisle. But when I turned, the slut from the restaurant was standing there. Didn't see the gun until she shot me. Right in the stomach. The last thing I saw in life was my white gown turning red. My last living emotions were shock and fury."

I almost gasped aloud. The temptation to hug Emily was strong, but my own desire to remain unpunched overruled it. I replied, voice low—it was such a sad tale, "I'm so sorry…"

She looked down at her open palms, voice thick with pain. "I sat alone in my anger for a long time when I first got here. I've focused on the bad memories of my death so much I can barely remember the happy ones anymore. It actually feels nice to finally tell someone." Her mouth curled—an almost-smile. "I'm grateful you actually stayed to listen. Maybe you're not a *complete* waste of space."

I SHOOK MY head as she left, amused at her openness to me despite her demeanor. I wondered if she would ever be able to make real friends. Mindi passed me, walking to where Emily stood. I headed toward Pete, who leaned against a tree at the opposite end of the campsite, whittling a stick with a tiny knife.

"I didn't know you were artistic," I said, adding a teasing edge to my voice.

"Whittling's a good way to pass the time." Smiling at me, he fished something small from his pocket. "Sometimes I get creative." He held his hand open, revealing a simplistic life-size carving of a Monarch butterfly. It wasn't perfect, but the craftsmanship was undeniable.

I stared at the tiny object in wonder once he gave it to

me. "It's beautiful." I pressed a hand to my chest, unable to speak.

"I chose a Monarch because it's the first thing you made purposely with your abilities. And to be honest, you remind me of a butterfly. Beautiful and gentle. They're far from the strongest things around, but they try, in the end that's what matters to me."

His face blurred as tears brimmed in my eyes. "That's so sweet."

He leaned in, softly caressing my lips with his. "What can I say? I'm a softie."

I pocketed the gift and wrapped my arms around his waist. "Your secret's safe with me."

His voice rang with laughter. "Yeah, because I've got *such* a reputation as a badass to uphold."

"Hey, no selling yourself short. You're plenty tough in my eyes."

"I don't feel like it most days, but who am I to argue with a beautiful lady?"

"Now you're just sucking up."

He shrugged a shoulder. "Maybe, it depends."

"On?"

He waggled his eyebrows conspiratorially. "If it's working."

I shook my head, snickering. "Should've seen that coming."

He laced his fingers through mine. My skin tingled at the unfamiliar feeling. "Can we just stay here? Forget everything else?" he pleaded.

I sighed. "I wish we could. Maybe someday, when this is all over, we can relax without a sword hanging over our heads."

"At least now the sword doesn't look so sharp. We know the Coals can be destroyed, and maybe with these things you can do, the tide can turn."

We sat down on the grass, looking up at the stars. Moonlight shone through gaps in the trees, mixing with the red of their needles to color our surroundings with a faint, serene purple.

I rested my head on Pete's shoulder. "Do you think we would've gotten along if we'd met in the living world, without this mess?"

"Yeah, I do."

"Maybe you wouldn't even notice me. You were a popular track star; I'm a nobody."

"Now who's selling themselves short?"

"I only have one friend back home." I took out the butterfly, turning it over in my hands. "I sometimes wonder if I should even go back. Maybe they're happier without me."

"They're probably frantic. I bet they'll be overjoyed when you get home. I wish I could say the same for my friends and family."

"You don't think they'll want to see you?"

"No. One of the few memories I've still got of my folks," he sighed. His voice grew strained as he continued, "is being called a failure. Didn't even want to *be* on the stupid football team…"

I squeezed his hand. "Doesn't mean they don't love you."

Pete ran his fingers through his hair with his free hand. "I know. Rather not burden them, though. Especially since Spencer won't be with me. They'd never say it, but they'd always wish he'd come back instead."

"I'm sorry."

He shook his head. "Don't be." His tone was nonchalant, but I could tell he was masking how he truly felt. His eyes gave it away. "Made up my mind a long time ago, around the time I lost him, that I'd start a new life if I got out of here."

"You could stay in Idaho with me," I suggested, but worries about the realities of how we'd get back started to crawl into my mind. "We could enroll you in the school I go to. I'm sure we could find you a place to live, too." *Could we actually do it? Should we?*

Pete smiled. "I'd like that."

We sealed our agreement with a kiss, and spent the rest of our night stargazing.

CHAPTER EIGHTEEN

A YOUNG GIRL'S cries roused me from sleep. Bursting from my tent, I drew my pistol. "Lily? Are you all right?"

The plea I heard next pulled the ground from under my feet. "Anna! Anna, please help!"

I gasped. "Isabel?"

My legs pumped as I darted through the forest toward her voice, but no matter how fast I ran, her voice still sounded so far away.

"Slow down, I can't keep up," I shouted into the morning mist.

After a while, I couldn't run anymore. My lungs burned. It was too early for this. The campground was nowhere in sight. Leaning against a tree, pistol in hand, I panted. All the oxygen in the world wouldn't have been enough.

"You are much too easily deceived," came Death's

voice, an amused lilt to it.

"How dare you trick me that way!" I said, mustering up as much disgust as my voice could through my wheezes.

"What choice was there? You hold nothing but contempt for me."

A tiny, crazed part of my mind wanted to argue—why, I didn't know. Thankfully, my sanity won out. I pushed myself off the tree, mostly recharged. "Well, I'm listening. For now. What is it?"

"Our bargain. Do you truly intend to not fulfill your role in it?"

"I'm not doing your dirty work."

He shook his head. "I would not consider that a wise decision," he said, using the tone of a parent scolding a misbehaving child.

"It's not your call."

"Be mindful of what you say. Before one of us takes action *you* will regret."

My hand twitched. I raised my gun ever so slightly. "Are you really threatening an armed woman?"

"Your bullets would be wasted on me." With a haughty air he turned up his chin. "No, I am merely giving words of sage advice."

I lowered the gun with a grunt, my brow furrowed. "You're right."

He let out an obviously exaggerated sigh. "It is a shame. You are causing pain to not only one of your families, but two."

A pressing weight crushed my chest. "Don't say that."

He approached me slowly, a sardonic spark in his eye. *I don't like that look…* "Say what? The Jerbins will despair because their dear Annabeth does not wish to come to them? Or the Kützs will forever mourn their beloved Heather, aligning herself with scoundrels rather than returning home?" He spoke like someone giving a eulogy at a funeral. *My* funeral.

"Please…don't," I whispered, barely able to form the words.

He walked toward me, a plea in his expression. "Spare your families such misery. Do what you agreed, and all will be well."

Frozen by the emotional turmoil he brought on me, I weighed my options. No matter the decision, I would suffer. Or those I cared about would.

Taking a deep, unsteady breath, I spoke slowly. Deliberately. "If either of my families were here right now, they'd understand why I can't do what you're asking of me. Even if it meant they'd never see me again. Those so-called scoundrels aren't what you think they are. They deserve a second chance." I raised my voice, feeling more confident. "So I'm going to help them, and go back where I belong. Without your help. Without compromising who I am."

He blinked in disbelief. "You are willing to sacrifice everything, yet again?"

"Yes. Because it was the right thing to do then, and it's the right thing now."

"What if you are wrong?" He raised an eyebrow. "What if you are re-making a horrible mistake?"

I stood straight, doing my best to appear confident. "Then I'll admit I was wrong, and do what I can to fix things."

He slowly came closer, a look of desperation in his eyes. "Please, see reason, Annabeth. Do not follow this path. It leads only to agony."

I held my breath, unable to move when Death reached for my arm. My stomach fluttered briefly. *Whatever that means, it needs to stop.* I took a step back.

"There *has* to be a way to give them what they want without hurting the balance," I insisted.

"There is not. You must end this nonsensical crusade. Please, heed my warning." He looked away for a moment, not letting me see his face. "I do not wish harm to come to you."

My heart skipped a beat. *Stop it!* I told it, *Don't let him get to you.* Thinking of the ravens, and everything else I'd been through, I said, "You're a little late to stop me from being harmed."

Death let out a long, rueful sigh. "I know. It troubles me."

Could've fooled me. "Didn't seem to at the time. Honestly, it's hard to tell what's *not* a charade with you. Is there a genuine bone in this body you've created for yourself?" I gestured at him.

He blinked, tilting his head like a confused puppy. "I do not understand."

I sighed. "I know you don't. Maybe you never will." I spun, and began to walk away.

But he materialized in front of me, his eyes tense with anger. "Do *not* depart while I am still speaking."

I took a step back, managing by some miracle to not show the panic stabbing at every inch of my body. "You don't control me."

"Even if I said, 'leave now and I will send my entire army to that campsite to lay waste to everything and every*one* in sight'?"

My leg muscles tightened. I considered running, to warn the others. "Don't you want this to end peacefully?"

"I do. But you try my patience. If there is no other method to coerce you into doing as I say, so be it," His threat lingered in the air.

The urge to flee grew stronger, but I held my ground. "I'm not a puppet you can just toss around."

"I do not desire a puppet. All I ask is for you to desist with this childish stubbornness and keep to the conditions you agreed to," he demanded, running a hand through his hair in frustration.

I declared, "*You* agreed to this *for* me. I'm leaving now. Don't try to stop me, and don't follow me." As I brushed past him, I found myself smirking inside at his dumbfounded expression.

MY FOCUS WAS awful while Pete and I sparred with swords later. I spent more time scrambling to fetch my weapon than holding the damned thing. My mind lingered on my conversation with Death.

"What's with you today? Grip the hilt tighter," Pete commanded. "If I were a Coal, you'd be dead by now."

"If I grip it any tighter my hands'll bleed," I grumbled, snatching up my blade for the millionth time.

He shot me a devilish smirk. "Hey, you suggested sparring today."

"Shut up," I harrumphed.

"Romance for the ages right here, folks."

I chuckled, despite myself. I winked before charging at him, aiming for his torso.

He easily blocked the blow, maneuvering his stance until he pinned me against a tree. My pulse raced as he leaned forward. While we kissed, he subtly nudged my sword from my hand.

"Not fair," I accused, breaking the kiss.

"I fight dirty, what can I say?"

I leaned to pick up my weapon again. "Good thing you're funny. It's why I'm letting you live. For now."

"Well, that works out, since I'm already dead and all."

I snapped my fingers in mock disappointment. "Damn."

Pete cleared his throat. "Okay, time to get serious. See

how I'm holding my sword?" He held it up to demonstrate. "Like this."

Mouth curved downward, I looked down at my sword. "Isn't that how I'm holding it?"

"No, you're holding it like a hot potato that's gonna burn you any second. It's not like you. Thought we'd gotten past that…"

"It's just been…hard. After you-know-what, combat freaks me out even more than it did to start with." My teeth pressed my bottom lip. "I don't know how I'm supposed to be okay with killing."

"You never become 'okay' with it. You learn to accept that this situation means either taking a life or losing your own."

The memory of killing the ravens flashed, making me shudder. "I guess."

"It's not pleasant, I know. But it's what it'll take to get where we want to be."

"If something makes killing and violence necessary, is it worth it?"

Pete stood quietly for a moment before replying, "In this case, I think so. We'll find out soon enough."

"If that weren't enough, Death was messing with my head today."

Eyes wide, his free hand twitched by his holster. "He was *here*? Dammit…"

My gaze drifted downwards, as if weighed down by my potential guilt. "He told me if I help you guys go back, whatever happens after will be my fault."

"That bastard," he snarled. After he sheathed his sword, he gently reached for my face and pulled my chin up so I had to meet his eyes. His tone was softer. "Heather, even if it all goes to shit after we go back, it won't be your fault. *We're* the ones that want this. You're just kind enough to help. If anyone would be to blame, it'd be me."

I shook my head. "I'll still have a part in it, no matter what."

"That still doesn't make you solely responsible."

His words didn't comfort as much as I would've liked, but I took a deep breath and nodded. "Okay."

He craned his neck from side to side, cracking it. "Enough about that asshole. We've got more important things to think about. You're getting pretty good with weapons, but what about those special abilities of yours? Have you practiced at all?"

I hadn't told anyone about practicing with my abilities—I still worried about what they would think. I sheathed my own sword before replying. *But Pete's different.* "I try not to push myself too hard—I don't want to end up in agony—but I do practice simple stuff. Small animals, y'know? I'm learning how to intentionally create things, but it's still a struggle."

"Like that wolf?"

I grimaced. "Yeah."

"You'll get it in time," With a reassuring smile he asked, "Want to practice now?"

"I guess."

He gestured a few feet ahead of us. "Let's try teleporting first. Should probably make it a short distance, though, so it hopefully doesn't hurt you. Try going past that tree over there." The tree was split in two, its branches sprawling upward like a person throwing their hands toward the sky.

"Right," I said nervously. "If I end up flipped inside out en route, I'm blaming you." I closed my eyes, imagining myself standing where he'd pointed. A gust of air rushed past me. I let it fill my lungs as I took a deep breath.

"You did it," he cheered. His voice sounded further away than before. My eyes flew open. He was right.

A dull ache pounded in my head, but I ignored it. "Still feels weird doing that." I patted myself down. Everything was as it should be. "My head hurts a little, but not too bad. Maybe traveling so far is what did it last time."

"Doing it twice in a row probably didn't help either. How about we move on to animals? Try making a squirrel."

Closing my eyes again, I envisioned a squirrel in a nearby tree, happily eating an acorn. I could almost hear it squeaking at me, feel the bushy fur of its tail…but then the image of that horrific wolf entered my mind and refused to leave. What if I made something that wretched again?

Pete made a retching sound and my eyes flew open.

"Oh God…"

When I dared to look into the tree, *something* oozed off a branch. It did have two beady, uneven black eyes. And four little twigs for legs. A matted, ratty thing that must've been a tail stuck out from one end of the gelatinous brown blob, twitching.

An acidic taste scraped its way up my throat. I slid my hands over my face. "What the hell is wrong with me? The poor thing…"

"Calm down." Pete held me, gently rubbing my back. "You're still learning how this works."

"Should we put it out of its misery?" I asked.

"You made it, so it's your decision. Do you want me to?" he asked, looking at me with sympathy.

A hot tear rolled down my face as I nodded. Pete slowly raised his gun, firing at the monstrosity. Letting out a hideous, gargling squeak, it fell in the dust with a *plunk*. Chunky bits splattered all over. I wrapped my arms tightly around Pete and sobbed, mourning the short, miserable life I'd created.

CHAPTER NINETEEN

LILY SAT BY Hazel, showing her a doll while Tina kept a watchful eye. Wes and Kay were in the throes of a passionate make-out session, not bothering to move behind a tree. Ollie and Megan sat by the fire, speaking animatedly about something I couldn't hear while she hand-wove a basket. The camp buzzed with activity. Mindi slowly approached Emily as she sat by the fire, holding up her hands as a show of peace. Emily's posture tensed as Mindi sat next to her, but, surprisingly, she didn't immediately start swinging. They spoke quietly, so I couldn't make out their words, but it seemed a lot more amicable than it had been.

Pete gave me a quick peck on the cheek before going to chat with Greg, who sat alone.

Jason caught up with me and fell into step as I walked to my tent. "Miss? I have obtained more information from the book you gave me."

"Yeah?"

"In this text—it appears the young lady spoken of may be the one to lead us to the land we seek." I turned to him, my curiosity piqued. "Follow me." He led us to a secluded place about thirty feet from the camp. Pulling the book from his satchel, he flipped through its pages until he landed on one. "Roughly put, it states, 'she brings the still to motion.' This may be false, but I found it noteworthy."

"Does it mention *how*?"

"In a fashion. Shortly thereafter, it says 'life must be consumed to be restored,'" he replied, once again translating from the book.

My eyebrows knitted together as I tried to understand. "They don't make any sense."

"Agreed, in those two lines, nor does much written here. My efforts to decipher will continue, however."

"Thank you, Jason."

"My pleasure." He bowed his head, closed the book, and departed.

Another puzzle piece I needed to make fit. Could *I* really be the one to bring these wandering spirits back to the living world? My eyes swept over everyone's faces. Would that be the best decision? These spirits were undoubtedly my friends now. I wanted them to be happy. But if Death was telling the truth, helping them spelled doom.

This situation gets messier by the day. I need to clear my head.

Going for a ride on Hazel seemed like a perfect way to relax. I waved to Lily and Pete, making my way across the campsite to Hazel's tree. She whinnied, bouncing with excitement when I approached.

A chuckle rumbled in my chest. "That's right, girl. We're going for a ride."

Hazel knickered happily as I untied her from the tree and hauled myself into her saddle. After I gently nudged her ribs with my heels, Hazel took off. A charge of exhilaration rushed through me. Trees became nothing but blurs in my peripheral vision as we left the campsite behind us.

The sunlight warmed my skin. A floral-and-pine perfume filled the air. We circled around the area about a mile from camp, easing into a gentle walk. Everything felt peaceful. Still. The stress weighing down on me lightened for the briefest of moments. Everything fell away.

A bellow on my left broke the silence. "Halt, girl! My master wishes to speak with you."

Slowing Hazel, my stomach tightened into a knot. Standing a few feet away, holding the reigns to a horse, was a Coal.

Shit. How did I not notice him?

"I've got nothing to say to him, or to you." I spat, "Leave me alone." My voice was surprisingly strong despite the boulder-sized lump in my throat.

"You have no choice in the matter."

Drawing my pistol, I considered firing at him. *What*

are you doing? You're not good enough yet to take on a Coal. Quickly shoving the gun back in its holster, I nudged Hazel's ribs with my heels. "Like hell I don't!"

"You will regret this," he snarled.

Hazel screeched in terror, launching herself into a gallop toward camp. With no time to call for backup, the Coal gave chase alone.

"Coal!" I hollered when we'd ridden close enough to the camp. "Coal on my tail!"

While I dismounted, everyone burst into action, drawing their weapons.

Within seconds, the Coal reached our camp. We fired a barrage of bullets and arrows the instant he came into view. All of them merely bounced off his armor. Ignoring them, he dismounted his horse. Drawing his sword, he barreled straight at us. His footsteps were unsteady, but still he came on.

Emily, Greg, Pete, and Mindi charged, their blades swinging at wherever they could reach on the Coal. Emily thrust her sword at the Coal's chest, howling in rage. As he swung at her, she jumped back, barely evading his attack. Greg used this distraction to make his move, slicing at the Coal's right side. The Coal grunted, haphazardly swinging his sword. Greg easily dodged while Pete came at the Coal from the right. After a while, the unrelenting attacks became too much. He fell to his knees.

"Grab him, quick," Pete cried.

We all grabbed the Coal's arms, restraining him as

best we could. Emily pulled out her machete, holding the blade against the armored being's neck. We'd never been this close to one before.

Pete held up a hand. "Not yet. First I want to see what's under their helmets." He grabbed hold of the towering metal helm and pulled, struggling with it until it finally came free.

Deafening silence engulfed us all.

Underneath the helmet was a man close to Jason's age. His eyes shone pure obsidian. An expression of unadulterated rage and hate lurked on his face.

Jason dropped his sword, mouth agape. "Reginald?" he whispered. The man gave no response. Jason knelt in front at his side. "Reginald, what has become of you?"

In the shouting bellow of a drill sergeant, he replied not to any of us but to the sky, "Our master chose me for a higher purpose. One of honor and glory. You rebellious imbeciles know nothing of such things," he spat, finally acknowledging Jason's presence by turning to face him.

"Do you not know me?" Jason asked. "It is Jason Rowbury," he tapped a hand to his chest. "We were boys together. We perished together in the war between France and Scotland."

Reginald looked into Jason's eyes, his mouth curling into a baleful snarl. "You are no friend of mine, traitor."

Tears streamed down Jason's wrinkled face. "Please, Reginald...please remember me. You are my last connection to my former life. My most trusted friend……"

The Coal looked away, instead focusing on a nearby tree. "I do not align myself with slanderous filth such as you. All of you soil the good name of our benevolent leader and master." He spoke of Death in an awestruck tone usually reserved for a deity. Speaking of someone who had done the horrendous things Death had done in such a way made my stomach turn.

Jason grabbed Reginald's shoulders, choking on a sob. "I swear, whatever Death has done to you, it will be reversed. We will return you to your former self. Your *true* self."

"*This* is my true self."

"It is *not*. Please, Reginald, let us aid you."

"I would rather burn."

"For your sake, for mine, I implore you to see reason," Jason pleaded, shaking Reginald's shoulders.

"Nay," his old friend replied, snapping his mouth shut, saying nothing more.

Pete looked to Jason, his voice trembling. "I'm sorry, Jason…we can't let him go like this. He could hurt Lily… I don't know how to fix him. I don't know if he *can* be fixed. If he won't accept help, there isn't much choice." Jason hung his head, unable to speak.

Pete drew his sword. The metallic scrape it made sliding from its scabbard hit me like a blow to the gut.

Jason stood, laying a hand on Pete's shoulder. He shook his head. "He is my companion. It is only right that

I am the one to do this…"

Pete hesitated, lowering his sword ever so slightly. "Are you sure?"

Jason nodded, a heavy sorrow in his words. "Aye. Reginald—the *true* Reginald, not this abomination wearing his face—*he* would prefer it."

Pete stepped back, nodding.

Jason eased his blade from its scabbard, his hands trembling. With a deep, labored breath he took one last glance at his old friend, before raising his weapon. "Forgive me," he whispered shakily, voice breaking.

I turned my head when the strike came down, unable to bear the sight of more death. A disgusting thud punched though the air, then all fell silent. A dense, black fog blew past us before vanishing.

When I finally turned back, my eyes fell upon Jason, holding himself up with his weapon. No one moved or said a word. Ollie first looked away from Jason, who wept openly at the empty suit of Coal armor. Then, he broke the silence, "That rat bastard thinks he can snatch us up and make us into those things? He's not getting away with this. We'll make him pay for what he does."

Jason looked to him over his shoulder, red circles around his eyes. "Hold your tongue, Oliver. There will be a time to decide what action to take in response to this, but it is not now."

"You can't be serious."

"I'm entirely serious."

"What about the rest of ya?" Ollie spun, staring at each of us. "Do you agree with him?"

No one spoke.

Ollie growled, "So that's it, then? You're gonna let him do this to us?" He'd stood and kicked a nearby rock. "We could be next, you tosspots!"

Greg's head shot up. "Can we breathe for a while?" he muttered in a barely-restrained tone. "For God's sake, Ollie, it hasn't even been ten minutes."

"Best time to strike, I say. Show 'em what we think of this shit."

Greg rose, towering over Ollie, snarling, "The only thing your plan would do is get us all ghosted."

"Piss off, we're smarter than that. *I'm* smarter than that."

"Everyone who tries to be a big shot says something like that. The story always ends with empty clothes and grief," Pete muttered, holding Reginald's helmet, staring at it for a moment before throwing it down.

"How do you know? And Greg," Ollie shouted, "all you do is sit on your arse all day mopin' about your brother. Don't tell me what I should do."

Greg clenched his shaking hand, drew it back, and punched Ollie in the face. Howling in pain, Ollie leaped at him in a futile attempt at a tackle. As he came at him, Greg kicked at Ollie's chest, knocking him on his ass.

"*Enough*," I yelled, rushing to Ollie and kneeling in front of him. "You're angry, I get that. We're *all* angry, but we can't take it out on each other. And we can't blindly seek revenge—we need a plan. Death won't get away with this, I promise, but revenge needs to be done with the right amount of preparation."

He spat in response. The revolting blob clung to my cheek. I wiped at it, forcing my expression to remain smooth. Ollie stood up and ran off, his silhouette eventually blending into the shadows around us.

CHAPTER TWENTY

THE DETERMINED GATHERING of misfits I'd come to know were replaced by a group of listless zombies. The trauma of knowing the true origin of one, if not all, of the Coals, had deflated us all. The following two weeks were shadowed with an undeniable aura of melancholy. Our daily routine continued as usual, but it felt hollow. Pointless. No one mentioned going out on recon missions. Nobody showed interest in leaving the camp at all.

I found a light in the darkness in Pete. We spent hours talking together at his oasis. With him, there was no need to pretend I was fine; the tears could flow freely. After a while, I could smile again without guilt gnawing at my soul.

It was in a quiet moment that Pete suddenly blurted out, "I love you." Three words a non-relative had never said to me. "It's probably nuts to say that. We haven't been together very long, and with everything going on, and—"

I pressed my mouth to his, silencing him. "You worry too much." I murmured with a smile once our kiss ended, "I love you, too."

He smiled sheepishly. "How I could've made it through all this without you, I'll never know. Don't really think I want to, either."

"I would've gone crazy a long time ago if you weren't here. Well, crazier, at least."

"Things have been nuts lately, that's for sure," he mumbled, shaking his head.

"How are we supposed to deal with this Coal thing, Pete?" I whispered, the fear I so often tried to hide breaking through in my voice.

He looked up, watching one of the birds I'd created fly past. "I want to say it changes nothing, but it'd be a lie. From now on, every time I face a Coal, part of me will wonder if it's someone I know."

"We can't let this stop us. Otherwise, *he* wins."

"I know," Pete said with a sigh.

"Any word from Ollie?"

He rubbed a hand over his face "Nothing. It's like he fell off the face of the earth after his temper tantrum."

"I hope he didn't do something stupid. His anger over what happened was justified, at least to a point."

"I just wish he'd used it in a more constructive way."

I nodded, picturing the last time we'd seen Ollie, the hurt and anger in his eyes before he'd left. "Yeah."

We left the oasis and headed back to camp. The others

were engrossed in their own activities, but one sight in particular stood out. Mindi and Emily sat close together by the fire, their knees almost touching, whispering to each other.

Pete nodded in their direction. "Weird, isn't it?"

Squinting to get a better look, I jerked back. "I'd say. Is she actually… *smiling?*"

"Looks like it. Guess it just goes to show, you never know who someone will turn to in times of darkness."

I smiled up at him. "Yeah, you never know."

"I keep thinking if I turn away for a second, you'll disappear. Everyone'll tell me I imagined you," he chuckled, though a twinge of genuine worry crept into his tone.

"Funny, I worry I'll wake up alone, horrified that I only dreamed you."

"If I dreamed, I don't think I'd come up with someone like you," he whispered in my ear, making me shiver.

"Trying to fatten up the mice again?"

"I'm gonna put them in a diabetic coma."

We were still laughing when Lily ran up to us. Her long, blonde hair had been tied back in a braid.

Pete scooped her into his arms, hugging her. "What are you doing, munchkin?"

"Megan and Tina did my hair! See?" She shook her head, letting her braided locks swish back and forth.

I gave her a warm smile. "They did a good job. You look very pretty."

She flipped the braid over her shoulder, pointing at a vibrant red feather attached to the tie holding her hair in place. "Look! They put a feather in there too, from those pretty birds. Megan said she used to put them in her hair too when she was little."

Pete beamed. "Looks like we've got some fashionistas around here."

Lily took hold of her braided hair, twirling it around a finger. "Do you think Mommy will like it? I wanna look special when we go home."

Pete and I shared a look, then I slowly began to speak. "We aren't going just yet, sweetie. First we need to figure out *how* to get home."

Her mouth drooped as she looked at Pete. "Tina said we're leaving soon, going to the place where the living people are."

Pete nodded. "We are. But 'soon' doesn't mean 'now,' Lily. We *will go*, though. I promise. And your mommy will give you lots of kisses when we do."

Her eyes began to water. "Do you think her and Daddy even miss me?"

"Of course. Who wouldn't miss such a sweet little girl?" he replied, tickling her stomach.

She threw her head back, howling with laughter. It was impossible not to join in. She squealed, "Hey, stop it, Petey! Not fair."

I piped in, "All right, tickle monster. Time to stop torturing children."

He set her down. "It's about time for your lessons, anyway."

Her nose wrinkled. "Do I *have* to? It's so *boring*," she whined, pretending to retch.

Pete knelt down, looking her in the eye. "You don't want to be behind when you go back to school, do you?"

Letting out an exaggerated sigh, her face scrunched with frustration. "No."

"Exactly. Now, please find Jeremy and go with him to Tina for your lessons."

We watched her go, snickering at the melodramatic way she trudged to Jeremy's tent; a convict walking to the electric chair.

"If she's this bad now, imagine her as a teenager," I observed with a smirk and a mock shudder.

"She'll be a handful for her parents, that's for sure."

"Do you think you'll start aging again once you get back?"

Pete shrugged, his posture suddenly tense. "We hope so, assuming we make it back."

I turned to face him. "You're losing faith?"

"It's been hard to hold onto hope these days." He stared down at his boots, nudging a piece of bark with his foot. "I haven't given up—I believe we can do this—but, you know, with everything going on, doubts come creeping in." His expression lightened when he looked back at me. "When they do, I look at you, or any of the others, and I kick those stupid thoughts out of my head.

Because I know all of you believe in me, are counting on me. If I lose hope entirely, we're screwed."

"Maybe just a little," I teased.

He slid his hand into mine, squeezing it tightly. "It really helps to know that others believe in me, even when I don't believe in myself."

I ran my fingers through his velvety hair with my free hand. "You're more capable than you realize. Somehow, I'll convince you, even if it takes the rest of my life."

How ever much longer that is.

He grinned. "I like the sound of that."

"So do I," I whispered, kissing his cheek. "Can I ask you a question?" Unsure how to begin, I bit my lip. "If I… didn't live long after we got back to the living world, what would you do?"

His brows rose. "What a weird question."

"I know. But humor me, please," I begged.

Time had to have passed in the living world since Death brought me to the Land of the Dead. I wasn't sure how much. No matter my stay's length, my current life would be over not long after we returned. *I need to know he'll be okay without me.*

He mussed my hair with a smile. "I wouldn't off myself, if that's what you're wondering." His expression grew earnest. "I'd be devastated, and miss you like crazy, but I couldn't throw away all we're working for. I'd try my best to get on with my life, waiting for the day we'd meet again."

Finally releasing the breath I'd been holding, I squeezed his hand. "Not a bad answer."

"Why?"

I evaded his gaze. *If I tell him now, he might freak out. I've waited too long.* "No real reason. I just wanted to be sure you'd be able to go on should the worst happen."

"That's logical, I guess." He held me close to his chest. "You worried me for a second."

"Don't worry. I'm not going anywhere. Not for a while, at least." Enjoying being in his arms, I let my eyes close.

His stiff posture relaxed. "Good. I've dealt with enough loss for three lifetimes."

"Feels more like eighteen for me."

He squeezed me gingerly. The security his touch brought made my worries vanish, even if only for a moment. "It'll be behind us soon."

Will it? I thought.

Greg's voice boomed from the direction of the practice area. "What the hell? Where is it?" Pete and I ran, skidding to a halt when we reached him.

"What is it, Greg?" Pete asked, his eyes searching the perimeter for signs of danger.

"One of the Coal's suits of armor is missing," he replied. He gestured, and we looked down at the light indent on the ground next to the remaining suit.

Like a cop doing an investigation, I folded my arms, looking to Greg. "Do you know who did it?"

"No idea." He shook his head. And growled, "Then again, it could've risen by itself and walked away. For all we know, those bastards could regenerate."

"This can't be good," Pete mumbled to himself before turning to Greg. "Let's increase our security. Have a couple of us patrol at night, switching every few hours."

Greg nodded. "You read my mind. I'll talk to some of the others, sort out a schedule."

"Good thinking. Did you notice anything else?"

Greg walked over to the pile of weapons, gesturing to them. "Someone came after practice and messed up *all* the bows, not just the ones from the last batch." He picked one up, pointing to various spots up and down the bow's face. "Like this one. There's little cuts everywhere. It'll fall apart if you put too much pressure on the grip." He set it down and leaned down to reach for another. "The string notch on this one has been cut away…" His left hand curled into a fist. "Just like Shaun's was."

Letting out a restrained sigh, Pete pinched the bridge of his nose. "All right. We'll make a new batch of bows, and keep 'em in my tent."

Trying to diffuse the situation, I nudged Pete, joking, "I'll keep an eye on him, Greg, don't worry."

Greg's lips curled into a smirk. The first time I'd seen him smile since he'd lost Shaun. "I'm not worried at all. Those bows will be safer than in Fort Knox with Pete. I trust him with my li—er, afterlife."

Pete gave him a fist bump. "Back at ya, bro."

"'Bro'? Oh, so it's about race now, huh? Because I'm black, I'm your 'bro'? Why you gotta be like that, man?" he replied, feigning offense.

Pete's eyes widened for a few seconds before he broke into a snicker. "You almost had me."

Greg shook his head, letting out a gut-busting laugh. "I can't believe you fell for that. You'd think it'd sink in after the first million times." He grinned. "You don't need to be so paranoid. Calm down. I know you're not like that."

Pete wrapped his arms around Greg in a huge bear hug. "It's good to see you being yourself again."

"It's nice to feel more like myself. I still miss him, but he wouldn't want me being miserable forever."

Pete stepped back, patting Greg's shoulder. "You're right. He'd want you to be happy. So when we blow this Popsicle stand, you should live it up for the both of you."

He nodded. "I will. But right now I'd better figure out the patrol schedule. Have fun, don't be too loud when you're going at it." he laughed as he left.

With the two of us alone again, and Greg's words echoing in my ears, I stared awkwardly at the ground.

"What is it?" Pete asked, concern in his voice.

"Well, um, Greg said… and I noticed we haven't… I mean, you haven't tried to, you know…" My pulse thudded faster than a heavy metal drum solo.

Pete's eyes widened. "Oh. *That.* See, well… there's an issue."

"Don't tell me you're celibate."

He laughed, shaking his head. "No, no. Are you *kidding*? I'm an eighteen-year-old guy! I mean, if you didn't want to, or if you weren't ready, then I'd respect that. But right now it doesn't matter, because I can't."

I tilted my head, raising an eyebrow. "You can't? I don't understand."

"You've had 'the talk', haven't you?"

I nodded, blushing already. "Yeah."

He wrung his hands anxiously. "Then you know guys have to… do a certain thing, for that to happen."

My cheeks were on fire. "Uh-huh?"

He looked at the ground, grimacing. "Well, being dead, I…can't. You kind of need your heart to be beating for it to work."

Everything suddenly clicked. A sickening whirl smacked me in my stomach. "Oh."

He kicked a rock. It smacked a tree with a *plunk*. "It's frustrating as hell. I want to, God knows I do, but it's literally impossible right now." He met my eyes. "I hope you aren't too upset."

Rubbing my hand up and down his back, I smiled at him. "It's not your fault. Besides, we can always give it a try once we've left this place."

He smiled back, the anxiety in his eyes evaporating. "Thanks. Wasn't sure how you'd react. That's why I haven't brought it up before now. And, I mean, if you really wanted to, we do have some options. I could…"

I shifted uncomfortably, interrupting him. "Um, I don't know if I'm quite ready for that, if that's okay."

"Of course. There's no rush."

"So, have you ever… you know?"

"Yes." He winced, looking into my eyes like he expected my judgment.

I kept my expression smooth. He'd already mentioned other relationships. His answer wasn't a shock.

"I used to think my death was punishment for my misdeeds in life—teasing Spencer, sassing my parents, neglecting the girls I'd been with. Now, I think maybe my experiences here are teaching me to be worthy of the right kind of girl." He looked down at me pointedly, wrapping his arms loosely around me.

He leaned forward, giving me a knee-tremblingly tender kiss.

"I don't consider myself someone a person needs to be worthy of," I said after a moment. "I've caused a lot of trouble for you guys."

He held me tighter. "I told you, it's nothing we can't handle. That includes you."

I squeezed my eyes shut. "With how insane things are getting, I don't know how much more time we've got unless we have some sort of breakthrough," I whispered, hating myself for saying it.

Pete pulled me close, his voice tense. "I know."

CHAPTER TWENTY-ONE

I N BED THE next morning I lay awake, wondering about
the missing Coal armor, when my tent suddenly
vanished from around me. In fact, *everything* from the
Land of the Dead seemed to vanish—I couldn't see except
for an inky blackness. I tried to call out to Pete, to Tina,
anyone, for help, but my voice had vanished too. Then, bit
by bit, I noticed familiar shapes emerging from the
shadows.

A bed.

A wardrobe.

A bookshelf.

My bedroom in Idaho Falls. If someone told me before
this chaos began that I'd weep at the sight of this house, I
would've called them crazy. But I did.

My relief at being in a place I called home felt tainted
by my desperation to have the group of spirits with me.
We'd made plans to return together to the living world.

Had it all just been a dream?

I couldn't have made him up. I just couldn't.

I launched myself from my bed and ran through the house, hardly believing I was really back. But something wasn't quite right. The furniture wasn't where I remembered. Dust and clutter coated every surface—except in my room, which seemed spotless.

Wandering the dim hallway toward Mr. and Mrs. K's room, I heard shouts echoing from inside.

"Don't start this again, Andrew," a voice I recognized immediately as Mrs. Kütz screeched. "It isn't my fault she's missing."

I listened outside the slightly ajar door. Mr. and Mrs. Kütz stood by their bed, faces red with anger.

"If you hadn't coddled her, maybe she wouldn't've bailed at the first sign of pressure," Mr. Kütz yelled.

She jabbed her finger against his chest. "Well, you're so strict I wouldn't be surprised if she ran off with a stranger."

He took a step back, sneering. "Didn't realize setting limits made me a tyrant."

"There are limits, then there's an eight o'clock curfew. What kind of lunatic puts such a harsh restriction on an eighteen-year-old?"

He smacked the back of his hand into the palm of the other. "The kind who wants his child safe."

She sighed, sitting down on the bed. "I want her to be safe too, but she's legally an adult now, Andrew. She needs the freedom to explore the world, to experience it. Maybe she'd still be here if she'd been freer."

He folded his arms with a glare. "This isn't just about Heather, is it?"

She nodded, wiping her eyes. "I need you, Andrew. Our daughter's disappeared. Why are you spending all your time at the office when I need you more than ever?"

He threw up his hands. "Excuse me for making money to pay for the search."

"You make more than enough money. You don't have to neglect me like this."

"I'm hurting too, okay?" Mr. Kütz cried. "You aren't the only one missing her! But all you think is 'poor, poor Abby'. Am I wrong? I *dare* you to tell me I am."

She looked down, biting her lip.

"That's what I thought." He barreled into their walk-in closet, tossing a suitcase onto the bed, carelessly flinging clothes into it before slamming it shut. "I don't need this shit. Heard it a million times since she disappeared." He hissed, "I'm sleeping at a motel." He charged out of the room, toward me.

I tried to call to him as he approached, but he passed right through me.

Gut-wrenching wails distracted me from my panic. I looked back into the bedroom; Mrs. Kütz had fallen to her knees in front of the bed, clasping her hands together. Her eyes looked up at the ceiling. Tears rolled down her face. "Please God, please just bring her home," she sobbed.

"We're falling apart without her. Please bring back my little girl…"

Her desperate prayer stabbed at me. My face fell into my hands. Consumed with guilt, I sobbed too. Suddenly, her crying stopped. Mrs. Kütz was gone. Red paint bled down the walls of the house, completely covering their normal beige tint. I watched in horror as black stripes formed through the red. Dark grey carpet grew from the hardwood floor like grass.

What the hell is going on? The Kütz's hallway changed shape around me until it formed a moderately-sized room. A bed, dresser, and other furniture came into view. After a while I recognized Alex's bedroom.

Alex lay on her bed in Carl's arms. Dark circles hung under eyes. The vibrancy I used to see in her was now hardly noticeable.

"What if something awful's happened to her? She's been gone for so long. It's not like her to simply vanish."

Carl caressed her back. "It'll be okay, Alex. I promise," he replied, a note of genuine concern in his voice.

She shook her head, looking up, though her eyes focused on nothing. "I could've prevented this whole thing. She told me something was going on. I shouldn't have assumed she'd work it out on her own, that things would go back to normal. Maybe if I'd tried to help her—"

"You don't know that," Carl said comfortingly.

"I'm so scared that I'll never see her again," she whispered shakily.

"Alex!" I called to her. "I'm here, I'm okay!"

Neither of them reacted. Carl pulled her closer. "You've just gotta have faith that they'll find her," he said.

She wiped her nose on her sleeve. "They can't look for her forever…"

"You're right, but that point isn't here yet. She could turn up before then."

"I know. It's just so hard to keep hoping. Especially s-since Grandma…" She cut herself off, putting a hand over her mouth.

He patted her leg, giving her a reassuring smile. "Don't give up, okay? Even though I didn't have much time to get to know her, I'm sure she wouldn't give up if you went missing."

She nodded, sniffling. "She wouldn't. Not for a second."

I nodded firmly. "Damn straight I wouldn't."

He pressed his lips to her forehead. "This'll be a crazy memory for you two to share before you know it."

She glanced at an old photo of the two of us she kept on her dresser, tears shining on her cheeks. "I hope you're right."

Before I could do anything, the room collapsed again around me, the familiar yellow-and-green interior of my tent taking its place. Pain radiated throughout my body. Collapsing on my cot, I clenched my jaw to hold in the screams. Red droplets splattered on my blankets.

I touched my face, staring at the blood smeared on my

fingers. My hands shook.

Another nosebleed?

Only after the pain subsided could I slowly rise to wipe my face with a cloth I'd made from a spare shirt. Once I was clean, I emerged from my tent to find everyone gathered around the campfire.

Pete smiled when I approached. "Morning, Heather. I was about to check on you. We're having a meeting."

I sat down, face hot. "Sorry for holding things up."

Megan shrugged. "It's fine. We weren't waiting long."

Emily leaned her head on Mindi's shoulder, smirking at me. "If you call three hours 'not long.'" Though her tone was light, I detected a definite undercurrent of annoyance.

I didn't snap at her, though. How could I be mad, knowing the story of her death?

Emily'd been through a horrible ordeal. It was little wonder why she was so angry at the world.

Pete cleared his throat loudly, dragging me back to the present. Everyone's focus returned to him. "We've been through a lot lately. But we can't let it stop us. If we forget what we're fighting for, *he* wins."

He slammed his fist into his palm. "It's about time we get back in the ring. Ollie was wrong about a lot, but he was right about one thing—we can't let Death get away with this."

"Mess with one spirit, you mess with us all," Greg agreed.

Emily rubbed her chin, seeming to ponder this. "We

could teach him that lesson."

"We've gotta do this right," Pete continued, "Storming the castle without a plan is a quick path to failure. Gotta start simple, get updated intel. Find out if anything has changed. Once we know his plans, we'll hold the ace. We'll surprise him, spoil his game."

A hopeful grin began to spread across Jeremy's face. "He'll have no choice but to give us what we want."

"What if he makes more of those ravens?" Tina piped in. "We'd be screwed."

"That's just it. If we get strong enough intel, we'll know his contingency schemes too, and can prepare for them," Pete replied.

Around the circle everyone chimed in again, "I've heard worse ideas," Greg noted.

"If it means I won't lose another arm, then I'm in," said Jeremy.

Mindi locked eyes with Emily, then gave a small nod. "You've got our vote, mate."

"Then we're in agreement?" Pete asked.

A sound of assent passed through the group.

He beamed. "Great. Then we'll leave soon. Greg, Jason, Mindi, Emily, and Heather, meet me at the training ground when you're ready. The rest of you keep an eye on things while we're gone."

WE SET OUT a short time later. We each brought some easily concealed weapons, in case things got heated. We walked for hours through the early afternoon until we reached the houses.

Pete turned to us once we'd taken cover behind a cluster of bushes. "All right, here's the plan. We're going to split up and see if we can recruit some more informants. Heather, you can be lookout. If you run into trouble, you know what to do."

I nodded, giving a little salute, and our group parted ways.

I wandered aimlessly around the nearly endless, perfectly even rows of duplicate houses. Every single one had wooden siding, colored perfectly white, with beige curtains in every window. The area was deserted. Completely silent. I still kept my guard up, just in case a Coal decided to surprise me.

This place gives a whole new meaning to 'suburban hell'.

Then I stumbled upon a house that didn't quite look like the others. It was painted blue, with a row of Carnadia blossoms planted on either side. An older man stood with a watering can to soak them.

Something elusive tugged at the back of my mind when I saw him.

I swear I know this man.

The realization hit like a heavyweight's punch. This was the principal of Idaho Falls High School.

I blinked, frozen with shock. "Mr. Advani?"

Staring at me, it took a moment before recognition

dawned in his eyes. "Heather Kütz?"

I nodded as I approached, stepping onto the lawn. "How did you get here?" I asked, jumping in before he could ask the same thing.

Setting down the watering can, he sighed. "My heart finally decided to quit. But I'm sorry to find you in this place. I truly hoped you'd be found alive."

"Found?"

"You were reported missing quite some time ago. Your poor parents are frantic. They convinced every police officer in Idaho Falls to search for you. They even asked the ones not officially working your case to help in their spare time."

I bit my bottom lip, but that didn't stop it from trembling. "They'll probably give up the search soon, won't they?"

"I'm afraid so. Shortly before I died the chief mentioned on the news they may need to."

Taking a deep, shaky breath, I looked up at him. "What about Alexis Mordaw? Is she all right?"

"From my understanding, she visits the on-campus counselor daily. But she's been absent from her classes regularly. With everything going on, you disappearing, and the awful situation with her grandmother, it's not difficult to see why."

"What happened?"

"I'm afraid she passed away. Her house is about a block away from here, actually."

I sniffed, tears beginning to form. *She needs me and I'm not there.* "Thanks for telling me."

"You're welcome, Heather," he said sadly. "I wish I bore better news."

"So do I." I gazed at the flowers to calm myself. "Is the afterlife treating you well?"

He shrugged. "I can't complain. I've got the stamina of thirty men, a beautiful land to explore, and a lovely garden to tend to."

"It's coming along nicely."

A small smile curled his lips. "Thank you. The days are always so nice it almost feels like cheating. I discovered these gorgeous blossoms on a hike and simply had to harvest some seeds to grow my own. If only troublemakers would stop tampering with them," he harrumphed. "Every morning I discover whole clusters missing."

"That's a shame," I mumbled, sure of the identities of troublemakers he spoke of. "At least it's not like the time the basketball team broke into the school greenhouse and stole all the vegetables."

He laughed, but then shook his head, a hand over his heart. "That was tragic. I slaved for months over that garden. Those delinquents were lucky they only got detention."

"Do you miss your work? Do you miss seeing the kids?"

Mr. Advani pursed his lips, thinking about my words before responding. "At first I did miss it. Part of me always will, I think. But I lived a good, long life. The students are in good hands with Ms. Peppern." He smiled serenely. "I'm at peace."

Once the words left his mouth, his hands began to vanish. Slowly. First his fingertips disappeared, then his arms up to his shoulders.

"Mr. Advani?" Horrified, I asked, "What's going on?"

He only closed his eyes, sighing contentedly while he disappeared inch-by-inch before my eyes, until only a pile of clothes remained.

My knees shook as I stared at the shirt and pants and his belt. Mr. Advani had moved on. He'd looked so happy. Content.

The peace he'd come to at the end was something I hadn't known for centuries. Was moving on something we needed to embrace rather than fear? Was our war with Death pointless?

AFTER MEETING WITH the others, I silently followed them back to camp and shut myself in my tent. I lay on my makeshift bed for hours, staring at the slope of the tent silently.

No matter how I tried, my conversation with Mr. Advani refused to leave my head. Alex was a wreck. My heart screamed at the thought of my best friend being beyond my aid. Mr. and Mrs. K were on the verge of divorce, and yet I was stranded worlds away, forced to watch it all happen.

A while later someone tapped on my tent. "Heather, sweetheart, are you in there?" Pete's voice asked.

"Yeah," I said, my voice hollow.

Pete slowly crawled inside. "Is something wrong? You were really quiet on the way back."

I sat up, tucking my knees against my chest. "I talked to the principal of my high school." My voice cracked. I couldn't come out and say, *My life is falling apart without me. Everyone I care about back home is a mess. I don't even know how long I've been gone.*

Pete's face sunk with a frown. He sat with me on my cot.

I gave a bitter, sardonic smile. "Oh, it gets better. He moved on right in front of me. Disappeared bit by bit. It's not at all like you said. And it wasn't like being ghosted. He looked so happy. What I saw wasn't a person vanishing into non-existence or going to some awful place."

"Heather, his happiness doesn't mean anything. People on drugs seem happy, but it doesn't mean heroin or cocaine, or even Carnadia blossoms are good things."

"This is different and you know it, Pete," I snapped. Mentally shaking myself, I looked at him apologetically, setting a hand on his knee. "This whole conflict, this group's unwillingness to *move on*—what if *we're* in the wrong here?"

"Maybe both sides are wrong in their own way, but I

want a chance to *know* who's right."

"This gets more complicated by the second," I sighed, wiping my eyes.

Pete nodded, his voice grave. "I know."

I raked my hands through my hair, lowering my forehead to my knees. "I wish we could leave now. Just the two of us."

"Sometimes I want the same thing, but we can't abandon the others. They need us. Leaving without them would be one of the most selfish things we could do."

I nodded, looking up at him. "You're right, of course. I'd never be able to go through with it. The eternal guilt wouldn't be worth it."

"We *will* get out of here, Heather. But it'll be on our terms."

"We will," I whispered, scooting forward to wrap my arms around his waist. "Did you guys find anything useful out there?"

He shuddered. "There's a lot of talk about Death considering setting fire to whole sections of forest to smoke us out."

I blanched. "That's bad."

Pete wetted his lips. A breeze shook the tent around us. "We need to act before he gets desperate and considers that a good move."

"Do you think we can be ready in time?"

"Yeah, if we can get the information we need quickly enough."

"Is there anything you need me to do?"

After a long, silent moment, he looked into my eyes. "Right now I need you to help me tune it out, just for a little while. Please."

I pulled his head toward mine, kissing him forcefully. My breathing came in wild gasps. My fingertips dug into his back as he lay us down. He held me tightly, his lips traced frosty kisses over my neck.

I pulled his shirt off, trembling as I kissed his bare shoulder. His hands greedily explored me—my hair, my waist, my back, my legs. His skin was freezing, but it did nothing to soothe the inferno raging in my chest.

I snaked my fingers through his onyx tresses, each kiss growing more intense, more impatient. We couldn't get close enough.

"Damn," he panted in my ear as he pulled back, "You don't make this whole 'lack of blood flow' thing easy."

"Sorry," I gasped, "I don't know what came over me."

He grinned, kissing me hard once more. "I wouldn't mind one bit if this came over you more often."

The hotness in my cheeks revealed my embarrassment. *Damn my stupid mortal quirks!*

He kissed my forehead. "I love you."

"I love you, too."

He rolled to my side, wrapping his arms around me.

I scooted next to him, sighing contentedly. "You're more than I deserve."

"You've got it backward."

"How about we just agree that we make one another happy?"

"Sounds perfect."

I fought the creeping urge to yawn. "I don't want you to go. Will you stay tonight? I know lying here all night while I sleep isn't very exciting, but…"

"Sure, I'll stay," he answered, a smile in his voice.

Sliding up the blankets, I kissed his cheek. "Thank you."

"For?"

"Existing."

"*Now* who's fattening up the mice?" he teased.

"Shush," I mumbled sleepily.

"Get some sleep. I'll be here when you wake up."

Resting my heavy head on his chest, I let my drooping eyelids close.

CHAPTER TWENTY-TWO

S UNLIGHT BEAMED DIRECTLY in my eyes, bringing my slumber to a harsh end. Pete's cool body still lay next to mine, so I snuggled against him with a barely-conscious grunt.

"Good morning." He ran a hand gently up and down my back.

I slurred, "Mornin'."

"Sleep well?"

Sitting up with a stretch, I nodded. "Best I've had in God knows how long."

"I'd say. You snored all night."

My cheeks stung as I blushed. "I did?"

He grinned. "It was so loud I think the living could hear it."

My hand smacked his arm. "Jerk."

He pressed his lips to mine with a chuckle. "Maybe, but I'm *your* jerk."

"Damn skippy. And don't you forget it."

He chuckled. "I wouldn't dare."

The two of us climbed out of my tent to find the campsite mostly deserted except for the well-known sounds of fight practice echoing in the distance.

"Looks like I slept longer than I should've," I noted.

"Don't worry about it." Pete smiled, squeezing my hand. "Listen, I promised I'd meet with an informant this morning. I'll be back later, okay?"

With a girlish giggle, I gave him a quick peck on the lips, ruffling his hair with my free hand. "Okay."

I grinned, sitting by the fire to watch him go.

Megan approached a couple of minutes later with an eyebrow raised. "Are you all right? You look strange."

I turned to face her, frowning with confusion. "I do?"

"Your cheeks are bright red, you've got this silly expression…" Her eyes grew wide. "Oh! I know what's going on. I should've guessed. The way he looks at you…" She looked me in the eye, her mouth taut. "I really don't want to stain your happiness, but there's something you should know about Pete."

My face fell. *Was something wrong?* "What?"

Megan looked at me hesitantly before continuing. "He has a certain reputation around here. Every of-age girl who joins our ranks eventually becomes a target for his charms."

I stood, shaking my head. "I don't believe you. Why has no one else mentioned this?"

"Has he taken you to his 'oasis' yet?"

My heart skipped a beat. "B-but… I thought…"

"You were the only one he'd shown it to? Heavens no. He's taken every girl he's *set his sights on* there."

"He said—"

"He couldn't 'rise to the occasion'?" She folded her arms, sighing heavily. "That's something else he tells them. Then, after enough time's gone by, he says the girl's love has caused a miracle, making it possible. Usually, he butters them up with a gift first. Has he…?"

I slid a trembling hand into my pocket, showing her the carved butterfly.

Her shoulders sunk. She rustled through her bag until she produced a small wooden carving of a doe. "He said he chose a doe because of all the stories we'd shared of our fathers' hunting escapades. And because I reminded him of a deer: sensitive, gentle, nurturing."

I bit my lip hard to hold back tears.

She stood, affectionately rubbing my back. "Oh, honey. I'm so sorry."

"I love him, Megan," I squeaked, barely able to form words.

She sighed, her eyes filled with sadness. "So did I, once."

"I should've known better," I whispered, my voice shaky, uneven. "Why would anyone want a—" I tried finding the right term, "—*thing* like me?" I paused, my breath came in hitching gasps.

"Don't blame yourself, Heather."

Holding up my hands, I took a step back. "I need to be alone."

"Of course," she whispered, leaving.

For a while, I just stood where I was, staring at the fire. Until Pete came up to me.

Gently, he shook my shoulder, panic in his voice. "Heather, what's the matter? What's happened?"

I looked him in the eye as I backed away. My voice was cold, vicious. I snarled, "Are you going to pretend you don't know?"

He raised an eyebrow. "Seriously, I've got no idea what's going on."

He stepped toward me, but I pushed him away. "Megan told me your dirty little secret. I know all about your reputation."

"Huh?" He blinked, still playing dumb. "Reputation?"

"She filled me in on your scheme. Seduce every girl that joins, treat them like nothing once you're done," I snarled.

He shook his head, looking at me like I was insane. "What? I've never been with any girl in this camp but you. Okay, I flirted sometimes before we met, but that's all. Mixing work and pleasure isn't usually my style."

I glared at him, counting his lies on my fingers. "Then explain the wood carving she says you gave her. How she knew about your oasis."

"I don't know how she knew about the oasis, but the

doe was a gift. A way of saying thanks for all her help around here. I give 'em to all my friends. Ask Greg. He's got a bear, and Shaun had a panth—"

Head swirling with conflicting versions of one story, I held up a hand, silencing him. "Just stop. I can't take one more lie from you."

Megan came out from behind a tree, tutting. The judgmental curve of her mouth reminded me of a teacher scolding a pupil.

"Heather, hun, are you really criticizing him for lying? I don't think you should be the one casting stones here."

"Leave us alone, Megan. This has nothing to do with you," Pete snapped, not taking his eyes off me. The burning fury he sent my way with his look was unlike anything I'd ever seen from him.

"It just doesn't seem right. She's been lying too, if not more so."

He finally let his rage find a new target. "What are you going on about?" he growled.

"I hate to do this, Pete. I know how much you like her. But I just can't cover for her anymore." Her folded arms said more than her words. "Remember the legend about that girl who's reborn every time she dies? Pete, she's real. She's Heather."

He scoffed. "You're crazy." He glanced at me, a touch of doubt in his next question. "She's crazy, right?"

The ground fell out from under me. I took a deep, unsteady breath. "It... it's true. I don't know how she found out, but it's true."

He whipped around, turning his back to me.

After taking a slow, barely controlled breath, he faced me again and continued, "So you're standing here acting all superior over a rumor, while hiding something like *that* from me?"

Stepping back, eyes downcast, a longing for a hole to bury myself in filled my shattering heart. "I'm sorry… at first I didn't tell you or the others because I didn't know you well enough. Wasn't sure I could trust you. Then I didn't tell you because I was afraid of your reaction."

He snorted, shaking his head. "You didn't just keep a secret, you outright lied. Get out."

I froze. "What?"

He stepped closer, looming over me. "I said, get out. Pack your shit. Get the hell away from my camp. Never come back."

Gritting my teeth, I forced my eyes to remain dry. "Fine."

Storming to my tent, I shoved my things into my bag. Memories of happy moments with Pete cycled through my mind on a loop. Every kiss, every touch, every laugh we'd shared. I was dizzy from the pain of it. Standing unsteadily, I pulled my bag roughly over my shoulder and took a shaky breath.

MY FEET WOULDN'T move when I reached the edge of camp. I couldn't make myself take the first step.

Megan approached, offering a deep sigh. "I'm so sorry things went this way. Those secrets were eating at me. I couldn't keep them anymore"

I swiped at my eyes, wishing the tears would stop. "Why didn't you talk to me first, before blurting out my secret like that?"

"Honestly, I tried—many times. The timing was never right, and I had no idea how to approach you about it. Then everything was happening and it just…slipped out."

"I guess it was only a matter of time before it all came out anyway. Secrets and lies have a way of catching up with you."

She nodded, her expression grim. "I suppose you're right."

"At least I found out about Pete before it was too late."

Her hand gently patted my back. "If any good comes from this, let it be that."

"How'd you know, though? About me?"

She shrugged, looking up at the orange-purple sky. "I heard you talking to Jason about some book about the girl from the legend. The look on your face said it all. Either you had some unhealthy obsession with her, or she was you. Just made a lucky guess."

Am I really so obvious?

I sighed. "Well, thanks for everything. Tell everyone I'll miss them… I hope you all reach the living world someday," I said with a sniff, my voice cracking.

She nodded firmly. "I will."

My feet dragged across the dirt as I walked away. I left Hazel behind—hopefully Tina would let Lily care for her. My eyes stayed locked straight ahead, not daring to take a backward glance. It wasn't till I'd gotten half a mile from the campsite that I sunk to the ground. A cold, burning pain throbbed in my chest. Sobs tore through me then. In a flash of anger, I chucked the wooden butterfly. A soft *thud* echoed from the trees when it landed in the grass.

We're in the middle of a war, these spirits are dropping like flies, and here I am wailing like a baby over my stupid love life!

My self-flagellation was interrupted by thick, gray smog enveloping the area. The air grew icy.

An all-too-familiar presence lurked behind me. "Oh, Annabeth. I tried to warn you to not become too attached, to not let their words sway you."

"Don't you dare tell me 'I told you so,'" I hissed, not turning to look at him. Shame and anguish coursed through my veins.

Death knelt in front of me, eyes downcast. "I shall refrain from such things. If only there were something I could say or do," he sighed.

"Take me back to the castle," I muttered, barely audible.

"Pardon?"

I sobbed. "Take me away from here!"

He nodded with something akin to sympathy in his eyes. "As you wish."

He took my hand. The coldness of his touch reminded me of the once-exhilarating chill of Pete's touch. More salt in the wound. Instantaneously, we stood in the castle's main foyer.

"Here you are," he announced gently, letting go of go of my hand. He leaned down to take my bag.

I snatched it up before he could. "Thanks. I'm going to bed." Numb, I walked away, not even waiting for a reply.

Once in my room, I let my bag slide from my hands. It fell to the floor with a soft thud. I collapsed on the bed, hugging my knees to my chest. It was all too much: losing Pete, everything I'd seen and experienced since coming to this terrible world. The emptiness in my heart threatened to swallow me whole. There wasn't a point in fighting. I closed my eyes, letting the darkness consume me.

CHAPTER TWENTY-THREE

T HE SKY GREW darker. It didn't matter. Death sent servants to check on me regularly, probably hoping their presence would break my catatonia. I refused to move. Part of my mind screamed at me to stop being so pathetic, but I tuned that out. I was acting stupidly, that wasn't some great secret.

At some point one of them placed a plate of food on the nightstand. I could barely stand to look at the thing. All it did was remind me of the meals Pete cooked for me, the laughs we'd share while he prepared them.

After a few hours, Death came into the room, sitting on the edge of the bed. "Annabeth, please, eat. My servants worked quite hard to make you one of your favorite dishes: something called 'stir fry'? I noticed you really enjoyed it before you came here, so I hoped—"

"I don't want it," I murmured, turning from him.

"Surely you would not waste a meal after the time my

cooks spent on it..." he replied, an obvious plea in his voice.

"I. Don't. Want. It."

"Maybe they could make someth—"

Jolting upright, I smacked at the plate Death held, knocking it to the floor. Vegetables and soy sauce flowed on the carpet. Hopefully it'd leave a stain. I shouted, "I'm not hungry, okay?" Each of my words were icy venom. "I don't need some pity meal because you think eating it will suddenly make me all better. What I need is to be alone. *So get out of here!*"

He sighed, slumping his shoulders as he pushed himself to his feet. "Very well. Perhaps you will change your mind later."

Laying back down, I ignored the closing door and his echoing footsteps, getting further away down the hall. Shoving my face into my pillow, I let myself sob and scream. Terrible things repeated in my memory ad nauseam: Jeremy losing his arm, his keening screams still echoed in my ears. Killing those monstrous ravens— would I ever stop feeling that strange black liquid on my hands? The abominable wolf and squirrel I created. My last moments with Pete—his blue eyes aflame with the anger and hurt I'd put there.

God, I'm an idiot. Expecting a picture-perfect fairytale... This is more my fault than his.

I remained motionless, but not sleeping, in bed until once more sunlight streamed through the curtains. A servant came to my bedside without a word, leaving a plate of eggs, bacon, and a small bowl of fruit on the nightstand.

Let it rot.

I rolled over to avoid looking at the stupid food. Exhaustion finally caught up to me. Hesitantly, I allowed sleep to come.

I WAS SITTING in a small rowboat on a lake by a flowery, sunlight-filled meadow. Glancing around, my heart clenched. Each in their own boats—Alex, the Kützes, Isabel, my original parents, and all of the spirits in the group I'd left behind. In my boat, my hand shot up, covering my mouth, when I saw who sat across from me.

"Pete," I whispered, my voice strained, a stabbing pain in my chest. "I've missed you so much!" I choked, "I'm so sorry for everything..."

He stared. Without a word, Pete leaned closer. My pulse began to race, but instead of kissing me, his arms gripped my shoulders and he violently began trying to pull me to the left. He was trying to shove me off the boat! I tried to break free of his grasp, but he was just too strong. He successfully knocked me overboard, eyes cold, empty, with a mirthless smile. I sank down into the watery darkness. My lungs were flooding... I couldn't breathe...

MY EYES FLEW open. I gasped for air, screams tearing at my throat. Hyperventilating while my tears continued to flow, I barely noticed Death rush to my side. He pulled me into his arms.

"What has happened?" he asked, voice frantic. He called over his shoulder toward the open door at someone I couldn't see. "Guard! I want four soldiers posted at every door. Inspect the entirety of the castle! If you find an intruder, dispose of them."

"Yes, sir," the voice of a Coal replied.

"No," I sputtered through sobs and gasps. "Not an intruder. No one's harmed me. A nightmare…"

"It is all right, none of it was real. You are safe," Death whispered, his voice calming me for once.

He remained in my room for the rest of the night, sitting at the vanity table. Nightmares plagued me again and again, but whenever I woke screaming, he was there to do his best to settle me.

Days went by, every one almost exactly the same.

ONE MORNING, I opened my eyes, the nightly visions of how the Kützes and Alex fared without me replaying in my mind.

I can't keep feeling sorry for myself like this. They need me.

I began to get out of bed. The servant permanently stationed to my room jolted to its feet, fussing over me as usual.

It tried pushing me back onto the bed. "Miss… it is… all right… please…… remain calm," it droned, as it had many times before.

Struggling wasn't very effective. Lack of food and sleep had sapped my strength. "I'm fine." The servant let me go, and I stood again. "I've just decided to stop moping around," I said, my voice cracked from lack of use. "Will you help me get dressed? And make me breakfast?"

It nodded, rushing to the closet. Upon its return, a flowing blue sundress lay in its hands. Surprisingly, I could actually breathe while wearing it. The color helped distract from my splotchy, puffy face, and helped me look like less of a train wreck. The servant twined my hair into a relaxed, comfortable bun, then spirited me away to be seated in the dining room. More servants set heaping plates of food before me. My appetite hadn't fully returned, but I decided to nibble on some buttery rolls and sip from a glass of water.

Death sat across from me. "Good morning." His voice sounded carefully controlled, but it hardly masked the anxiety in his tone.

"Hi," I mumbled, gazing down at my plate.

He watched cautiously, probably expecting me to collapse into hysterics again. He offered another roll, smiling pleasantly at me. "It is good to see you out of your bedroom."

I took the roll, turning it in my hand. "It feels weird to be doing something other than crying. How long was I," I paused, struggling to find the right phrase, "out of it?"

"Today would have been the seventh day."

Leaning on the table I set my face in my hands, I couldn't help groaning. "You probably think I'm the weakest mortal you've met. Ever."

"Not at all. Being distraught because of the wrongdoings of others is *not* weakness."

I lifted my face, staring like he'd grown three heads. "I wasn't just 'distraught'; I shut down."

"Yet despite what you have been through, which I must remind you is more than most, you have stood back up. Yes? Resume your life now." My glance drifted to the window behind Death, which showed nothing but a light blue sky.

Before Death brought me to the Land of the Dead, the words might have given me some comfort. Now, I just felt more guilt. I stared for a few moments in silence before speaking again. "I don't know how long it'll take for me to be 'okay' again." I couldn't get Pete's blue eyes out of my head. "Hell, I may never be 'okay.'"

Death sighed, dejected. "Perhaps I should never have brought you to this realm. I should have taken care of this nonsense myself. Let you be."

While what I'd experienced in my time in Death's

world was often painful, filled with fear and uncertainty, deep down I couldn't bring myself to entirely reject it. I had regrets, sure, but they'd taught me valuable lessons I'd always carry with me.

My hands shook for a moment. Then I looked away. "It's fine. You did what you had to."

He rose from his chair. "I will leave you in peace. When you are finished, would you like to meet me in the garden? For a stroll?"

I shrugged. "Sure."

Once he left, I half-heartedly poked at my food for a minute or two before pushing myself from my seat.

HE WAITED BY a rosebush. "I hope some fresh air will help raise your spirits."

Taking a deep breath, it was impossible not to enjoy the garden's sweet, floral aroma. "I won't lie; it's nice to be outside."

He plucked an aquamarine rose, tucking it behind my ear. An all-too-familiar warmth began to rise in my chest. I pushed it out of my mind, disgusted with myself.

With a timbre of sadness, Death said, "I have decided I shall return you to your own world. However, there is much business I must attend to over the coming days. I will not be able to return you until that is done. Is that acceptable?"

It didn't matter if he was lying or not. I needed more time to get my head on straight. I plucked a flower of my own from another bush nearby, staring down for a moment. The bloom was the same shade as Pete's eyes. Pain scraped at my heart. I shook myself free from memory, and set down the rose.

I'm going home. I should be happy. We walked together along a stone path snaking through the garden. "Yes. Thank you."

Gesturing to the flowering plants around us, I asked, "What will you do with this once I'm gone?"

"Demolish it, I would imagine." Death snatched an apple from a tree, admiring it quickly before casting it aside. "I may leave the flowers. They are quite fetching, don't you agree?"

I studied the nearest rosebush. Lily's bright eyes and warm smile flashed in my mind. *Please stop*, I begged myself. *I can't handle it.*

Clearing my throat, I did my best to sound casual. "I'm still amazed you made this garden just for me. You could've only manifested food each day, but instead you created this spectacular garden."

His eyes fell on me, a slight curve forming on his lips. "You are worth the effort."

I stepped back, raising my hand. "Don't."

Death gaped at me, bewildered. "I beg your pardon?"

"Don't. Please," I repeated. "I'm *not* worth the effort. All I do is cause problems, whine, and hurt people. Every time I move, or speak, I cause damage." Unbidden, I imagined the devastation my numerable deaths caused to the families I left behind. "No matter how hard I try not to." The inconsolable tears of my mothers, the agony in the eyes of my fathers. I sighed, hesitating on the next part. "We're very similar, Death. More than I'd like to admit. Both of us want to be accepted rather than hated or feared." I looked around Death's garden once more. "Both of us long to create something beautiful, so everyone will finally see we aren't monsters." Memories of Pete, Lily, Tina, and the others flooded my mind. "But in the end, destruction and pain will always lie in our wake."

Death stared in silence. As though, for once, he had no words to say.

I walked back to the bedroom, leaving him there alone.

MY HEAD SWAM. I needed to be by myself. Sitting on the bed, I instantly regretted how harsh I'd been, but bitterness and anger overwhelmed any desire to do a thing about it. At least, for the moment.

CHAPTER TWENTY-FOUR

T HE NEXT MORNING, I made my way stiffly to the dining room. This after being forced into another moderately comfortable silk sundress, and having a thick layer of makeup plastered on my face. The awkward cut of my shoes pinched my toes with every clicking step. My only consolation was I'd soon be sitting down for breakfast; my feet would get their reprieve.

Once at the table, a servant dumped a steaming pile of various fruits onto my plate. Stabbing my fork at a piece of apple, I took a hesitant bite while the servants' blank faces stared. The food was unlike any other I'd experienced. Every warm bite jam-packed with more flavor than I thought possible.

I wolfed down this meal like I'd never eaten before in my existence. Each bite tasted better than the one before. After a third helping, my roaring stomach finally felt satisfied.

"You are enjoying the food, I take it?" Death hesitantly lowered himself onto the chair next to mine.

I nodded, pushing the empty plate away. "It's delicious. I didn't expect your staff to be so skilled. It's not like they've had a lot of practice."

"That is because they consumed the souls of many world-famous chefs."

I retched, nausea bubbling in my stomach.

Death threw his head back, laughing. "Merely a joke."

"That wasn't funny. After—" I stopped myself before mentioning my knowledge of Reginald's fate. Starting an argument with Death didn't seem like a wise choice.

"After what?"

"After the stress of these past few days, a joke like that seems inappropriate."

He winced, seeming contrite. "Perhaps you are correct. My apologies."

"It's fine." I stared down at the table. "Please give my compliments to your servants for a wonderful breakfast."

"I shall," he said, waving the ones waiting away.

"About yesterday…" I sighed, looking to him from under my mascaraed lashes. "I wanted to say sorry for what I said. Hell, for almost *everything* I've said to you over the past week."

He shrugged. "Do not fret, your words did not bother me. In fact," a mischievous smile curved his lips, "they inspired me. I will be holding a masquerade this evening as a gesture of good will to the residents of this realm. You are more than welcome to attend."

"Aren't you worried someone will attend just to cause trouble?"

"Armed guards will be posted at every entrance to the castle, and outside the ballroom."

I paused for a moment to deliberate. Was going to a ball a smart decision? One hosted by the enemy of those who once considered me friend? Going to this ball would feel like a betrayal. On the other side of the coin, my absence would potentially cause Death to become suspicious that I still held some fondness for the rebels. The last thing I wanted was a paranoid Death, misguided, hurting the spirits I'd left behind. Especially in revenge for some imagined slight. The choice was as easy as it was foolish.

"Fair enough. I guess I'll attend."

He beamed. "Excellent." Reaching into his pocket, he fished out a long, thin black box. Opening it revealed a dazzling diamond bracelet. In his palm it cast rainbows in the light.

I couldn't help but gasp. Instead of reaching for it I placed a hand over my heart, "It's beautiful. Are those…"

"Real? Yes. Eighteen of them, signifying the eighteen lives you have lived thus far."

"You know how many lives I've lived?"

He looked pointedly into my eyes. "Of course."

I stared at the bracelet, unable to speak.

He watched expectantly. "Do you not like it?" His

voice rose with apparent anxiety. "If you do not, then I will make something else."

"I like it; I just didn't expect it, that's all."

"Will you wear it?"

Taking the bracelet and securing it around my wrist, I smiled. Bashful. "Thank you."

"You are most welcome." The relief was obvious in his tone. "I am afraid I must take my leave now. There is much to do before the proceedings begin." Taking my hand, he gingerly pressed his lips to my knuckle. "Until tonight, I bid you farewell." Then he vanished.

STUFFED INTO A puffy, black and white ball gown, I shoved my way across the overcrowded dance floor. I felt so ostentatious. Swirling classical music rang out around the ballroom. The tune was beautiful, but lacked feeling. It wasn't surprising to see a small orchestra of servants sitting next to an ornate painted screen, mechanically playing instruments.

Everyone attending the ball was elegantly attired in jet-black tuxedos or shimmering dresses, most likely a result of Death's intervention. The jewel-encrusted walls shone, polished so thoroughly everyone's reflections danced in them.

As Death had assured, Coals stood, armed, at each of the hall's arched entrances. They didn't move much, only occasionally turning their heads to watch the room. If I hadn't seen them in action before, I would've assumed they were statues.

Eventually, I found Death at the opposite end of the floor from where I'd entered. He stood in the midst of conversation with a spirit. He laughed at a joke I couldn't hear over the chatter of the crowd. His golden hair was slicked back. His frame dressed in a black three-piece suit, paired with a red tie.

Death politely removed himself from the spirit's presence and turned to me, a delighted grin spreading across his face. "You came."

I shrugged. "I said I would."

"I did not expect you would keep your word."

"Well, I did." My mouth twitched into a slight smile. "Besides, it's not like I had much else to do tonight."

The music slowed, it became a waltz. Death extended his hand. "May I have this dance?"

A fluttering feeling swam in my stomach as I slid my hand into his. "Um, I don't really know how to waltz, but sure."

He chuckled huskily. "Do not worry, I will make sure you dance flawlessly."

He lead us to the floor and placed a hand on my upper back, holding me close. I tried to remain calm. Placing a hand on his shoulder while he took my other hand, clasping it firmly. "You still find ways to surprise me," he murmured in my ear.

"You know what they say about books and covers."

He tilted his head slightly in confusion. "Of course.

Reading is one of my favorite activities."

"I never would've guessed, with the enormous library you have," I said dryly while he turned us around the edges of the dance floor.

He let out a low chuckle, his chest vibrating against me as he leaned me in a dip. "How witty you are. I still expect my book to be returned, while we are on the subject."

"I'll give it back once I've learned all I need to from it." Death didn't need to know that it was still with Jason. I defiantly raised my chin, which distracted me, and I lost my footing.

He caught me, and his move made the entire slip seem like part of the dance. "You certainly seem confident this book contains the information you seek."

Trying to settle the ever-present fluttering in my stomach, I swallowed. "It's been a valuable asset thus far."

He spun us with a flourish, the jewels in the walls looked like beads of twirling light around us. It was dizzyingly beautiful to watch. "I'm curious what you will do once you understand what you are, the things you are capable of."

My heart raced when he pulled me closer. His cold hand drifted from my waist up my back. "You'd find out quicker if you were more forthcoming with answers," I murmured. My cheeks grew hot as I took a small, self-conscious step backward.

He grinned, a glint of something—devilish—in his eye? "My amusement at your ignorance outweighs my curiosity."

To steady myself I took a breath. "Lucky me."

His voice became earnest. "You actually *are* quite fortunate. You've seen and experienced things no other living mortal will."

I paused. "Most of what I've seen is heartbreak, pain, and fear." Death twirled me again, "I won't lie, though. Being here has given me some amazing experiences."

"I am not solely speaking of coming to my realm. Your many lives enabled you to watch history unfold. Your memory goes further back than anyone else alive."

My eyes darted to my reflection in the polished wall as we danced. "I appreciate that, but sometimes I wish I was normal. That this life was the only one."

"If you saw things the way I do, you would never want to settle for less."

I raised a brow. "Who says I'd be settling?"

Death sneered. "Mortals spend their short lives in misery, slaving away at menial, pointless tasks, all the while wishing desperately they could do something that brings satisfaction. They attempt to fill gaping voids with material objects—anything to make others think they are happy. Of course, it all only forces them to spend more time laboring at what they despise."

He tipped his head slightly. "I acknowledge some mortals do not conform to this. Indeed, some truly enjoy their existence. But they are exceptions."

Adjusting my skirt to make the dance easier, a tingling

pricked at my fingertips. Struggling to find the words to respond proved useless. I stared at him, defiantly letting my knotted brow say what I couldn't.

Death's gaze met mine as he grimaced with disgust. "Do you truly *desire* such an existence? Do you truly *want* their fate? Why? You'd return to your world, one that's scarcely done more than mocked and rejected you?"

My dress brushed my ankles when I twirled away, then rejoined him in our dance. "It's the world I come from. Where I belong. There are people I care about there. I want to see them again. Sure, I'm not well liked, but so what? There will always be people who don't like me."

"I still do not fully understand, but there is plenty of time to persuade you."

"Can I…ask you something?"

He nodded. "Certainly."

"Why make me that offer all those years ago?"

Death looked away, his gaze seeming to drift back in time. "You saw me. Before we met, only the dying detected my presence. Your desperate pleas for me to spare Isabel genuinely moved me. And you spoke to me. Looked directly at my corporeal form. I knew if I let you simply continue an ordinary mortal existence then any chance of discovering how you could see me would die with you. It became clear what I needed to do."

"It wasn't purely selfish."

He returned to the present moment. "Perhaps it *was* partly done out of selfishness. It is true I always hoped you would assist with those rebellious spirits—they were already a nuisance by that time, although on a lesser scale. But I truly did desire to help your sister, for your sake."

"For the longest time I wondered if you'd tricked me. Taken her anyway."

He looked straight into my eyes, speaking sincerely. "I kept my word. I cured her ailment. She went on to live a long, happy life."

Warm tears threatened to stream down my cheeks. "You actually did it? *I* did it? Everything I've gone through wasn't in vain?"

He stopped our waltz to pull a handkerchief from his breast pocket, offering it to me. "No, not in vain."

A strange sound, half sobbing, half laughing escaped me. "She made it. For once, something I did helped someone I love."

"Isabel's descendants live today. She had children. And those children bore children as well."

Everything spun around me. "They do?"

He nodded, deftly swirling us to avoid collision with another dancer. "You may meet them one day, if you have not already."

Dabbing at my eyes with his silken handkerchief, I muttered, "Thank you for telling me. It means a lot."

He smiled, wrinkling his nose. When had we moved to such a secluded corner of the dance floor? "It is strange. This may be one of the first civil conversations we have had."

My head swam. "They've been rare, haven't they?"

"I know it is most likely far too late, but will you give me another chance?"

Thinking about his treatment of my friends, about Reginald, I said, "It's hard. You've done some heinous things. Things I can't easily forgive." Then I imagined Isabel's children, her children's children, and continued, "I'll need some time to think. But if circumstances stay like this, I could see it happening. Possibly."

"That's fair. I'll do everything in my power to earn your forgiveness." He looked directly into my eyes, drawing close again to resume our dance. "You look positively divine this evening. This gown suits you well."

My throat grew scratchy. "Thank you."

He leaned closer, his expression shifting to something I couldn't define. My mind began racing quicker than my pulse.

Is he trying what I think he is? Should I slap him? What about Pete?

Before I could respond, a shadow fell over us. Death abruptly stepped back, ceasing our dance. Turning, I saw a Coal standing beside us.

"What is the meaning of this? Return to your post, soldier," Death commanded, his tone sharp.

Ignoring the command, the armored figure removed his helmet.

My muscles tensed. *Ollie?*

He reached into his satchel and fished out a small,

dark object. Laughing, Ollie yanked a metal pin from it before dropping it at our feet. "Long live the king."

With a thundering boom and a scorching, bright flash of light, we were violently tossed several feet.

The last sounds before darkness fell around me were screams of terror.

CHAPTER TWENTY-FIVE

E VERY INCH OF my body burned. The only sound was a loud, piercing ring in my ears. When I could finally open my eyes, everything seemed like a white blur. Fiery agony stabbed through me when I tried to move.

This is it. I've died and gone to hell, I managed to think.

Someone must have picked me up from the hard floor, I felt them gently lifting me into a seated position. Every touch felt like a hot poker being jammed into my flesh. My back arched and I screamed.

Slowly, first colors, then shapes returned. Who was holding me? The loud, piercing ringing in my ears subsided; it was Pete, in a set of Coal armor, sobbing.

I began to hear more: the chaos of spirits screaming as they fled from the ballroom. From the corner of my eye, I could see those that hadn't been ghosted in the attack were literally crawling over one another to get away, shoving their way through the archway. An elderly woman knelt about thirty feet away, firmly gripping a suit jacket to her chest as she sobbed uncontrollably. A little boy, who couldn't have been older than three despite his miniature tuxedo, stared wide-eyed at a scorched ballgown, calling for his mother. Unable to move, unable to help, I groaned, the only sound my cracked vocal chords could make.

Pete's shoulders were heaving as he wept, his words becoming clearer. "Heather, oh God, Heather I'm so sorry. This is all my fault. If I hadn't been so stupid…"

"Are you all right? How badly are you hurt?" Death appeared by our side. His voice frantic.

"Everything hurts," I wheezed.

Death's gaze, aimed at Pete, was an expression of recognition, before it quickly turned into a furious scowl. "*You.* I should have known this was your doing."

"I didn't do this!" Pete protested.

"*Silence,*" Death shouted. The entire room shook with those syllables. "Do you think me a fool?"

Pete scooted back, pulling me with him, anxiety creeping into his voice. "No. I came to find Heather. To apologize for being an asshole." He winced. "Then Ollie……"

"You're on a first-name basis with the terrorist. Am I to believe you two were here by mere happenstance? At the same time, both disguised as my soldiers?"

"It was just an awful coincidence."

Death gestured to the rubble surrounding us. "Look at

the damage caused by this. What about the spirits lost in one blast of destruction? The chaos I'll have to inflict upon the living world to bring the balance back into equilibrium? What about the suffering Heather now endures? This atrocity has shown me how naive it was to consider seeking peace." He turned to the Coals standing nearby. "Guards, take this monster to the dungeon to await execution. Perhaps these fools will finally stop when they see their leader decapitated in front of them."

"No," I cried with my broken voice. I'd just gotten him back…I couldn't lose him again, not this fast.

Pete rose swiftly, with me in his arms. As we retreated, I watched Death make a motion and then frown, staring down at his hands. We flew through the hallways of Death's castle, an increasing number of Coals chasing us. He ran as fast as he could with me clinging to his neck as strong as I could bear. Leaping down the main staircase, grunting from both my weight and the armor he wore.

We reached the foyer, only to be surrounded Coals.

"Shit," Pete muttered, frantically searching the area for an escape route.

"Chandelier," I croaked, raising my arm to gesture painfully above us. It felt like a ridiculous idea, but I wasn't sure we had any other option.

"Atta girl." Drawing his pistol with his free arm, he fired at the chandelier. As the heavy structure came crashing down on a cluster of soldiers, Pete kicked open the unlocked front door.

Pete let out a high-pitched whistle. "Hazel! Bring your bony ass over here! Now, please!"

Hazel came running. Hoisting himself onto her back, still cradling me against his chest, he sent her into a gallop. The Coals weren't far behind, though it had taken them longer than expected to get up; I could hear their armor rattle, angry shouts, and whinnies from their horses growing closer by the second.

While Hazel dodged around the houses, Pete mumbled, "Gotta lose 'em. Gotta hurry."

DESPITE PETE'S BEST efforts the Coals remained on our tail. Pete kept maneuvering Hazel through the trees as quickly as he dared to push her.

Our luck worsened once we got to the river. Hazel, digging her hooves in once she saw the water, skidded to a stop. Pete tried to goad her on, but she let out a terrified screech, protesting. The thunderous sounds of the Coals' horses were coming up behind us. We'd managed to elude them for the moment, but it wouldn't last long.

Clutching me tightly, Pete dismounted, desperately looking for an escape. "This isn't going to feel good, but it's our only chance." He looked over, patting her rump with his free arm. "Hazel, lead 'em on a chase, then go to camp once you've lost them."

She snorted, and barreled off westward, following the flow of the river. Pete set me down on the riverbank and frantically began tearing off the armor. His gaze was constantly shooting over his shoulder, warily keeping track of how much time we had left.

He took a deep breath after picking me up once more. "Here we go," he whispered, and we dove into the water.

He was right. It didn't feel good. The water stung every burnt inch of my flesh. I tried screaming, but it poured into my nose and mouth, choking me.

The current violently tossed and spun us, dragging us down into its depths every few feet. The river kept trying to rip me from Pete's grip. He did his best to keep my head above water, struggling against its force, until finally we reached the shore, throwing ourselves onto it coughing and sputtering.

Gasping for air, Pete asked, "Are you okay?"

"Lot of pain," I moaned, "but I'm alive."

He pushed himself to his feet, dragging us away from the river. I clamped my teeth down on my fried lip until it almost bled to hold in a scream. Pete winced. "Sorry. That probably hurt like a bitch, but it worked. We lost them." He stood there dripping, looking up river. "And we're really close to the campsite."

"Great," I wheezed.

He picked me up, wrapping my arms around his neck as we gingerly headed north. "For someone who should be dead, you don't look *that* bad."

Taking a glance at my arms, my throat clamped shut. If I possessed the strength to vomit, I would have. The flesh was bright red and peeling in most places. My elbows were charcoal black, with jagged cracks spreading all over. My dress was now a mass of tattered, scorched rags barely covering my body. The water hadn't helped. "Lucky me."

"You're pretty badly burned, but you've got all your limbs. Your heart's still ticking, so all in all, I'd say you're coming up roses."

I kept silent, unsure if I could agree. The blessings he counted felt so minimal compared to the agony radiating through every inch of my body. The pain increased tenfold every thirty seconds or so, but then would taper off to a lesser degree of torture. Everything felt prickly and hot, like the worst sunburn imaginable. Even a bath in a glacial pool wouldn't cool me down much.

"How *are* you alive, anyway?" And that stopped us both for a step. Pete said, "I mean, I'm glad you are, but Ollie dropped a bomb at your feet. You should be a crater."

"I don't know. Maybe it's because I was right by Death, could he have protected me somehow? Maybe I can't die here."

He jutted out his lip, considering this for a moment. "Makes some sense."

When we reached the campground, Megan was the first to see us. Like a cyclone, the shock cascaded over her face. She ran over to us, tears in her eyes. "What happened?"

"Ollie set off a bomb at Death's ball." Pete set me down, running a hand over his face. "She was right by him. Death blames me—" Megan's hand shot over her mouth, her eyes wide and scared. "And by extension, us, for what happened."

"How awful," she cried, delicately patting my head. "Are you okay?"

I mumbled with a cough, "Other than being burnt to a crisp, I'm just peachy."

"I think I've still got some burn ointment I made." Megan offered, ordering Pete to bring me along. "From the castle's garden. Leaves and herbs. Let me look. Then I'll see what I can do about her hair." She let out a heavy sigh. "Sadly I don't think most of it is salvageable. I'm so sorry, Heather."

In a bright red tent, Pete gently laid me down. Other than a makeshift bed of a few blankets, wood shavings and half-finished carvings littered the floor. A couple weapons I recognized as ones he'd used lay propped up in the corner.

"Why does Megan have burn cream?" I managed to ask.

He shrugged a shoulder. "We might heal pretty quickly, but being burnt doesn't exactly feel good. So she has ointment to make things more comfortable in the meantime." He carefully fluffed my pillow, and crouched, stroking my hair. "Get some rest. I'll snatch the cream from Megan and we'll go from there, okay?"

I closed my eyes, and tried to let sleep claim me. It wasn't easy with the pain, but eventually I managed to slip into a light slumber.

CHAPTER TWENTY-SIX

I WONDERED IF it was the first time Pete had looked in on me. I didn't open my eyes. I was too weary for that. I heard him close the tent's flap, but not his footsteps heading away to the campfire. Then, voices outside the tent roused me. It took a minute of listing to the intense debate to realize it was Emily, Greg and Mindi. They were ganging up on Pete.

"... but you keep bringing her back here," Emily's voice spat. "You're an idiot."

"She's trouble, mate," Mindi added.

"She lied about some major shit." Greg said.

"I don't give a rat's ass," Pete snapped. "I know she lied. Never denied that. But she's saved us all more times than someone with malicious intent would. Despite everything, I want to try to forgive her. You all should do the same."

"Oh, so now you're telling us what to think? Bernard

would be so proud," Emily accused.

"Don't you *dare* compare me to him," Pete bellowed.

"Then stop acting like him," she replied, each word venomous.

"You don't *have* to agree with my choices," said Pete, "but can you at least respect them, and her?"

"She had my respect," Greg interjected, "but then she turned out to be a snake in the grass."

Pete grunted irritably. "Look, arguing is pointless. Things are about to get worse in this war. We need to stand together. I want her to stay, so she's staying. It's not up for discussion."

"Fine," came Emily's voice, "I'll keep my mouth shut, but if she stabs us in the back again, I'm done." Her footsteps faded as she stomped away. The others followed suit.

Pete came back some time later, kneeling next to the bed. "How are you feeling?"

Gritting my teeth, I eased myself into a seated position. "Better, but I still feel like a KFC combo. And now I've got G.I Jane hair."

He carefully took a seat next to me, shoulders slumped. "I'm so sorry. I overreacted and got us into this mess."

I did my best to arrange my toasted face into some sort of reassuring expression. "You didn't overreact. You were right to be angry. I kept a large part of myself hidden from you, and lied about it. Should've been honest from the beginning."

He looked up at me, seeming less dejected. "You probably should've, but it's in the past now. I can kind of understand why you did it. You were afraid. But you don't need to be anymore." Pete shifted his weight so he leaned over me, *it was kind of nice, kind of strange.* "Never be scared of being honest with me, okay? Even if it's bad, I'd rather know the truth."

"Wish I'd learned that sooner," I muttered, staring down at my hands.

"I forgive you. I'm probably an idiot for that, but I don't care."

I managed to smile without my face feeling like it was going to fall off. "Thank you."

He ran his fingers through his hair, smirking with embarrassment. "I was sort of a mess after you left. Like every clichéd romantic comedy you've ever seen. Only thing missing was the bucket of ice-cream."

I let out a rattly, coughing chuckle. "Funny, because it was almost exactly the same for me."

"Now I feel even more like an asshole," Pete groaned.

I wished I could reach forward to pat his shoulder, but moving still made every inch of my skin sting. "You aren't an asshole. If anything, I am."

"Can we not do the whole 'it's my fault,' 'no, it's *my* fault' thing?"

A grin cracked on my face. "You've got a deal."

He glanced behind him at the tent flap. "I should warn

you, not everyone's happy you're back."

I sighed. "I know. I heard the ruckus outside."

He turned back with a sigh of his own. "Yeah, it wasn't pretty. I think they'll cool off after a while. Most of them aren't the grudge-holding kind."

"I hope so. I really don't want everyone hating me again."

"Not everyone hates you. Megan and Lily are overjoyed you're here. Jason's glad you're back, too. Translating your book gave him purpose, which he didn't have after he lost Reginald."

"At least I'm not a complete black sheep."

He smiled, gingerly patting my leg. The blankets covering me lessened the pain from his touch. "See? There's a silver lining. It's not the brightest one I've ever seen, but it exists."

"You're right. There's plenty to be positive about."

He slowly leaned forward and carefully stroked the buzz cut that now adorned my head. Megan had managed to do something with the scorched disaster that had been my hair. "Yeah, there is. And as for the 'do, you still look beautiful to me."

I smiled again, this time without excruciating pain.

Fumbling in his pocket, he pulled out a butterfly carving, now with a sturdy piece of twine threaded through it. "I made you a new one. Found some twine to turn it into a necklace."

Carefully slipping it over my head, it fit nicely. "It's

perfect. Thank you."

He grinned. "Glad you like it. I would've preferred a normal chain, but those aren't easy to come by around here."

"I'd love it no matter what."

Pete smiled, holding my gaze a little too long. He looked down at my wrist for a moment, eyeing the bracelet that still hung there. His jaw tensed, but he relaxed it and turned his focus back to me. "Are you hungry? I could whip up something for you."

I nodded as enthusiastically as possible without causing further pain. "Sounds great."

Taking my hand, he helped me to my feet and led me outside. My legs were extremely stiff, but walking wasn't as hard as I feared it would be. "I hope you don't mind being by the fire," he said as he helped me sit.

The heat stung my skin a little, but the pain was tolerable compared to everything else. "No, it's fine."

"All right. One 'Pete's Special' coming right up. Grabbed some more food while you were out. It wasn't easy, Coals were everywhere, but somehow I got lucky and didn't get caught."

"So, what do we do now?" I asked, handing him the empty wicker bowl once I finished.

He watched the fire for a long moment before replying. "Train as much as we can, and hope we're ready when the storm hits."

My stomach tightened. "This is going to be it, isn't it?"

"Yeah. It's coming, I can feel it. Don't tell anyone, but I'm scared out of my mind." He looked at me, eyes wide with fear. "What if we lose?"

"If we lose, then we'll go down knowing we did everything we could, until the end."

He took my hand. "If we go, we go together."

I met his gaze, squeezing his hand with a mirthless smile. "Absolutely."

He pressed his lips to the top of my head, avoiding any burned places. "I'm grateful we've had this time together." He sighed, voice growing sad. "I just wish it hadn't gone by so fast."

"So do I. It feels like I blinked and it all sped past me."

"If you die here, will you be reborn again?"

Using my shirtsleeve, I dabbed at my tears. They stung my scorched cheeks. "Most likely. If I am, I'll look for a way to find you as soon as I'm old enough. Wherever you are."

"I'll hold you to that," Pete murmured, leaning toward me.

"I'd expect no less."

Our lips met. It was a kiss with an unspoken promise, one that betrayed our fear at how little time we had. I held him close, ignoring the stinging pain on my skin. I could've bled out from a stab wound. I wouldn't have cared. The only thing that mattered was the two of us.

MY INJURIES MADE training harder than usual, but with time, I continued to heal. As the days went on, my skin eventually stopped looking like an overcooked marshmallow. A few red patches still lingered, but they mostly looked like I'd been sunburned. It didn't take long to get back into my old rhythm. My muscles hated me after each practice, but I carried on. Some things were more important than comfort.

Pete sat by Tina and I while everyone took a break, leaning back against a tree. "Tina, I really think we should teach Lily a few self-defense maneuvers, just in case. Or at least some survival skills. It might not be all that effective, with how small she is, but it'll at least up her chances of making it through an attack."

I kept out of their discussion. The angry glint in Tina's eyes said it all.

Tina folded her arms, puffing her chest out defiantly. "I can protect her."

"What if something happens to you, or to the rest of us? Don't you want her to be able to take care of herself?"

She looked away for a moment, stubbornly clenching her jaw. "I've arranged a place for her to go to if that happens."

"What if that falls through?"

Her gaze snapped back to his. Standing up to loom over him, she tightened her fist. Was she going to hit him? "Enough," Tina snarled. "She's not fighting, and that's final."

"If you're sure, then I guess I won't argue the point anymore." Pete shook his head, conceding. "If you ever change your mind, just let me know."

She stood, walking over to Emily to spar.

Pete sighed irritably, turning to me. "I don't even know why I bothered. We've had the same discussion at least a hundred times since Lily came to us."

I rested my head on his shoulder. "Well, I've never known you to be a quitter. And you're right. Lily should be able to take care of herself in an emergency."

"Doesn't matter what we think. What Tina says, goes. I tried sneaking in a lesson once—Tina caught us and broke my arm."

"Don't expect me to try my hand at convincing her."

Laughing, Pete ran his fingers through his hair. "No worries, you're off the hook. You're a great girl, but a miracle worker, you ain't."

I chuckled. "Not even remotely."

"I'll figure something out, don't worry," he grunted, hoisting himself to his feet and drawing his sword. "Ready to jump back into the action?"

I stood, stretching before grabbing my own weapon "Ready as I'll ever be."

He charged at me with his blade, aiming for my stomach. I parried his strike, spinning to the left.

"Not bad, but how about this?" He leaped at me, striking at my head.

"Easy," I breezed, blocking the blow, and stepping out

of harm's way.

He nodded, pursing his lips. "I'm impressed. Took at least a thousand whops on the head for that to sink in with me."

"Guess you're a slow learner."

He gasped, placing his free hand over his heart like I'd stabbed him. "Ouch. My poor ego will never recover from such witty barbs," he joked.

I winked, making a sweeping strike at his legs. "I think your ego could use the bruising."

He jumped, evading my attack. "Then I wouldn't be able to get on your nerves. What fun would that be?"

I thrust my sword at his chest, an attack he easily dodged. "You're in a mood today, aren't you?"

He guffawed, swiping at my arm. "I will neither confirm nor deny your allegation." He moved quickly, gracefully. It was impossible to keep up.

"Hold still, dammit," I whined.

His mouth stretched into a wide, playful grin. "Not a chance."

We continued like this late into the afternoon.

After practice, he twined his fingers through mine once I'd put my weapons away. "Good work today."

"Really? But I missed about a million times."

"You did fine. Your defense was stronger than your offense, but you managed to get a good move in now and then." He held his other arm for me to see. A few rapidly-healing wounds scraped his bicep and shoulder.

I let out a quick bark of laughter. "Damn. It doesn't hurt, does it?"

He grinned proudly. "Nope. Great job, sweetheart. You'll have the Coals crying for their mommies before long."

He brushed his lips against the nape of my neck, muttering, "You know, I'm glad you're back."

I tilted his head back, kissing him fiercely. "So am I, because being away from you for even a second is agony."

His eyes lit up. A teasing grin spread across his face. "My cheesiness is rubbing off on you."

I giggled. "Maybe. It's okay to be a little schmaltzy sometimes. But it doesn't mean we need to be one of those couples who are always latched to one another, cooing about their oh-so-perfect love."

Pete wrapped his arms around my waist, pulling me close. "I hate to break it to you, but we might be one of those already."

WE WERE SITTING by the fire, enjoying the peaceful silence, when footsteps came from behind us, followed by a familiar voice. "Oi, ya bastards! Did you miss me?"

I turned, my heart skipping a beat.

Ollie.

CHAPTER TWENTY-SEVEN

"**G**OT A LOT of nerve coming here after the stunt you pulled," Pete snapped. We'd both leapt to our feet. Pete took a small step, placing himself in front of me.

"You're not happy to see me? I'm hurt. Truly, I am."

My fingernails dug into my palm. "Get the hell out of here."

Ollie leaned against a tree, holding his hands behind his head. "Think I'll stay, actually."

From nowhere, Emily charged at him, pressing her machete to his Adam's apple. "Give me one good reason I shouldn't slice you like a Thanksgiving turkey."

"Your gal Mindi wouldn't be too pleased if you offed her best mate," he replied coolly.

"You're damn lucky." Emily pulled back her weapon with an angry grunt.

Greg, hearing the ruckus, emerged from his tent, marched up to Ollie, and slammed a fist into his gut.

"She's got a reason not to beat your ass, but I don't."

"Don't know what you're upset at me for." Ollie coughed, gripping his stomach. "Least I *did* something, rather than sitting here doing bloody *nothin'*."

Pete growled furiously, running to Ollie. He punched him square in the jaw, knocking him off his feet. "We were waiting for the right time, you impulsive asshole! Thanks to you we're on constant alert because Death thinks *we* did it."

"Bollocks! Both you lot and the pretender king needed a kick in the pants. Maybe now we can get back to the living world faster."

Mindi and Wes approached Ollie, both looking him dead in the eye.

"What are you on about?" Mindi asked. "There's no 'we' anymore, Ollie."

"You went an' set off a bomb at Death's ball," Wes added. "That sort of shit got us killed in the first place."

Ollie balked, pushing himself to his feet. I watched him not taking a step to defend himself. I read his eyes— he knew he couldn't take us all on. "Tryin' to pin that one on me, are ya? Who provoked the cozzers at the concert the night we died, Wes?" His gaze flew to Mindi. "Who'd been mouthing off at 'em the whole bloody time? I was first to hit one, but I didn't start it."

Wes folded his arms. "Didn't like how they were lookin' at my Kay."

Mindi leered, throwing up two fingers, faced at Ollie.

"Piss off! I get feisty when I'm off me arse. You were sober, Ollie. You knew what you was doing."

Ollie shoved Mindi then, his eyes alight with rage. "I'm not responsible for you. Sure, I was a right wanker that night, but don't say it's all my fault."

In return, Mindi shoved Ollie. "That's *exactly* what I'm sayin'. Get out of here. No one wants you 'round."

Ollie stepped back, glancing at each member of our group. "I try to help, and I get this. Tossed out by my friends and blamed for everything."

Unable to hold my tongue any longer, I got in his face and jabbed my finger into his chest. "How was setting off a bomb at Death's feet supposed to help?" I couldn't help it, I screeched. "All it did was make our situation worse. Death might torch the forest, just to smoke us out and annihilate us in front of all the other spirits so *they* don't get any ideas. Is that what you wanted? *Is it?*"

Ollie's eyes widened. "He might? No one told me…"

"Yes, Ollie. He might."

He stared at the ground, trying to process my words. "I—"

"Save your excuses. Just leave," I interrupted.

After taking another lasting glance at each of us, Ollie vanished into the forest once again.

THAT AFTERNOON, I lay at the edge of the campsite, looking at the sky to calm myself. There weren't any clouds, as usual, but looking at the blue of the sky mixed with the red of the pine needles proved a fascinating distraction. Part of me held a little sympathy for Ollie, despite the atrocious action he'd taken. In his mind, he'd done something good. He'd tried to take down, in his view, a tyrant.

What would've happened if he'd succeeded? If he'd managed to destroy Death? I shuddered. The consequences were too large to imagine. Though the concept of death unnerved me, I could at least admit it was a necessary part of life, whether or not there was a 'balance' involved.

I heard undergrowth snapping nearby. Jerking upright, gun drawn, I found Lily. *Thank God.*

"Whatcha doing?" she asked, laying down next to me.

It's not Death. I let myself relax once more. "Looking at the sky."

She looked up, watching a bird fly. "I used to look at clouds when I was alive. There's never any here though."

"I miss them, too."

She fiddled with her necklace. The clear gem threw rainbows while she played with it. "I bet they feel like cotton balls."

"Maybe they do. I've never felt one." My gaze wandered to her fingers. "Where'd you get your necklace?"

Lily scooted closer, whispering conspiratorially. "Promise not to tell?"

"I promise."

"The bad man gave it to me when I first got here." She

turned the crystal over in her hands as she spoke. "When I woke up, I was scared and all alone. Then he came. He said he was really sorry for what happened. I asked when I could see my mommy and daddy. He told me if I was patient and good, I'd see them soon. He gave me this to help me feel better 'cause I started crying." She held up the necklace, the gem shone in the sunlight.

I blinked in surprise. "Really? Doesn't sound like something he'd do."

"That's the only time I've seen him. When Tina found me, and I talked about him, she got really mad. She told me he was bad and mean. That he took her away from her family. I got confused. He seemed so nice. Then we found these guys, and they told bad stories about things he did. I still don't understand. If he's so mean, why did he give me this necklace and act so nice?"

I looked back at my interactions with Death. His malicious cruelty toward these spirits I'd allied myself with, the undeserved sympathy he'd shown me during those dark days after my return to the castle. "I've had a hard time figuring that out myself. He's done some awful things. But when I was at my lowest, he took care of me. I don't know how I'm supposed to feel either. Should I hate him for the terrible things, or should I be grateful for the good?"

She shrugged. "I dunno. Maybe it's a little bit of both?"

"You could be right. We've got to look at the whole picture rather than focusing on certain sections."

"Am I bad for keeping this?" she asked, clutching the necklace tightly.

I shook my head. "It's beautiful. If I were you, I might keep it too. In fact, I *did* keep a piece of jewelry he gave me." I held my wrist out, showing her the sparkling bracelet. It'd been singed a bit in the explosion, black spots dotted its facets, but it was still an impressive sight.

She gasped, staring at it in wonder. "Wow, that's really pretty."

"I know. I probably shouldn't be wearing it, but I couldn't bear to throw it away."

Her expression grew worried. "You're not going to go away again for lying, are you?"

I sat up, fidgeting with the bracelet. "No. If anyone asks, I'll tell the truth. It might make some people mad, but no one will be able to say I wasn't honest."

Lily wrapped her arms around me, squeezing tightly. "Good, because I'd miss you if you had to leave again."

I returned the hug, kissing her forehead. "I'd miss you too."

"I should probably go before Tina wonders where I went."

"Might be a good idea."

She stood and ran back to her tent. And I returned to gazing at the sky, but after a few minutes, I pushed myself to my feet. Yet another one of the birds flittered from tree to tree, and that brought an idea.

I haven't practiced my freaky powers for a while. Maybe

I should.

I looked around the area for inspiration. My gaze fell upon the boots I wore, worn and paper-thin.

I closed my eyes, envisioning a brand new pair of boots, identical to the old ones. Sneaking a peek, they sat on the ground right in front of me, just like I'd imagined. When I slid them on they fit perfectly. If my feet were sentient, they'd thank me.

I PUT A little distance between myself and the campsite.

Maybe I should try something a little more complex and useful than a pair of boots.

This time I pictured a steel bow and arrow set, one that couldn't be tampered with. Looking down, I saw it shining on the ground. A dull throbbing ache pounded in my skull, dampening my excitement.

One more time, then I'll stop. Should I dare…?

With a deep breath, I pictured a chipmunk. After a few seconds, I heard squeaking, but I hesitated to look down. Then, a rush of excitement flowed through my body. There stood a tiny chipmunk, precisely how I'd imagined. As I crouched down with my hand extended toward the chattering little guy, its breath quickened. Its eyes darted in fear.

In my most soothing tone, with the calmest smile I could muster, I crooned "Don't worry, I won't hurt you."

Looking up at me, its breathing slowed. It stopped panicking and cautiously walked onto my palm. Calmly.

Like it knew I was its creator. Then it stood, rubbing against my fingers like a cat.

I giggled at the tickling sensation. "All right, all right, that's enough for now. Go do whatever adorable rodents do," I whispered, letting it crawl out of my hand.

Disbelief and awe sank in watching it leap from one tree to another. I'd actually managed to deliberately make an animal that wasn't a horrific monstrosity. I was no longer a Dr. Frankenstein!

Returning to camp, I couldn't help but notice Jason desperately rummaging through his tent, mumbling to himself.

I approached, peering beyond him into his tent. "Did you lose something?"

"I am afraid so. The book you bequeathed to me has vanished. I do not know what happened. It was next to my other texts when I departed for practice," His voice rose, frantic. He didn't even spare me a glance.

"Who could've taken it? Was anyone here alone?"

"Not that I can recall. Megan and young Miss Lillian tend to stay within the confines of this encampment." He continued to search. "But this day they went swimming in a nearby lake before I took my leave."

Our argument from earlier flashed in my mind. "What about Ollie?"

Jason stopped his hunt for a moment to consider this. "It is possible, but Nathan and his maiden Katherine were guarding the perimeter. If Oliver or some other bandit had come, they would have sounded the alarm."

"Maybe someone just wanted to read it and forgot to ask first?" I suggested.

He finally looked at me, shaking his head. "Nay. Most of the others believe the book is cursed and will not touch it." Jason stroked his beard. "It is hard to deny trouble has befallen us in the time since it came into our possession."

"Yes, but how is that the book's fault?"

He brushed some dirt off the knees of his hand-sewn leather pants. "They are merely superstitious. Under normal circumstances, I would think the same, but that book has protected me."

I tilted my head, intrigued. "Really?"

"Indeed. When those vicious birds attacked, one of them nearly took hold of me. I came down upon its head with that text, and it made a hasty retreat." He stood a little taller as he spoke, obviously proud of his ingenuity.

"I'm glad it helped."

He smiled. "As am I."

"I guess we can start looking for it. Where do you think we should search?"

He fished out of his satchel a torn piece of paper, on which he'd drawn a crude map of the Land of the Dead. His gaze swept over it while he talked. "The surrounding area. That would be a good place to begin. The houses might hold answers, but it is far too dangerous, my lady, with Death so irate with us."

I sighed, folding my arms. "That's a light way of

putting it."

Jason returned the map to its original place. "I am hopeful his temper will abate and we will be able to resume our usual activities."

The two of us searched the entire camp, looking, with permission from their owners, through every tent. The book wasn't in any of them.

"I don't see it from up here" I called from a tree, slowly climbing back down.

When I landed on the ground, Jason was rubbing his face in agitation. "This is quite worrisome. I was very close to unlocking a vital piece of information."

"You were?"

He groaned, nodding. His mouth's downward curve broadcasted the guild he felt. "Aye. How you would be able to help us return to the world of the living."

My heart skipped a beat. "Wait, I can get you guys back there?"

"If my translation is correct, yes. All that remains is the specifics of how."

I looked at my hands, turning them over. "I didn't realize I possessed so much power."

"You have more than you know. According to Mr. Moritsa's notes, you already returned the dead to life while in the living world. Doing the same for us could be difficult, but you were able to once."

The frog. Zoology class.

"Death didn't do that?"

"It was you, Lady Heather."

I fell back against the tree. "My God…"

Jason gently patted my shoulder in an effort to comfort me. "There is no need yet to become overwhelmed. I am still to learn how you will do this, then we will prepare accordingly."

I covered my face with my hands, groaning. "I didn't ask for any of this. I only wanted to be just like everyone else."

"Fate cares not if you wished it to come into your life. Unfortunately, many of those whom destiny called feel likewise. There is no choice in the matter. What you *can* choose, however, is what you *do* with that destiny once it finds you."

"I want to do the right thing, but it gets harder by the day to see what the right thing *is*!"

"Follow your instincts. You will do what is best. I have faith in you."

I laughed sardonically. "Why? All I've done is cause trouble for you all."

With his thumb he lifted up my chin while he spoke. "You protected us from harm many times. You also made Sir Peter happier than I have ever seen him since his arrival in this God-forsaken place. You helped Miss Emily to leave her past behind. You have made mistakes, as everyone does, but do not let those steal your focus from the good you have done and the good you will do."

My gaze turned downward. "Sometimes it's easy to

forget I haven't done everything wrong."

"Well then, it is good you have friends and a suitor to remind you."

I grinned, wrapping my arms around him in a hug. "Thank you, Jason."

He patted my back. "You are most welcome. Now, let us go and check the training area."

We turned the practice ground upside down, but the book wasn't there either.

With a frustrated grunt, I kicked a nearby pinecone and watched it bounce away. "How hard is it to find this thing? It's not like it's a small notepad, it's *huge*."

Megan approached, placing a freshly made set of arrows with the rest. "You know, I think I saw it at the houses, the last time a group of us left to interrogate some spirits." she noted.

My fingers pinched the bridge of my nose. "Great. It's probably sitting out there somewhere."

"Have you tried using your abilities? To bring it here?" she offered.

"No." I took a deep breath. "It's worth a try though." I held my hands out, and closed my eyes, trying to envision the book in my grasp. Stinging pain scratched at my skull. When nothing happened after a few seconds, I concentrated harder. The more I tried, the worse the pain became. Still nothing.

"Don't push yourself too hard," Megan's voice tensed with concern.

My eyes flew open. "I can't get it. Weird. That's the first time my powers haven't worked."

"Perhaps it is too far away for you to transport it?" Jason suggested.

"Not a bad theory. But it doesn't help us find the book."

"I hate to say this," Megan began, her nose wrinkling, "but if you can't find it that way, we'll need to send you with a team to search by the houses ASAP. Someone might find it and take it if we wait too long."

I shot her a look—*You've got to be kidding.*

She held up her hands in defense. "Hear me out. If our strongest fighters go with you, there's a smaller chance of any attacks taking you by surprise."

"I find this plan foolish." Jason stroked his wrinkled chin. "But she does make a point."

I sighed. "Yes. She does. I'll talk to Pete. See what he thinks."

Jason turned his gaze to the lowering sun. "I would hurry, Miss Heather. If we are to do this, then it must be before nightfall." He pointed westward. "The sun will soon be setting."

CHAPTER TWENTY-EIGHT

ETE WAS SKEPTICAL at first, but even he had to acknowledge the importance of finding the book. The five of us—Pete, Emily, Jason, Greg, and I—crept out of the camp's safety shortly thereafter.

Emily spun when a twig snapped behind us, poising to strike with her bow. No Coals, only Greg. "I don't like this," she whispered. "They could be anywhere."

"I don't either," I admitted, "what do you suggest? We can't give up. It could be the key to ending this."

She disarmed her bow with a grunt. "I'm still not convinced Jason isn't going senile," she murmured, careful to speak quietly.

Pete adjusted his gear. "He isn't going senile, and you know it. We don't change once we're here. You just don't want to admit Heather's important."

She glanced over her shoulder, leering. "Or maybe you're biased, so you're grasping at straws."

Pete took a deep breath before he spoke again. "Look. We've got to be quiet or they'll hear us."

Part of me wanted Emily to be right. I didn't want to be important, be the center of attention. But a different, quieter voice in the back of my mind wanted to prove her wrong and rub that in her face. The jury was still out on which one I'd go with.

We stood at the edge of the tree line, taking cover while we talked. "Where do we start? This place is huge," I whispered, gazing warily at the houses about half a mile ahead.

Pete shrugged. "We go row by row, I guess."

Emily shot him a death stare. "Seriously? That'd take months. Years, even. Coals would take us out before we found it."

"Well, what's your suggestion? I'm all ears."

Greg piped up. "How about checking our informants first?"

Pete nodded. "I like that idea, but what if it's not there?"

"Then we go through with your stupid-ass plan to search every row, and most likely be ghosted in the process," Emily sneered.

Pete, speaking soothingly, told her, "Calm down. No one's getting ghosted. If we hear Coals, we'll hide in a house. There's empty ones waiting."

"Sounds like a plan," I admitted.

She turned, looming over me. "Of course you love his

idea. Pete can do no wrong, can he? If anyone else came up with it, you'd call them an idiot."

I stood straight and tall, forcing down my bubbling anxiety. "Maybe you're right, but so what? I haven't heard you give any alternatives."

"My alternative is to forget the damned book."

Impatiently, Pete tapped his foot. "So we should abandon our biggest chance of getting what we've worked for? This could be the key to living again, seeing our families."

She stabbed her finger toward me while looking at Pete. "She's not the answer, Pete! There's a way, but this compulsively lying bitch isn't it."

I sighed, my shoulders slumping.

"What's gotten into you?" Pete asked.

She turned away, not meeting his eyes. "Nothing."

Pete placed a hand on her shoulder. "Emily, don't lie. I can tell. What's bothering you?"

She jerked away from his touch. A rumbling growl broadcasted her frustration before she finally blurted out, "I'm scared, okay? Of losing Mindi. That Heather might really be the key to us going back and she won't take me. That in the end it won't work at all."

He reached to pat her back, but changed his mind at the last minute, and withdrew his hand. "It's okay to be anxious. You aren't the only one."

I smiled, speaking sincerely. "Of course I'll take you back with everyone else. Do you really think I wouldn't?"

Emily eyed me, appraising. "I don't know what to think anymore."

I adjusted my bag. "Well, we're even there."

Greg gave a firm nod, looking to Pete. "Right. Where do we start, chief?"

"At April and Geoffrey's place."

We crept between houses, keeping weapons drawn just in case. Everyone constantly scanned for Coals. With the houses as cover, they could've been anywhere, ready to overwhelm us. We finally came to Geoffrey and April's house without trouble. No one relaxed once we arrived.

It's too quiet.

All of the windows stood open, causing the inside's horrific stench to radiate out. The fumes were so potent it had turned the outer edges of the windows brown. Everyone else could hold their breath indefinitely against the noxious fumes. I wasn't so lucky. Every time my lungs begged for air, the wretched smell suffocated me.

We circled the house three times, combing the overgrown lawn surrounding it. Every blade of grass. We even searched twice around the houses to the left and right. No sign of the book.

"This is a bust," I choked with a gasping breath.

Emily folded her arms. "She's right. It's obviously not here. Where should we check next?"

"Bob's place?" Greg suggested.

Pete stroked his chin with a nod. "Bob won't want to talk with us, but we don't need to talk to him to search his house."

Jason piped up, his eyes sad. "I very much doubt Robert will be bothered by our intrusion. None have seen him for three days."

"Death got Bob? Dammit," Emily hissed. "He's got kids here, for God's sake."

Greg swore. "Do you really think *he* gives a damn if Bob has kids?"

I suggested, "Maybe Bob's just moved on. Doesn't mean he's been Coalified."

Pete wrapped an arm around my waist. "She's right, guys. Jumping to conclusions just leads to trouble. Just look at Ollie."

SILENTLY, WE TRUDGED along, our posture rigid, listening for the tiniest hint someone or something waited nearby. Once again, there was absolutely no one around.

This isn't right. Spirits don't need to sleep, so where are all the homeowners? Finally, we reached the house with 3047 engraved on a gold plaque by the door. Bob's house.

"Praise be, I have found it," Jason called in a strangled voice from a few feet away.

He stood, holding the book, a huge smile stretching across his aged face. I returned his smile. He seemed about to say something else, but before he could, an arrow pierced his head. It protruded from his eye socket.

"Jason!" I screamed.

It was too late. He gasped for a moment, then vanished.

The book fell onto the pile his clothes left behind; open to a random page. Like a bookmark, the arrow that ghosted Jason dropped into the crease.

Trying to keep myself steady, I looked in the direction of the shot.

It was a Coal, emerging from behind the house a few doors down. And it wasn't alone. Ten more of them showed themselves, all with weapons drawn, aiming at us. Another arrow darted past our heads. In my peripheral vision a tall, thin figure with green hair and wearing a long, dark jacket ran toward the woods, his back to us.

Ollie, you coward!

As the Coals charged us, Pete shouted at me, "Grab the book and run!"

I snatched it up and ran in the direction of the woods. Glancing over my shoulder, I drew my pistol to fire, but stopped myself. It wouldn't do any good. Pete and the others, however, fired like crazy. All that did was cause a couple of them to stumble in their pursuit.

One of them cocked its gun, and fired a shot. I peeked over my shoulder, horrified to find it'd struck Greg's ankle. He staggered, and howled in agony. He painfully tumbled into a heap behind us. Pete rushed back to his side, using his body as a stand-in for a crutch.

We skidded around a street corner, losing the Coals long enough to scramble into an empty house.

The interior seemed eerily sparse. The rooms were veiled in shadow, giving off a foreboding air. Sliding down the living room wall, sweat rolled down my neck. Once I could finally breathe again, I clutched the book tightly, struggling to keep back the tears pooling at the edges of my eyes. The others just stood there, unable to speak.

Pete sat next to me after helping Greg. Nothing hung on the walls. A lone table and couch sat in the living room we now rested in.

Thunderous, marching footsteps sounded outside, growing ever closer.

Emily crept to the window, sneaking a peek through tan curtains. "They're going the wrong way." The final rays of the setting sun shone on the wall, dyeing the room a reddish gold. "We've lost 'em," she whispered.

But there was no sigh of relief, no smiles at our success. For a long time, there was only silence.

Pete spoke first. He looked to Greg, his voice an empty monotone. "Are you all right? Will you be able to walk back to camp?"

Greg nodded, gritting his teeth. "Yeah, I'll be all right."

"I told you so," Emily said, on the verge of tears, though none fell. "Now the oldest member of our group is gone. Who, may I add, was the only one who could read the stupid book. Was it worth it, Pete?"

"Can we go five minutes without you blaming me for something I have no control over?" Pete fired back.

She ducked her head.

Pete's voice broke. "I could've—don't make me feel worse than I already do, Emily. Jason was like a grandfather to us." He let out a sob. "No matter how hard I try to protect those I care about, I just can't."

"What do we do now?" I asked, rubbing my wet eyes on my sleeve.

"I don't know." With a sigh Pete leaned his head against the wall. "We'll stay here until morning. The sun's almost gone."

I nodded. "We need to get a message to the others that we're okay until tomorrow."

Carelessly, Emily tossed her weapons onto the leather couch, narrowly avoiding hitting Greg. "How do you suggest we do that? You whip up a carrier pigeon with three eyes and six legs who can't even fly?" A teasing lilt hung in her voice, though with her tense posture there wasn't any mistaking a genuine bitterness there.

I chuckled. "You've got me there." My gaze turned humorlessly to the window. "It'd be best not to worry them back at camp. They might come looking for us. Run into Coals."

"Why don't you teleport back and tell them?" she asked.

I rubbed my eyes, doing my best to fight the incoming wave of exhaustion. "My powers are too much of a wild card. I've never teleported that far on purpose before. What if I end up in some random location and get lost forever? Or the trip fries my brain somehow?" My gaze drifted to Pete. "Not only would I lose you, which would be bad enough, but if the book was right, then it would end your dream of getting back. Sure, maybe I'd reincarnate eventually, but how would I get back to this world without Death? I doubt he'll bring me again."

Greg's head shot up. "We could each take lookout shifts. Then, when the coast is clear, we send one of us back, let everyone know what's going on."

Pete nodded. "Good idea. After Bernard, it's cruel to not tell them we won't be back right away. Emily can be lookout first, then me, then you if your leg's up to it."

"What about me?" I asked.

"You're the only one who needs to sleep. You look about ready to drop. Besides, I don't like the idea of you being out there alone now that night's come."

"I'm not a porcelain doll, Pete. I can take care of myself."

He half-heartedly smiled, wrapping an arm around my waist. "I know you can, believe me, but I'd rather you got some rest. If you're determined to help, how about you take the last shift, early tomorrow, before we all head back?"

"I guess that's a decent compromise."

He kissed the top of my head. "I'm glad you think so."

I scooted closer to him, lying down to rest my head on his knee. Sleep took a while to come, and when it did, it wasn't peaceful. Nightmares tormented me, each filled with screaming and blood. The scene of Jason's final moments repeated continuously.

CHAPTER TWENTY-NINE

P ETE STILL LAY next to me when I opened my eyes the following day. He looked down, trying his best to give me a smile. "Good morning."

"Hey. How did last night go?"

"Everything went great. There wasn't a single peep the whole time. Emily left a few hours ago to tell the others what happened."

I stood, stretching my arms. "Good. I guess it's my turn to be lookout, then?"

He rose with a grunt. "Yeah, you can take over for Greg until we're ready to leave. I'd make you breakfast, but I was a dumbass and forgot to bring food for you. Didn't think this was gonna be an overnight thing."

"I could try making some food with my powers."

"You sure? Don't want you to hurt yourself..."

"I should be okay."

Letting my eyes slip closed, I held out my hands and

imagined they were filled with strawberries. Tried to visualize the specific weight and feel…

"Holy shit! Not sure I'll ever get used to that."

I glanced down at my hands. Despite the throbbing headache pulsing behind my eye, I manage to smile with pride at the cluster of strawberries.

"Now for the taste test. Here goes nothing." I muttered before hesitantly popping the fruit into my mouth, chewing for a moment or two.

"Well?" Pete asked, eyes alight with curiosity as he stepped closer.

"Not the best strawberry I've ever tasted. It's kinda bitter, but it's not absolute garbage." I replied as I ate another.

"That's great! Now if we run out of food for you, we aren't screwed."

I leaned my head on his shoulder, hoping it would dull the creeping ache in my skull while I continued to eat. "Yep."

He turned a strawberry in his hands, looking to me with a plea in his eyes. "Do you think they suffer when they… you know…"

I took the tiny fruit from him, staring at it for a moment before I could speak. "I don't really know. I'd like to say no, they don't feel a thing, but there's no way to tell. I just hope they're somewhere peaceful, quiet, doing whatever makes them happy."

He let out a heavy sigh. "To rub salt into the wound, I

realized Emily's right. Our chances of being able to use the book to get back are pretty much gone without Jason. Who else can read Latin?"

"Maybe he left notes."

"We'll figure it out when we're back at camp."

I tossed the strawberry back to him. "I'll take the next watch while you and Greg make sure we're ready to go."

"Yes ma'am," Pete joked, saluting, though the sadness hadn't left his voice.

Greg sat on the porch, his eyes sweeping over every possible angle an attack could come from. His ankle looked good as new.

A grunt escaped when I helped him up. "You're off the hook."

He rubbed his eyes. "Thanks. Been watching for Coals so long I'm seeing them everywhere. Almost sounded the alarm over a leaf rolling by."

"That would've been good." I grinned. "Given us a good laugh back at camp."

"It actually might've. Laughs are hard to come by these days."

"War tends to do that."

"Don't I know it," he sighed, then limped into the house.

Diligently keeping watch, my eyes scanned every square inch of the grassy avenue. A gentle breeze danced through the cool morning air, raising goose bumps on my skin. Spirits in the surrounding houses went about their business, their doors quietly opening and shutting. A child's laughter echoed from far away. A floral and pine scent came to me on the wind, most likely from the woods.

The door behind me squeaked open. Pete and Greg stepped outside, blinking in the sun's light.

"Ready?" I asked with a yawn.

Pete stretched. "Yeah."

Once we were beyond the perimeter of the house, and turned a corner, a booming, marching rhythm shook the ground. Pressing myself close to the nearest wall, I dared to peek around the corner. A battalion of Coals, at least twenty, walked down the street in V-formation.

We scattered, making it harder for any Coals to take us all out at once. I signaled to the others to hide, mimicking soldier's gestures I'd seen in movies. My attempt left a lot to be desired, but it got my message across. The others ducked behind the house closest to them, drawing their weapons. My hand hovered over my pistol, ready to grab it if I needed to.

The Coals marched closer; my pulse raced. I wiped sweat-soaked hands on my jeans, but they were damp again in seconds. My eyes darted to Pete. He gave me a grim smile, tightening his grip on the handle of his sword.

Peeking again, they'd changed direction, heading directly toward the house where I hid. My throat clamped shut.

Think, Heather, think, I shouted mentally.

It took some effort to close my eyes, but I managed it.

Please, get us out of here. Please, don't let them find us.

My racing mind did its best to visualize the three of us safe at the campground. Cold air scraped at my skin. A force pulled me forward. *The Coals. They'd grabbed me.*

"Holy crap," Jeremy's forever 'changing' voice squeaked. "They just came out of nowhere."

When I dared to open my eyes, a shaky laugh passed my lips. It wasn't a Coal! All three of us were safely back at camp.

I've done it! And my brain isn't a plate of scrambled eggs!

Relief was quickly replaced with pain as a throbbing ache stabbed at my head. It was so intense it almost made me vomit.

Pete bounded to me, picking me up when my knees buckled from the pain. He wrapped me in an embrace. "Have I ever told you how amazing you are?"

"At least once a minute," I joked, wincing at the pain driving into my brain like nails.

He set me down, eyeing me. "Are you all right? You're really pale."

"I'll be okay, I think. Like I said, never gone this far on purpose before."

"I'm sorry. Thank you for what you did."

My legs wobbled. "…wasn't about to let them get us," I mumbled, leaning against him so I wouldn't fall.

"Let's get you to bed. We'll talk more later."

"M'kay."

IF THERE WAS a higher power, they must've liked me. Jason had left bright red notes in the book's margins. His thin penmanship stared up at me, scratchy, daring me to understand it. I groaned. *Like a doctor's handwriting,* I thought, *only ten times worse.*

Reading this chicken scratch wasn't simple. Turning back to the first page, it seemed more worn than the others. Written on it, at least I guessed, was Richard Mortisa's list of every life I'd lived thus far, including birth and death dates.

How could a stranger know all this about me? I wondered. *I'd never heard his name before we found this thing.*

I flipped through the pages; there were a few sketches by both Jason and the mysterious Richard which gave some clues. One drawing near the back caught my eye—a flower weaved in and out of Jason's notes, like it was created by the words themselves. The shape of the petals didn't look like any flower I'd seen, but it was impossible to deny the sense of familiarity. I stared at Jason's notes by the drawing, willing myself to understand what they said.

Pete and Lily crawled quietly into my tent, trying not to bug me.

"Hey, honey," Pete said, sliding to sit next to me, "Decided to check on you. You didn't get up, we got worried."

I gave him a quick kiss before turning back to the book, flipping through it once more. "I'm fine. Just trying to make sense of these notes. Jason's handwriting is awful."

Pete ran his fingers through his hair, sighing deeply. "I really miss that old man."

"Is he coming back soon?" Lily asked.

I closed the book, biting my lip. "He's... not coming back, Lily."

Her brow furrowed, her gaze fell. "Oh."

"Why don't you play with Megan?" Pete suggested. "Heather and I need to talk alone."

Lily nodded, crawling out of the tent without a word.

I glanced down at the book, my breath catching. "I still can't get the image out of my mind. That arrow," I whispered, "going right through his head." A shudder raked my body.

"I know. He was a good fighter, a good man. If just one of us could make it back, my vote would've gone to Jason. He deserved life more than most of us."

I ran my fingers over the book's worn leather cover. "He always had faith in us, in what we're trying to achieve. We need to make it back, Pete. For him. For everyone we've lost. Otherwise, everything we've done in this place will mean nothing."

"We will." He nodded firmly, trying to force his expression into something more peaceful, content. "So, is there anything interesting in Jason's notes?" he asked, picking up the book.

Pointing out the flower sketch, I glanced from it to Pete. "Ever seen a flower like this?"

He looked at it for a moment before shaking his head. "No. It sort of looks like a Carnadia blossom, but the stem is too thick, and the petals are *way* too long."

I turned a few pages, tapping my finger on the paper. "Richard Mortisa drew a similar one, see? This flower is important. I just wish we knew why."

Pete closed the book, kissing my cheek. "Why don't you take a break for a while? I'll make you some breakfast. You can study this after fighting practice. A tasty meal and some exercise always worked for me when I needed to figure something out." He shrugged. "It still does, I guess, minus the food."

AS USUAL, PETE was right. Breakfast and practice helped a ton. My mind felt much clearer as I sat down again with the book. Jason's handwriting was still atrocious, but I could actually make out some words now. By the flower sketch, I deciphered the word 'home'. *Do we need something like the flower to get back?*

I also managed to read an odd phrase—*Mother Ca...* The rest was a jumbled scribble. Mother what? *Mother Cancer? Mother Catwoman?*

The answer hit me harder than a bird hitting a freshly cleaned window—Mother Carnadia! Every plant had an original, spawning the rest. Was this the Carnadia blossom's? Had Jason believed it held the key to returning to the living world?

My heart thudded against my rib cage. Barreling out of my tent, I skidded to a stop in front of Pete, who sat whittling. "I think I've got the answer," I panted.

His head shot up, eyes alight. "You do?"

I held open the book, jabbing at the flower sketch. "The flower Richard and Jason drew. It's called the 'Mother Carnadia.' I'm pretty sure it's the original that the rest came from. It could be the answer."

For the first time in a while, hope flickered across Pete's face. "Great! But where do we find it? Do you know?"

"No. But Jason was looking for it. He drew a map of this entire world in the back of the book with a list under it. See? There're places crossed off."

I pulled Jason's map out of the book, looking over it. My finger scanning the items on the list he'd marked off. "Somewhere in the houses, probably Mr. Advani's garden, and something about mountains." I looked up at Pete. "That's what's not crossed off yet. Are there mountains here? I've never seen any."

Pete rubbed the back of his neck. "There are, but everyone avoids them. No one who's gone there ever comes back."

"Fantastic," I quipped. "More danger to get into."

"If it means ending this, I'm game."

"So am I."

TO SAY THERE was some discord among the group about the mountains would be putting it lightly.

Pete held up his hands, taking a slow, controlled breath to calm himself. "Listen. This war's taken a lot from us. We've all lost someone important in the process. I think this Mother Carnadia can finally end it. I wouldn't suggest this unless I had the utmost faith in it succeeding.

"I won't say it'll be easy, because I know it won't be. But, we can't let this chance slip away. Especially not from fear. Now's the time to be the amazing, courageous people I know you are. Are you with me?"

Emily snorted, turning her head away with a sneer. "Do we have a choice?"

He balked. "Of course. I'm not going through with this unless *all* of you are okay with it."

Greg folded his arms, glowering. "Seems like an awful big risk for something that might not even work."

Pete scratched his chin pensively. "You're right, but hasn't that been what this whole thing has been?"

His eyes widened slightly. "Hadn't thought of it that way."

"And Emily, you can't tell me that it wouldn't be satisfying to be the first to make it to the top of that mountain."

She smirked ever so slightly. "Be that as it may, I still don't like this plan."

"Honestly, have you *ever* liked one of my plans?"

"Yes. Overthrowing Bernard was a good idea. Adding

Mindi to the group was," her eyes softened as she shot a glance at her, "smart."

"See? I'm capable of making good decisions. You trusted me those times, why can't you now?" Pete turned his focus to the others. "What do you guys say? Take this leap of faith with me?"

The rest of us nodded, ready to see this through to the end.

His eyes misted as he looked at us—his friends, his brothers and sisters in arms. "This is a lot to ask, I know. If it gets too hairy, I'll do everything I can to get us out. I promise your loyalty won't be in vain. I'll make you proud."

My hand slipped into his, squeezing it. "You already have."

A solemnity swept through the camp while we readied ourselves to leave. The couples—Emily and Mindi, Nathan and Kate, and Wes and Kay—held each other in firm embraces, giving one another kisses that might mean 'good luck' or 'goodbye' or something else entirely. Looking at Pete, I bit on my bottom lip. The idea of saying goodbye made my stomach twist. Watching Pete talk to the others, giving commands, I made a silent vow.

When shit hits the fan, if I can't save the others, I'll save you, Pete. No matter what.

CHAPTER THIRTY

A FEW ALL-TOO-SHORT minutes later, the time came for us to split up. Kate, Megan, Tina, and Lily stayed behind to keep an eye out for trouble. Nathan, Jeremy, Kay, and Wes left in the direction of the houses to find Mr. Advani's garden while Emily, Pete, Greg, Mindi, and I set off for the mountains. I elected against riding Hazel. She needed to stay in camp in case Lily needed to make a quick escape.

We followed the rugged dirt trail that snaked deep into the woods, which we'd avoided until now. As we progressed, it was easy to see why. The further from camp we walked, the taller and thicker the trees seemed to grow. Eventually, the pine needles blotted out the sun, leaving only thin streaks of light to see by. Being caught by a Coal here would be suicide. Pete and I walked close, holding hands, so we didn't become separated as the shadows engulfed the light.

"How far are the mountains?" I asked, squinting. It didn't help me see better.

"We've still got a way to go," Pete's scabbard nudged my calf with every step we took.

I asked, "No one's ever returned? Do you know why?"

"Some say there's horrible monsters up there," Greg replied, anxiety in his words. "With all I've seen, I believe it."

I bit my lip before asking, "Do you think we'll be able to handle whatever's up there?"

Emily chimed in. "Sure. I'm not scared of whatever *he's* got guarding the mountains. I say, bring it on. We—"

"Don't get cocky, darlin'," Mindi interrupted. "Too many good people don't come back from where we're goin', better fighters than any of us."

My grip on my sword tightened. A chill rattled my bones. "Encouraging."

"Didn't know you were a motivational speaker, Mindi," Greg added, his tone condescending.

Emily teased, "Thank you for thoroughly scaring us all, dear."

"Not sayin' I don't believe in us. I do. We just need to keep our confidence in check, or else we're askin' for trouble."

THE DARKNESS BECAME so severe at one point, the only way I could tell we were still on the trail was the crunch under our feet.

Pressing onward, we eventually emerged from the woods. The sun's warmth held me in its glow.

It's afternoon already? We must've walked for hours.

Closing my eyes to let them adjust, I took a deep breath and let the crisp air fill my lungs. Everyone else did the same, enjoying the feeling of being less restricted after the murky woods.

When I could finally see, the jagged stone mountains looming overhead immediately grabbed my attention. The distant peaks shone a bright grey-blue, stabbing through the ghostly mists that swirled around them.

Directly ahead of us, thick, spiked weeds shot up underfoot, twisted and tangled. They blocked our path, stretching to the base of the mountains.

"Wow," I gasped.

"It certainly is something to see, but those weeds look like trouble." Pete stroked his chin in concentration.

"Easy. Just hack 'em to bits to make a path," Emily suggested, unsheathing her machete.

One of the plants twitched. "Emily, don't," I cried.

Too late.

She'd hacked at the weed, easily cutting through it. But right as she struck, it began shaking and emitting a low, almost hissing sound. The segment she'd severed slithered across the ground, wrapping itself around Emily's leg; a snake ensnaring prey. Emily tumbled, wildly swinging her machete. Another tendril grabbed her as she struggled with the first, dragging her into the patch of waiting weeds.

Mindi immediately took off after Emily, bellowing as the weed's spikes dug into her flesh. The vines tried to grab at her, but Mindi bounded out of the way. Emily kicked frantically. The plant pulled her toward a Venus flytrap-like mouth rising above the weed patch. She held her machete high, then brought it down upon the gaping jaws. The quick motion freed her. Struggling against the spiked vine, she screamed a long string of obscenities before she could leap to her feet and run back to us.

We all stared, dumbfounded, at the chaos before us. The weed slithered toward Greg next, aiming to wrap around his ankles. With a startled cry, he side-stepped, slicing it apart with his sword. I pulled my bow off my back, taking careful aim at the weed's large 'head' before firing. The weed thrashed as the arrow hit home, letting out a terrible high-pitched squeal. Emily and Mindi, cussing and chopping, sliced their way to us. Its head fell limp. The rest of the weed grew still.

"They weren't kidding when they said some scary shit guarded these mountains," Pete mumbled, returning his bow to a strap on his back.

I panted, leaning on a tree for just a moment before jerking away from it. "No. They weren't."

"Is everyone alright?" Pete asked.

"My legs sting." Emily breathed heavily. "But I think I'm okay."

Mindi rubbed her arm, shrugging. "M'legs are

thrashed, but they've been worse."

"Didn't even touch me." Greg rubbed at his nose with an overconfident sniff.

My heart rate gradually slowed back to its normal pace. "What do you think? Should we keep going this way, Pete, or find another way up?"

He brushed a piece of the plant from his shirt. "It'd be stupid to look for a different path when we're so close, wouldn't it?"

I wiped my brow. Mindi said, "If it means not being attacked by another of those things, then it's not stupid."

Pete took a quick glance around before shrugging. "Let's just keep going this way. It's a straight shot. If another plant attacks us, we'll kill it, too."

THE REST OF our journey to the mountain was smooth sailing. We cut a path through more weeds, listening carefully for any sort of hissing, until we reached the base. An earthy, mossy smell filled the air. Emily and Mindi moved on ahead, trying to find the best path up the mountainside.

"Anyone got climbing gear?" I queried with a gulp, craning my neck to see the summit. I couldn't see all the way up.

Greg looked to me. "We hoped you'd create some with those powers of yours."

"I've never gone mountain climbing before. Only times I've ever seen the gear are in movies and on TV.

There's no way to properly judge the weight and feel."

He sighed irritably. "Great. We came all this way, now we're stuck."

"If you'd told me beforehand, maybe this would've gone smoother."

Pete nudged a rock with his foot. "Stop it. It's my fault. We had a quick meeting while you were getting into your combat gear. Didn't want to…uh…disturb you, so I left you alone."

"If you three are done yapping, we've got a mountain to climb. This looks like the safest path up," Emily called from about sixty feet away.

We began our ascent, keeping a watchful eye for signs of trouble. My hands gripped the cold, unforgiving stone as I hitched up my leg to press myself shakily upward. A breeze whistled through the slope, almost sounding like a bird's song. It would've comforted me if the frigid air wasn't stabbing at my face.

Another icy gust crashed against us like a wave. I flattened myself against the mountain's rugged face, licking my cracked, dry lips. The wind tore at my clothes, holding me captive until the blast passed.

My right leg swung beneath me, frantically searching for a rock ledge, a crack, an indent—anything. I jammed a foot into a hole, pressing so hard the circulation in my toes started dwindling.

Please be strong enough to support me, I begged.

Another few minutes and my fingers would be too

chilled to hold on, much less keep the strength to struggle against the fierce frozen crosswinds.

"There's a ledge right above us big enough for us to sit on." Pete yelled. "Try to get there so you can rest for a minute." Over my shoulder, his voice seemed barely audible against the howling of the wind.

I took a deep breath, coughing as granite dust shot up my nose. With one last burst of energy, I hoisted myself up to the ledge. Collapsing, my lungs screamed for oxygen in the thinning air. How did anyone survive mountain climbing? My head swam, the world swinging in circles around me. I felt like dust floating in the breeze, a tiny cloud of smoke. No more substantial than the labored breathes I took.

Pete leaned over me, his eyes wild, panicked. "Are you okay?"

"She's fine," Emily calmed him. "She's just light-headed from the altitude. Give it a little while. Her body will adjust."

"Climbed a lot of mountains, 'ave you?" Mindi queried.

Emily nodded, tightening her ponytail. "Went on a few climbs with Travis when I was alive. Wish I'd pushed him off, saved myself the trouble."

"When we get out of here I'm beating that bloke senseless for what he did. If he's even alive."

If I weren't already struggling for breath, the view would've taken my breath away. The entire woods spread out below us in the evening light, the distance blurring the trees into a big cluster of red. The castle stood proud and tall further back, a grayish speck, with a brightly colored speck next to it that could only be the garden.

"It all seems so insignificant looking at it from up here, doesn't it?" Pete asked, sitting next to me. He fished a few strawberries out of his satchel and offered me one.

I scooted closer to him, slipping under his arm while I nibbled on the fruit. Not far from the castle a series of white dots were perfectly spaced, assumedly the houses. There were a lot more of them than I'd imagined. "It certainly puts things into perspective. I wonder if this is how *he* sees everything, how he sees us."

"I wouldn't be surprised. I'll give him credit, though. He sure made a beautiful world. It's easy to forget how good this place looks with everything going on. As impressive as it is, though, it's nothing compared to the real one."

A rustle came from behind us. I peeked over my shoulder to find Greg pulling a red scrap of cloth from his satchel, securing it to a nearby rock.

I stared at him, eyebrows raised. "What are you doing?"

"It's a piece of Shaun's favorite shirt. Always ranted about wanting to climb this thing, but with all the talk of people not coming back, he never got a chance to do it." His eyes started to water. Greg watched the fabric wave in the breeze. "He would've loved this view."

Pete rubbed his nose on his sleeve, giving Greg a nod. "Yeah, he would've."

WE SAT ON the mountainside watching the world go by until everyone felt ready to continue.

Our path onward quickly became unsteady. The closer we got to the peak, the more rocks wobbled under our feet and hands. One of them gave way as Mindi pushed off it. She screamed, frantically clawing to regain her grip. Emily howled, her expression frozen with horror.

CHAPTER THIRTY-ONE

GREG CAUGHT MINDI'S wrist, helping her to a safe position. "Careful. We've lost enough people already."

Mindi paused, taking deep, shaking breaths. "Thanks, mate. Thought I was a goner."

"So did I, for a minute. Lucky I caught you."

"I won't forget this. Somehow I'll make it up to you."

"Don't worry about it."

Emily leaned her head against the rock face, cheeks wet with tears.

"You all right, dear?" Mindi asked, climbing with some effort up next to her.

"I almost lost you," Emily whispered, choking on her words. It was difficult for me to hear her words over the wind, but from my position I could read their lips.

"Hey, now. I'm right 'ere, sweetheart, safe 'n' sound."

She sniffed, nodding. "I know." She took a deep breath

to steady herself. "God, I haven't cried in over fifty years."

"If I have anything to say about it, Emily, you'll never be in a situation that makes you cry anything but happy tears."

She let out a single, barking laugh. "You're so sentimental."

Mindi grinned, carefully moving to kiss the top of her head. "And proud of it."

AFTER AN EXHAUSTING hour-long climb, we finally reached the top of the mountain. Rather than a sharp point, the peak flattened into a grassy, moss-covered plateau. Carnadia blossoms poked above the grass, their red petals complementing the various shades of green, reminiscent of Christmas. Towering bushes lined the whole plateau, creating the feel of a garden. Death, always the showoff.

"Do you see it anywhere, Heather?" Pete queried, his eyes scanning the area.

"Hard to tell. There's so many of them."

"Guess we'll examine them all until we find it. If it's not here, it might be at your principal's house. That wasn't crossed off on Jason's map yet."

Emily groaned. "Great. Staring at flowers all night is exactly how I wanted to spend my time."

"Relax. We've got the advantage of numbers." Greg

cracked his neck with a grunt. "Long as we're focused, this'll be a snap."

As 'snap' left his lips, a twig did just that. My heart hurdled to my throat the second I saw what caused it.

A vulture, two times bigger than any of us, emerged from a bush, covered in matted, dusty feathers. Fangs protruded from its bloodstained beak, their color matching its red eyes. Talons the size of my arms scraped across the ground, tearing out grass and moss as it approached.

We drew our weapons in a flash and spread out, poised to attack.

"Does Death have some sick obsession with birds or something?" asked Pete.

The creature took flight, charging at Emily and Mindi, knocking them backward with its wings. I brandished my sword, ready to assist. Quickly standing, Emily and Mindi picked up their weapons, ready to fight before I could take a single step to aid them. The vulture tried to snatch up Greg, but he rolled out of the way, slicing at its left wing in the process. Screeching in pain, it fell to the ground. It turned to swipe its talons at us.

Running at the beast while it was distracted, I threw a rock, smacking the creature on its side. Mindi and Emily circled, causing the bird's head to dart left and right in confusion while it watched them.

Pete hacked at the animal's other wing with his sword, cutting it off. Black dust splattered everywhere as the wing fell, then withered.

Greg leapt into the air, bringing his sword down on the vulture's back, embedding it there. The bird collapsed, trying—and failing—to regain its footing. Mindi flew at the vulture and, before it could react to her charge, brought her sword down on its neck, catching it there. It let out one last gargled squawk, then was still. With another chop, the vulture's head was gone. The whole creature withered into dust, blowing away on the wind.

Emily sheathed her machete. Her posture still tense, ready for more of a fight. "What's Death sending next, a robin shooting bullets out its ass?"

"Wouldn't put it past him, honestly," Greg answered, wiping his dust-covered hands on his pants.

I moved to tuck some hair behind my ears, before realizing I couldn't. *Never going to get used to that.* "At least it's gone now. Hopefully, there aren't more."

"Okay, 'The Hunt for the Mother Carnadia,' take two," Pete joked, though his clipped tone lacked humor.

We combed every inch of the mountain's peak, carefully taking in each petal on every flower there. No stone went unturned—literally. When I paused to stretch my back and looked up, the sun was low in the sky.

It's evening? We've been at this for hours?

"Hey," Emily called. "Does this look like that drawing you won't shut up about?"

I lumbered over, weary of this task. When I saw the flower she knelt next to, my heart somersaulted. Long, silken petals draped over a sizable green stem. In every detail, rising from the earth, was a flower matching Jason and Richard's sketches.

"That's it," I stammered, blinking in disbelief. The petals were a darker shade of red than other Carnadias, with red spots on the lighter tips.

"So do we just pick it?" she asked. "Pull it out by the root, or what?"

"I'm not sure. We'll need to be careful so it doesn't die before we get back to camp."

"They don't die," Pete interjected. "I've kept ones I picked for April and Geoffrey in my bag for weeks. They were still fresh when I handed them over."

Mindi nodded. "Don't need water, neither, once they sprout." She took a step back with her hands up when we all shot her accusing stares. "Don't look at me like that—Ollie grew some for a bit. Never tried 'em though. I'm a vodka gal myself."

"We'll talk about this later," Emily threatened, carefully plucking the flower from the ground and handing it to me.

I stared transfixed at the flower. The simple plant I now held was the potential answer to giving everyone what they wanted.

Not everyone, part of my mind whispered. *Not Death.*

It took some work, but I managed to push away that thought.

"Ready to start heading back?" Pete asked. "It might

not be safe up here. Descending is going to be even harder. Especially in the dark." He peeked over the cliff's edge with a grimace.

Emily glanced over, too, before gesturing. "Unless Heather takes us back using those freaky abilities," she said with much less venom in her tone than I'd grown accustomed to.

Pete turned to me. "Do you think you can? Would that be too much?"

Could I? Well, they're counting on me.

"Yeah, I can." I twirled the flower in my fingers. "It'd mean I'd need to rest for a day after we get back before we start piecing together how this is gonna work, though. Would everyone be okay with that?"

Pete nodded. "We've waited to get to this point. I think we'll survive an extra day."

Greg shrugged his massive shoulders. "Long as we eventually get back, I'm cool."

"One day's nothin'," Mindi piped up. "Rather wait, that's for sure, than worry about climbin' down this bloody thing at night."

WHAT HAPPENED WHEN we arrived back at camp was a blur. My head pounded. The energy drained from my body. Emily and Mindi shook where they stood, faces wide with astonishment from being teleported for the first time, but I had no strength left to comfort them. I stumbled to my tent and fell onto the bed, claimed instantly by sleep.

THE SUNLIGHT STABBED at me when I emerged from my tent, forcing me to squint. Everyone was crowded around, their eager faces full of anticipation.

Had they sat out here all night waiting?

"Hi, everyone." I mumbled, wiping the sleep from my eyes. "Sorry to keep you waiting."

Tina spoke first. "Pete said you found the flower. Does this mean we can get out of here now?"

A rumble of *Yeah* and *Can we?* passed through the crowd.

"Not yet." I shook my head. "I still need to figure out what to do next. I think I get the main idea, but I'm not sure if it'll work for all of us, or just me."

Kate held her arms folded, firmly against her chest. "Like, what if it won't work for us?"

"We'll find another way. I wouldn't leave you guys behind."

Emily opened her mouth to say something, but hesitated and closed it when Pete gave her a pointed look.

Pete turned his focus to the rest of the group. "Come on, everyone. Let's leave her alone to focus." He leaned, giving me a kiss on my head, before leading the others off toward the training ground.

Sitting by the fire for hours, flipping through page after page of the book, I searched for any reference to bringing spirits back to the living. Jason's awful handwriting and the language barrier in Richard's notes proved a challenge, as always.

It'd be nice if the others weren't scared of this thing. They could maybe help a little.

I scowled in deep concentration. As I turned back to the first chapter for the millionth time, a commotion rang out behind me.

"Look who I found sneaking around," Emily hollered.

"I told ya, I was just passin' by," Ollie's voice whined.

"Right. And I'm Marie Antoinette. Stop lying before I chop your balls off and feed 'em to Hazel," she threatened, her voice a low growl.

He yelped. "I swear, I wasn't doin' nothing."

I slammed the book shut and marched in the direction of the noise. Ollie lay on the ground on his stomach, pinned under Emily's heel. He struggled, but to no avail. I knelt as the others, taking notice of the racket, surrounded us. "Now listen, you," I muttered into his ear. "You stole Jason's book, and I know it. I saw you running when the Coals showed up. The only reason I haven't told anyone is because I felt sorry for you. After you-know-what, I figured you had enough rage flying your way. However, if you keep lying—"

"—Get rid of him, Emily," Greg barked.

Nathan shouted, gripping the hilt of his dagger. "Last thing we need is this idiot causing problems! We're about to win this war."

A cacophony of anger ensued. It was hard to tell who called out what. I tried to get them to stop, but my voice was lost in the noise.

"He's probably a spy for Death."

"Murderer!"

"Don't trust him."

"Liar!"

"He got Jason ghosted!"

"Terrorist!"

Ollie's gaze shot frantically from one person's face to another before his voice rose in panic. "I didn't take the bloody book!"

Hands clenched, I spoke through gritted teeth. "I'm not stupid, Ollie. I saw your hair. How many spirits around here have their hair dyed bright green?"

"So now he's a thief, too," Nathan bellowed. And a murmur of fresh outrage spread around us.

Ollie's eyes grew to the size of small planets before he sighed in defeat. "Fine, I did it. Happy now?"

"Why'd you take it? Did you plan for Jason to be ghosted?"

He shook his head vehemently. "No. 'Course not. I liked the geezer. Stole the book to give to the prick who thinks he's somethin'."

That's not what I expected.

I froze. "Why?"

Brandishing her sword, Tina shouted, "He was trying to betray us!"

Ollie tried to scoot away from her but Emily's boot still held him captive. He kept babbling, "I hoped if he got his book back, he'd let us go home! Ya know? As a reward?" Emily leaned down and gave him a solid punch to the back of his head. "Hey! Was on my way to the castle when those armored bastards came 'round. Must've dropped the book when I ran!"

The crowd cheered Emily on. "You twit. Did you really think he'd do anything for you after you tried to blow him up? Even *if* you returned the book?"

Ollie rubbed the spot she'd struck, groaning in pain. "Yes?"

"Then you're even more stupid than I thought."

"It wasn't even m—" Another punch.

"I don't want to hear it," she snarled.

"Emily, stop. Ollie, it's great you wanted to repent by helping us. But stealing isn't any way to do it. You set us back a couple days. That book's what's helping us return to the living."

Ollie moaned. "Dammit. Even when I try to do something right, it's wrong."

Pulling a cloth from my pocket, I offered it to him to wipe some of the dirt off his face. "I'm gonna be honest, Ollie, you're not in the running to be one of our favorite people. But you made an effort to smooth things over with Death. It doesn't erase the past, but it's something."

He took the cloth hurriedly before Emily, or anyone else, could strike again. "Thanks. You probably won't want to hear this, but you're the one who inspired me to try an' fix what I'd done."

A shockwave of surprise rushed through my body.

He gave a slight nod, afraid to move too much. "Yeah, you did. What you said before I left last time really got to me. About him burnin' the trees down."

Everyone began shouting all at once again.

"He's lying!"

"Ghost him!"

"This is all his fault!"

Pete turned to face the mob we'd become. "Relax, guys. This isn't Salem. No witch trials, 'kay? We aren't going to string him up for an effort to do something right by returning the book." Pete gestured, "Look at him. Does this look like a criminal mastermind? All I see is a guy racked with guilt. If we execute him, we'd be no better than Death. Especially knowing he's seeking redemption."

Ollie sniffled, cheeks shining with genuine tears. "I'm sorry for what I did, all right? Seemed right at the time, y'know? I didn't understand—till it was too late. Didn't mean to hurt nobody, feel like a right shit about that. Was tryin' to make this place better."

Swiftly, Emily kicked his ribs, making Ollie cough and sputter again. "You can't just build a bomb then say you didn't mean to hurt anyone."

Ollie spoke through gritted teeth. "The bomb was only meant for *him*. I didn't know the others were just innocent bystanders. Thought they were his pompous friends, celebratin' their own bloody brilliance. Not like I'd really seen the bastard much."

I pointed to myself. "I was there. Shouldn't that've told

you something?"

Ollie blinked, his face falling with obvious shock. "That was *you*? I remember a girl next to him, but didn't recognize 'er. You looked so different…"

"Yes, that was me. And I looked like something from a horror movie for days afterward"

He sniffled again. "I'm really sorry about that, and, and everything else."

I crouched down, placing a hand on his shoulder. "Not quite sure if I'm ready to accept that, but I'm glad you apologized."

Tina stuck her sword into the ground, leaning on the hilt. "If we aren't going to hurt him for what he did, then what *do* we do with him?"

Pete stroked his chin, pondering for a moment or two. "I don't want to make anyone uncomfortable by having him stay here, but tossing him out on his ass just seems cruel."

"How about we give him his tent back and he can go where he wants?" I suggested.

Pete turned to the group. "Does everyone think that's okay?" No one spoke up, so Pete turned to Jeremy. "Jeremy, would you and Nathan go grab Ollie's tent?"

They nodded in unison, trotting off to camp.

Ollie spoke up. "That's why I came 'ere, actually. Was hoping you'd still have it. Not having somewhere warm at night starts to mess with your 'ead."

Mindi shoved her hands in her pockets, keeping her

head down. "Wes and I made 'em keep it, just in case you came back."

"You don't hate me?"

Wes shook his head. "Nah, mate. We were steamed, yeah. For the attitude you had last time you came 'round. We still are, but it doesn't mean we stopped carin'."

Jeremy and Nathan returned with Ollie's tent, carefully wrapped in an easily portable bundle. Emily took two steps back, giving Ollie room to push himself upright.

Holding his things close to his chest, he asked, "Am I still welcome to come with you lot? When you figure out how to get back?"

Pete patted Ollie on the back, a weary smile on his lips. "Yes. I promised you when you first joined our little gang. I keep promises. Just try to stay out of trouble, okay?"

"I will. Look me up when the time's right. Won't go far from 'ere." Waving farewell, he vanished into the trees like he'd done many times before.

CHAPTER THIRTY-TWO

I SPENT THE next two days raking over every page of the book, tirelessly trying to find answers. I remembered Jason saying something about life needing to 'be consumed'. Did I need to eat the Mother Carnadia? The idea made my stomach roil. I'd seen what addiction did to April and Geoffrey; would that happen to me, if I ate one to get us home? A chill rushed through me. A tangy, smoky smell lapped at my nose.

Is Pete making lunch?

"Oh, God. He's actually doing it, he's burning the forest down!" Kate screamed, running toward the camp. "Everyone *run*!" I immediately hopped up, dashing to untie Hazel before making my way to the campsite to put everything I could grab in my bag.

The smell grew stronger by the second. Smoke crept into view. Everyone scrambled about, gathering their things. The birds I'd made so long ago fled from the trees, screeching in terror. Pete was packing up his tent at record speed, his body taut with anxiety.

I barreled up to him. "Pete! What do we do?"

He answered, not even looking my way. "We've got to grab what we can and find somewhere safe. Now."

"He's trying to smoke us out. If we go anywhere beyond the trees, he'll send an army to take us down."

"He can try."

Tina called from across the campsite, "Lily! Lily, where are you? Please, don't run off, we have to go!" Her voice breaking. She ran up to us. "Have you seen her? She got scared and ran away."

My chest tightened. Dread crept up my spine. "I haven't seen her."

"Me either," Pete said.

"Dammit. Would you two help?"

"Of course," we replied in unison.

The three of us searched, scouring every inch of the campsite to find Lily. No trace anywhere. The blaze drew ever nearer, roaring and hissing. Charcoal grey columns of soot smothered the sun, leaving only a gloomy sky in their wake as ash fell like snow.

"You don't think..." Pete began, giving us a pointed look.

"She wouldn't have," Tina choked. "She's smarter than that."

"I hate to agree, but maybe we should check nearer the fire." I felt my blood running cold.

We hurried toward the flames, calling Lily's name, and careful to stay out of the heat's reach. Where was she?

My heart stopped when I spotted something glinting in the flames twenty feet away. The jewel from Lily's necklace was turning black under the all-consuming flame. A tiny piece of her favorite tennis shoes smoldered to ash right in front of me. The pink butterflies sewn into the side were barely visible.

Tina fell to her knees. "No," she gasped. "No, please God, *no!*"

I stumbled, it took all of my strength to not collapse.

No... not Lily...

Tears streamed down my cheeks but the heat of the backdraft quickly evaporated them. Pete stood frozen, his eyes wide with disbelief.

"He killed my granddaughter. That *animal* killed my granddaughter," Tina screamed, punching a nearby tree yet to be touched by the flames until her knuckles all turned red. "I planned on telling her when we got back...when we found her mother..."

"We can't stay here." Pete's arms shook as he reached to lift her from her knees. His voice wavered and trembled. "Tina, we—we need to go before the fire gets any closer."

She struggled against him, howling, "I won't leave her here!"

"You've got to or we'll burn up too!"

"Maybe that's what I want!"

He did his best to restrain her, but Tina continued to

fight his hold. "Tina, please. Don't give up. Don't do this."

"Spare me, it doesn't mean anything," she snarled, breaking free.

"Just calm down, Tina. It isn't fair, and it hurts like hell, but—"

"I don't want to hear it." She held up a hand. "I'm not staying after losing the one bright spot I found after being in this dark place for so long. Thank you for being a good friend, Pete, and helping to take care of her. Get that bastard for us."

"Tina!" Pete shouted, but it was too late.

She wrenched free and threw herself into the inferno, screaming and writhing in pain until she vanished. Her clothes left behind to burn beside Lily's necklace.

"No," I ran, unthinking, toward the fire.

I can save them. Maybe if I—

Pete snatched at me, holding me back. "Heather, don't. I….I can't lose you, too!"

"B-but Lily…" I sobbed. "T-Tina."

"I know, I know…" Pete held me close, our tears dampening my shirt.

THE FLAMES GREW closer every moment. We reluctantly left Lily and Tina's final resting place and headed back to camp, where everyone was finishing grabbing what they could.

Numbly watching the scene, I turned to Pete. "Should we tell them?" I asked, my voice hollow.

"Not yet. Let's get through this. Then we can tell them."

I knelt by his side. He asked, "Should I turn myself in? Maybe he'd stop…"

"That'd be a huge mistake. He isn't going to stop until all of you guys are gone. Can't you see that?"

Pete nodded, taking a long, slow breath, pushing himself up. "You're right. Let's just get out of the forest and plan what to do from there."

WE RUSHED AWAY from the fire. Hazel galloped ahead of us, whinnying nervously as burning trees collapsed behind us, booming crashes piercing through the fire's roar. The blaze picked up unnatural speed, destroying everything in its path with a ferocity that couldn't be from natural flame alone, even with the blanket of dry pine needles. My heart caught in my throat. Looking back while I ran, our abandoned tents fell to pieces in the flames, burning to ash. The flame's groan grew ever-louder, making my ears ache.

REACHING THE EDGE of the forest, we marched toward the houses to find temporary shelter. We'd only traveled a few dozen meters into the open field when I noticed everything had gone silent. The others were frozen in place, their expressions locked to the dawning realization of our reality.

Before I could wonder what was going on, Death stood by me, the light from the fire casting a crimson shade over his golden hair. I couldn't even bring myself to frown at him, much less be alarmed by his sudden appearance. "Here we are, at the end of this madness. I knew this would work. It was an extreme method, but you cannot deny it garnered results."

"Don't talk to me," I snapped, gritting my teeth. "Because of you, Lily's gone."

His irritated glare fell. His eyes widened. "What? Lillian is no more?"

"She burnt up in your fire. Tina threw herself into the flames when she discovered Lily's clothes. Their second deaths are no one's fault but *yours*." My shoulders quaked as I sobbed. "Is it enough now? Can this end?"

Death cleared his throat, trying to appear unmoved. "It will be ending very soon. My army is approaching."

"So, that's it. You're just going to have your army rip us all to shreds." I felt too full of despair to muster any of the anger surging in my veins.

His eyes softened. "All but you. Surely you understand they must be executed for their crimes."

"What crimes?" I screamed. "Wanting a second chance? Not bowing down to your will?"

"Is your memory so short that you have forgotten what took place at my ball?"

I threw my hand back, gesturing wildly at the spirits

behind me. "It wasn't *them*! That was one spirit, who made a terrible mistake. Ollie wasn't part of this group then."

He sighed in disappointment. "You are more conditioned than I believed."

"Think what you want." I looked away from him dismissively. "We'll be gone before your soldiers get here." I pulled out the book, slamming it at Death's feet. "Thanks to my good friend Richard Mortisa."

He looked down, smirking at the book. "It is ironic you call him a 'good friend.'"

His statement distracted me from my anger for just a moment.

"Because *I* am Richard Mortisa." For one short moment, I didn't believe him. "It seemed amusing to use a pseudonym."

My mind screamed that it *had* to be a lie. But another tiny voice in my mind whispered the truth—it made perfect sense for Death to be Richard Mortisa. Who else would've known such detail about my history and abilities?

Cupping my hands over my face, a deep groan escaped. "Of course. How could I have been so stupid? I suppose nothing in the book is true, that it was all a lie to give false hope."

"Every word is true. I honestly did not expect you to ever see this. Your resourcefulness is admirable. However, I must ask that you give the Mother Carnadia to me. I will return you to whence you came, but these spirits must not accompany you."

I took three steps back, shaking my head. "No. They're coming with me. I don't give a shit about the supposed risk. These spirits, these *people*, have gone through hell. They deserve to harvest the fruits of their labor."

"If you are uncooperative, then my associate will enact my contingency plan," Death threatened, though I perceived some hesitation in his voice.

I'd been stretched so thin I was past the point of feeling shock. "Associate?"

He let out a heavy sigh, giving a strange twisting hand gesture to the small crowd behind me, before snapping his fingers and vanishing without another word. Incredibly, the fire went with him, leaving a charred and demolished forest in its wake.

Everyone began moving again. Ironically, I was now the one standing frozen, staring at the ground. My mind spun, trying in vain to comprehend Death's parting words.

Suddenly, a sharp pain dug into my side. My focus snapped back to my surroundings, and I looked up to find Megan standing there, her hands wrapped around a blood-covered knife.

Wincing, I slid my hand to my side. Blood began seeping through my shirt. "M-Megan?" I sputtered, and crumpled to the ground.

Pete rushed to me, cradling me in his arms. "Megan," he bellowed, "what the *hell*?"

Greg's voice came from behind me. "Have you gone crazy?"

"Needed to make sure she was taken care of until this is over," Megan replied coolly, her expression hard as stone. "Don't worry, I didn't puncture anything vital."

"… what?" I gasped, clutching Pete's hand. Nothing alleviated the pain.

"He wanted you out of the way," Megan explained, slowly cleaning her blade with a rag she fished out of her pocket. "It's not a fatal wound. You'll live. Unfortunately, your powers will be too busy healing you. So the others won't have help to get out of here before the Coals arrive. I've just got to keep you busy until then. It won't be long." Her tone grew sad. "I don't enjoy this. I consider most of you friends, but there are times when you make sacrifices."

Pete tore off his plaid jacket and pressed the absorbent lining to the wound. "What did he offer you? What could be worth betraying your allies?" he demanded.

"Immortality. Shortly after *she* came and made it clear she wasn't on his side, he came to me. If I convinced her to help him, if I turned her against this group, sabotaged your plans, he'd make me like her. I'd live forever. He'd tried to make similar offers to other spirits, but they spurned him too fast, he didn't get a real chance to. Until me."

"Why would you want that?" I wheezed.

She stared at the ground, her brows knitted together in anger. "When I was alive, I was useless. My parents told me, my bosses, even my *husband*. They were wrong. I'd *prove* them wrong. I hoped I'd get my chance when my father received an inheritance. My hope was to borrow some money to start my own business. Surely someone who owned a successful restaurant was worthwhile."

Her grip tightened on her knife. Her hands trembled. "My husband, Otto, murdered me to get my portion of my father's money. I vowed to make it back to the living world, show them how foolish they'd been. Even if it took one hundred lifetimes to do it. No one would call Megan Byrd useless again."

Byrd. Bird. Oh my God.

My mind flashed back in time, recalling the moments that should've tipped me off.

"Champ said he heard some of those armored soldiers talking about this skirt that's giving them hell... said they mentioned birds. 'Bird this, bird that,' he said."

"A little birdie told me."

A rattling cough shook my chest. "So it was you. All along."

She looked at me with eyes void of emotion. "Yes. I sabotaged the bows. Everything Ollie did, I was privy to. Did you really think he was smart enough for all of that on his own? Stealing the armor, setting off the bomb—both my ideas. Guess all my work as an army nurse paid off in the end. I bet those stupid soldiers didn't even realize a 'little woman' like me would be curious enough to pay attention to their conversations and figure out how to make a bomb. Taught Ollie how to build one myself.

"After you sent Ollie away, he came to me, filled with guilt over what he'd done. The rest of you were off training or finding intel, I can't remember which. It doesn't really matter." She looked to Mindi and Wes. "He missed being your friend, just wanted to be accepted. I suggested he take the book from Jason to return it to Death. Then I informed the Coals. Thank you for making messenger birds, by the way." Her tone switched to the more innocent one we'd come to expect, "Telling Heather and Jason I'd seen someone go off with the book was too easy. The Coals were supposed to ghost you all."

Greg's eyes flamed with hatred. Shaking, he drew his sword. "You're why Shaun's not here." He bellowed, "You little bitch." He charged at Megan, sword poised to strike.

She straightened, looking into his eyes without even flinching. "Stop."

His eyes glazed over, and he skidded to a halt mere inches from her.

A horrified cry spread through the crowd—the whooshing pulse in my ear made distinguishing singular voices nearly impossible.

"Put down that horrible thing. You'll poke someone's eyes out," she said, still unnervingly calm.

Greg dropped his sword, it clanged on the ground. He blinked and shook his head, coming back to himself. "How…?"

"Death gave me some gifts to help me with my task.

Why do you think everyone trusted me completely, almost always followed my advice? Sure, being among you for almost twenty years was also useful, but this ability certainly didn't hurt."

My legs wobbled as I forced myself to stand, holding onto Pete's arm for support. "But you're the one who showed us Coals can be killed. Why would you do that if your job was to get rid of everyone but me?"

Jeremy chimed in, his trembling voice broadcasting his fear. "She's right. Makes no sense."

She shrugged, nonchalant. "Crisis of conscience. At one point, I told him I wouldn't do it, that he needed to find someone else. It was around then I figured out the Coals' weakness. Death and I had a good talk after that. He helped me see the error of my ways."

I weakly gestured to Emily, who'd drawn her bow. "What about Emily? She never trusted you. Don't your abilities work on her?"

"Never used them on her. If she said anything disparaging about me, you'd attribute it to her rotten attitude and ignore her."

Emily prepared her bow, pulling the string back with a sneer on her lips.

"Emily, hold your fire. Don't do something we'll both regret. Mindi, go to Emily. Stand in front of her. Don't move."

They both robotically did as instructed, their eyes clouding over. Emily put her bow and arrow down. Mindi stood directly in front of her, posture uncharacteristically rigid.

There was a twinge of satisfaction in Megan's voice as she instructed, "Emily, grab your machete and slit Mindi's throat."

Kay and Wes hollered, holding out pleading hands toward Emily as they desperately rushed toward her.

It was too late. Without a moment's hesitation, Emily unsheathed her blade and brutally dragged it across Mindi's throat. Her shirt floated down like a parachute after she disappeared.

Emily immediately regained control of herself and howled in despair. "Mindi…! What have I done?"

She clutched Mindi's clothes tightly to her chest, sobbing. Kay and Wes stood beside her, joining her in grief with comforting arms around her shoulders. Someone might've wailed behind me, but sound was getting harder to make out by the second.

Megan stepped in front of them, a harshness in her tone I'd never heard before. "Maybe that'll teach you to treat others with more respect in the future." Her focus moved to the rest of us when she got back to her feet. "Anyone else want to try to stop me?" she asked, half of her mouth curling into a cruel smirk.

"How 'bout me?" Ollie shouted, coming up behind her, tackling her and holding her arms behind her back.

Megan cried out. Ollie ripped through the seams of his shirtsleeve and stuffed the wad of cloth into her mouth.

He held his hand behind his ear as she let out muffled screams. "What's that, love? Can't hear ya. Such a shame, now you can't force us to do your bidding."

Megan kicked in random directions in hopes of getting out from under him as he used his belt to secure her wrists together.

She managed to squirm her way out from under Ollie, but before she could break free of her restraints, Greg charged her.

Holding his sword high, Greg swung at Megan's midsection, but she strafed to the left, avoiding the blow. He swept his leg under her ankles, knocking her, half-stumbling, onto her back. As he brought his sword down, she rolled, and used the momentum to wriggle out of Ollie's belt. Angry shouts burst out behind me. Gritting his teeth, Greg made another swing for her head. She spun again, managing to untie the cloth and free herself.

Pete's eyes darted between the group and me, teeth pressed down on his bottom lip. He took a deep breath. "This isn't going well."

"No…it's not," I coughed.

Tears began to well in his eyes. "I can't leave you like this…"

Smiling took some effort, but I managed to give my best approximation. "It's okay, sweetheart. I'll heal soon enough. The others need you more right now."

"Are you sure?"

"As sure as I've ever been of anything."

He gave me one final kiss, holding me as close as he dared. "I love you."

"I love you, too. Now go."

Pete drew his sword, running toward Megan at top speed. Everyone's fierce battle cries echoed through the field, drowning out individual voices in the cacophony. Megan hastily backed away from the others, heading toward me. This was my opportunity to strike. My wound stung so badly when I reached for my bow, making me hiss in pain. I wasn't in any condition for hand-to-hand combat, but doing nothing wasn't an option. It took everything I had. But carefully, pulling back the bowstring, I sent my arrow into the chaos in front of me, striking Megan in the shoulder.

She cursed, pulling it out with an ear-piercing yowl.

Using the distraction, Greg plunged his sword into her stomach. "This is for Shaun, you little whore," he growled.

As Megan lurched forward with gurgling cough, Emily took a wide swing at her neck. "And *this* is for Mindi and Jason," she screamed, voice wild, her eyes full of tears.

Megan's head tumbled from her shoulders, then vanished in midair along with the rest of her.

We stood in silence, unsure how to feel. The thundering of hooves rattled the ground, steadily growing louder. Soon the sound overpowered anything else.

My eyes met Pete's, and clarity hit me square in the face. This was it. My lungs shrank. The ability to breathe became a distant memory.

Pete's mouth drew into a straight line. He cracked his shoulders, swinging his sword. Everyone took a pointed glance at one another, silently saying their goodbyes, just in case. Keeping a death grip on my sword handle, I squeezed my eyes shut. If this had even been few weeks before, I would've collapsed in a full-on panic attack. That urge was non-existent now. There was too much at stake for me to be that girl anymore.

My eyes flew open, immediately a dark blur coming from the east caught my attention.

Must be them.

I glanced around quickly on the off-chance there was an escape route, a way to delay this confrontation just a little longer, a way to buy more time. All I saw was an empty, grassy field spread out in front of me. My wound ached and throbbed, the pain steadily easing.

The Coals surrounded us, all on horseback, numbering at least a hundred. Death led them. I looked straight into his fire-brown eyes, determination pumping through my veins.

He returned my glare, his mouth turning down slightly in what looked like an expression of sadness. That faded, and in its place grew a ferocious scowl. Death drew his sword, holding it high above him. "Charge," he bellowed.

We ran to meet the Coals, voices ringing out as a single cry of fury. Swords clashed and arrows and bullets flew, their clamorous sounds probably echoing for miles.

A Coal rushed by, trying to scoop me up, but I jammed my sword into a gap in its armor's codpiece. It screamed in pain, dropping me. I tumbled, gritting my teeth with a groan as the fall jostled my wound.

Standing, I came face-to-helmet with another Coal. As it swung its enormous blade at my ribs, I blocked the attack. Its strength outmatched mine, however, easily knocking me onto my back with a simple push. It moved to bring his sword down on top of me. Rolling to the left, I evaded that strike, the blade only leaving a scrape on my shoulder. Blood flowed from the wound onto the grass as I pushed myself up and grabbed the throwing knife strapped to my right calf. I flung it at the Coal with little time to aim.

The blade hit the black hole in this Coal's helmet, directly where I assumed its eyes were. The Coal fell backward, shaking the ground when it landed. Black smoke poured from every opening in the armor, then stopped.

Screams of rage and pain surrounded me. Everywhere I looked, my friends were in trouble. Jeremy, pinned under the hooves of Death's horse. Struggling frantically, trying to push the horse's bony leg off his chest, crying for help. I tried to run over to him, but my legs wouldn't let me move fast enough. Before I'd gotten halfway there, Death whistled inhumanly low, and the horse trampled Jeremy, stomping hard.

After a few seconds, Jeremy was gone.

Barreling toward Death, Emily's scream was like a banshee, her machete poised to kill. Death maintained a cool, collected expression, drawing his longsword with frightening speed, driving it into her shoulder. She managed to gurgle out a curse before fading away.

Our numbers were dwindling. Clothing I recognized as Greg's, Wes's, and Kay's were strewn on the grass like they'd simply blown off a clothesline. Empty sets of Coal armor lay everywhere.

Ollie held his own, managing to stay out of arm's reach. "That the best you've got?" he mocked a Coal with a sardonic chuckle.

While he laughed, another came up behind him, stabbing clear through Ollie's chest. The end of the sword split through the front of his shirt. Ollie's mouth was still upturned slightly from his final insult before he, too, was gone.

Nathan stood protectively in front of Kate, holding his sword out in front of him as three Coals closed in. "Stay away, you hear me?" he cried.

They didn't respond, stabbing him in the chest and twisting the blade.

Kate screamed, dropping her dagger and holding her hands over her mouth. "Nate..." She fell to her knees before them, clutching one of Nathan's boots. "Please, please take me too. I can't do this alone. Please. Just make it quick..."

"Kate, no," I screamed.

But her pleas must've moved the brutal Coals. One of them simply lifted her off the ground, took hold, and snapped her neck. Her final tear rolled down her cheek as she disappeared.

My lungs collapsed when I realized only one of the others was left. Pete. He skillfully engaged in a sword fight with two Coals, though the way his jaw clenched showed he struggled.

Ignoring my pain, I rushed to his side. "Pete," I screamed at the top of my lungs before it was too late. "Pete, run!"

He shot a momentary glance at me. His face fell when he saw no one else still standing. He frantically sidestepped away from the Coals. One of them reached out and grabbed him by the hair. He managed to yank himself free, losing a chuck of hair in the process. Finally he ducked behind a charred fallen tree. I charged, dashing to his side. "We need to go, now."

"But—"

"They're all gone, Pete," my voice shook. "All of them."

He hung his head, letting out a single sob. "We failed them…"

Gritting my teeth, I fished the Mother Carnadia out of my bag, holding it tightly in my hand. "We will if they get us too."

"Give it to me," Death commanded.

I clamped it tighter. "No. I just watched most of my

friends be destroyed at your hands. All of this could've been avoided if you'd just *listened* to each other. If you'd left well enough alone. I don't care about the risk. I want to go home." I looked straight into his eyes, hissing, "Get the *fuck* out of my life."

Gripping Pete's hand, I shoved the Mother Carnadia into my mouth. The taste was sour, and bitter on my tongue. The urge to spit it out became powerful as I chewed, but I fought it. My head felt empty, like helium was being pumped into my brain. Squeezing Pete's hand to keep myself anchored, I closed my eyes, picturing the two of us standing in front of my home in Idaho. The air swirled around us, nearly knocking me over.

"No!" Death cried.

Everything faded into beautiful, empty nothingness.

EPILOGUE

T HE FIRST THING I noticed was the cold. My flesh stung from its intensity.

This isn't right, I managed to think.

My eyes flew open. A few stars managed to twinkle through the dense clouds. Snowflakes gently danced in the frosty breeze, coming to a delicate rest on my cheeks. Head spinning, I gingerly sat myself up, then shakily hoisted myself to my feet. My heart caught. Pete lay motionless a few feet ahead, onyx curls peppered with snow. Eyes closed, his expression was smoothed into the picture of serenity.

I scanned for any sign of danger as I stumbled over to Pete, but all of the houses in my neighborhood were exactly the same as I remembered. Snow blanketed the quiet avenue, the sidewalks freshly plowed. The streetlamp at the end of the block flickered as it lit the darkened neighborhood, like always.

We had disobeyed Death, and there was no doubt in my mind that he would seek vengeance.

We were home.

Acknowledgements

My sweet, amazing fiancé Ian Juarez: When the world is a swirling vortex of chaos, you are my anchor. There is no one else I'd rather spend the rest of my life with. You inspire me every single day to be the best version of myself that I can be. I love you so much!

The incredible mountain of strength known as my mother: I can never put into words how grateful I am for everything you've ever done for me. It hasn't always been easy, I'm sure, but please know that it's truly appreciated.

My courageous, stubborn Grandma: thank you for always encouraging my love of books. Without you, I'm not sure I'd have the close relationship with literature that I do. Without you, this book might not exist.

My helpful editors, writer friends, and beta readers: Dakota Byrd, Holly Farrar, Taylor Kowalski, Nicolene Hale, EJ Runyon, Kathleen Lapeyre, Charles Alley, Dewi Ylönen, Lola Roberts, Keysha Mcmurtrey, Scarlett Dawn, Angela Smith Cappillo, Rebecca Hall. Thank you for helping make Eighteen Lives the best it could possibly be.

My incredible publisher Sara-Jayne Slack: I'll never be able to explain how much it means to me that you took a chance on me and my work. This has been my life's dream, and there are not enough 'thank you's in the world for making it real.

About the Author

Born in a small town in Idaho, Dove Calderwood has been passionate about reading and writing from an early age. From the short story about a knight named DeJel she wrote for her cousin at age eight, to the scathing satire of her elementary school she penned at 12, to the first manuscript she completed at 17, her pencil has never been still.

She currently resides in her hometown with her wonderful fiancé, their two cats, and dog.

Find the author via her website:

www.dovecalderwood.com

Or tweet at her: @DoveCalderwood